Baba's Story

Baba's Story

Mirjana Vinčić-Katić

IGUANA

Publisher: Meghan Behse
Editor: Mary-Anne Kanny
Front cover photo: Photo by Cristian Newman on Unsplash
Front cover design: Laurie Kallia and Meghan Behse

978-1-77180-340-3 (paperback)
978-1-77180-341-0 (hardcover)
978-1-77180-342-7 (epub)
978-1-77180-343-4 (Kindle)

This is an original print edition of *Baba's Story*.

Baba's Story *is in memory of my brave and wonderful sister-in-law Ljubica Vinčić, née Borkovic, and many other women who came to the city of Hamilton in Ontario, Canada, after the Second World War to marry men they'd never met before in order to have a better life.*

Ljubica came to Hamilton on New Year's Day, 1957. She married my brother, Dusan Vinčić. On October 13, that same year, she gave birth to their eldest child, son Stevan (Steven), who became the first-born Canadian in our Vinčić family. Two years later, Ljubica gave birth to twin girls, Lillian and Lydia. Another son, Aleksandar (Alex), was born later.

Ljubica and Dusan's marriage and their way of raising their children was an inspiration to all who knew them. They also sponsored many of their extended family members to come to Canada.

In the last few months of Ljubica and Dusan's life, their physical health was failing them. Their children and grandchildren each took turns to care for them. They both died in their own home in 2011, two months apart.

The Milutinovic Family

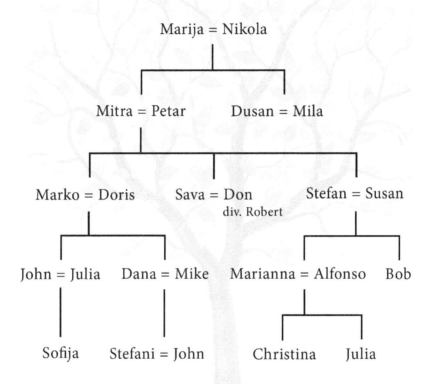

Foreword

In order for the reader to comprehend this story, some background might be helpful. The novel takes place in a remote village in the Balkan Peninsula, close to the Adriatic Sea. This area of the world has experienced so many wars and skirmishes because of different ethnicities and religions. The Ottomans were significant and long-time occupiers.

They ruled the Balkans for over 400 years.

The Ottoman Empire inflicted many harsh rules on the people. The most lamentable punishment was taking healthy male children from their parents; the Ottomans turned those children into their best warriors called "Janicari." The boys' identities were hidden from them. They were not allowed to have any relationships with women or marry while they were in their prime.

Parents who didn't want to convert to the Muslim religion and were afraid their sons would be taken away, escaped to remote mountainous regions to hide.

Due to that, they removed themselves from the modern world's progress and development, worked very hard to survive, and accepted their lives as normal because they didn't know any better. If they were not hungry or too cold, they were happy.

After the Ottoman Empire was defeated and the First World War ended in 1918, a new kingdom was formed, known as the Kingdom of Serbs, Croats, and Slovenes, called Yugoslavia. The new government built public schools up to grade four. Villages were small and one school served more than one village. It was also hard to find teachers who wanted to work in such remote areas.

Parents were not keen to send their children to school. They did not perceive the importance of education, especially for female children.

When the Second World War broke out, the young men from those villages were hunted down to join the fight. At first it appeared to be a united front repelling enemy forces from Germany and Italy. That all changed when Josip Broz Tito and his Communist followers created a civil war in Yugoslavia. It was such a confusing time, trying to figure out on whose side to fight on. Your worst enemies were your next-door neighbours.

There were big massacres among the major ethnic groups: Croatians, Serbians, and Muslims.

Tito won the war with Western support, taking over Yugoslavia and making the Crown capitulate.

Many young men from small villages were fighting against Tito and his Communists and were on the side of the kingdom of Yugoslavia and the Crown.

Once they lost the war to the Communists, they had to leave the country and retreat over the border to Italy to survive. Many of those who tried to return home were killed.

The League of Nations, now called the United Nations, set up camps for displaced persons in Italy where these young men, who were mostly 16 to 18 years of age, some even younger, were sheltered. Eventually, some of these young men came to Hamilton, Ontario.

There was a lot of work in two steel plants: The Steel Company of Canada and Dofasco. Since most of the new arrivals were mostly illiterate, they were assigned heavy manual labour. They were used to working hard.

Many had difficulty learning the language and assimilating into the Canadian culture. Their culture from back home reminded them that it's shameful to admit you don't know something, so they created their own community among themselves and considered this their family.

After becoming more comfortable with their new lives, these new Canadians wanted to start their own families. Some of them who were more outgoing married Canadian girls; others wanted to marry girls from their own villages. At that time, there were no match-making agencies. But many men still believed in their cultural motto, "Parents know best about whom their children should marry." Those young men put complete faith in their parents to match them with sensible girls. There was a problem of finding girls their sons' ages because all the girls who were good and healthy were married. So, parents matched their sons with girls who were often more than 10 to 15 years younger.

It is coincidental that *The Hamilton Spectator* published population statistics for the city on April 12, 2018, writing, "There are 12,000 more women than men over the age of 65 in Hamilton." It could be that those women who came after the Second World War contributed to this difference.

Chapter 1

One day, Sofija came home from school happily expecting to see her great-grandma, but when she entered the house, she found her sitting on the floor. She realized something was wrong with Baba.

Sofija asked, "Why are you sitting on the floor, Baba?"

Mitra saw that Sofija had turned white and was worried for her. Smiling at Sofija, Mitra told her that everything was all right.

"I slipped a little and slid to the floor. I wasn't able to get up and the phone wasn't near me. I am not hurt; I'm all right. Help me get up, won't you?"

Sofija threw so many questions at Mitra: "Are you sure you are not hurt? Why didn't you call us? Stupid me, you already said you were not able to reach the phone."

Sofija tried to help her baba get up, but even with her best efforts she could not. Sofija said that she was going to call their neighbour across the street.

"Yes, you can call if Clara is home, but don't call Adam," Mitra insisted.

"Why not?" Sofija asked, "He is much stronger than Clara."

"Please, no," Mitra said for the first time with a raised voice, "No."

"All right, Baba, I won't."

"The reason I don't want Adam to come is that I'm all wet underneath. That's why," Mitra admitted.

Sofija called the neighbour Clara who came right away. She moved the kitchen chairs to Mitra's side and asked her to put her arms on the seat of the chair and grab the sides of the chair to pull herself up. They turned Mitra on her side, then on her belly, but it didn't work. They tried to turn her on her side again and set her up.

Somehow, Mitra grabbed the chair and with all her might started to pull herself up. The two of them were trying to lift Mitra's bum and legs. Pulling and pushing, they eventually got her standing again. Sofija was still upset with what had happened to Baba. Clara helped Sofija to undress and shower Mitra and dressed her in clean, dry clothes.

The whole family was upset with what happened to Baba. The decision was made that Mitra could not be home alone anymore. She needed someone to look after her when they were away. Mitra's family hired an older woman named Zelma, who was still in good shape, to look after her when nobody was at home. Every time, when they asked Baba if the woman treated her well, she would always tell them, "Yes, yes, she does."

One day, immediately after Zelma went home, Sofija sneaked into the house to check on her baba. When she came close to her, she whispered, "Hi, Baba."

In fact, Zelma wasn't treating Baba well; however, she was treating herself very well by eating the good food, talking constantly on the phone, and reading books. Baba was very unhappy with the woman, but she did not want to upset her family, so she kept quiet. She didn't know what to do.

One day, she revealed her feelings to her friend Mara and asked what she would do in this situation.

"Do you think I should move into a retirement place? I hear people get treated very well there, and it would solve my problem."

Mara told her that she knew a lady who was in such care.

"She was my next-door neighbour. I go sometimes to see her, and she tells me she is happy with the place."

"Can you arrange for me to visit that place and see for myself?"

"Of course, I can. I will phone her tonight and ask her. Her name is Evica."

"Please call her."

Once Evica heard from Mara, she made inquiries on Mitra's behalf.

Evica told the assistant responsible for admissions that two ladies would like to come to check out the place. One lady was interested in moving in, if she liked it, she added. The establishment was always looking for potential residents.

The next day Mara informed Mitra that she could visit the establishment on May 5th at 1:00 pm, if that was agreeable with her. Baba told her family that her friend Mara would pick her up and they would go to visit her friend and neighbour, Evica, in Maple Retirement Place for seniors.

"Can you please call Zelma and tell her not to come tomorrow? I won't be home," Baba asked them, without mentioning what was on her mind. But her son Marko thought that she might be thinking of moving.

Mara drove Mitra there and introduced her to Evica and a manager. The establishment was very friendly and gave her lots of information; they even offered her drinks and some cookies.

Mitra never promised anything that day, but she was inclined to move into the establishment.

✳✳✳

When Mitra came back she spoke about the things she had seen. She told her family that the place was quite nice, the staff was very friendly, and the food was good. Mitra went a couple more times, to be sure about her decision. She found Evica quite friendly too.

One day, soon after these frequent visits to the establishment, Mitra told her family about her intention to move there. They were disappointed that she would do that. They liked their baba to stay with them because she was always fun to have around.

When the family started to question her about why she was doing that she said, "Please understand me. I like living with you and I know that all of us get along very well, but everyday, I am getting older and weaker in my limbs. I need someone to be with me all the time because I'm afraid that I might fall down again. I know you got Zelma to look after me, and I sincerely thank you for that. She cost you quite a bit of money, but she wasn't worth it. If you get another person, I am not so sure that person will be any better. For that reason, I've decided to go."

Mitra had common sense when it came to decision making, and when she decided to do something, she always carried through with it. She claimed this would be the best solution for her and for the whole family. They knew that Baba's decision was final, and she could not be persuaded to change it.

They felt guilty for taking her for granted. Her family considered her indestructible because she was such a strong character, and she'd taught them all to be strong and positive. Baba took care of them when they were growing up, but they let her down.

Marko fired Zelma instantly, despite her pleas that she would do a better job taking care of Baba. Mitra did not want to tie down Marko so she decided to move on May 25th.

When Sofija heard this, she cried; she did not want her baba to leave her. Mitra convinced her that everything would be fine.

"You have to be happy for me because I am going to have good care and be safe. It is not too far for you. You can visit me any time you want. I will always be happy to see you and talk to you, my dearest Sofija."

Marko, Doris, Stefan, and Sofija went to see where their dearest Baba was moving to. The staff received them pleasantly and showed them around the place. Baba's future room on the fourth floor looked very large and sunny. Marko asked several residents how they liked living there. Some of them told him they liked it, but a couple of men only shrugged and murmured with low voices, "not bad." Marko wasn't so sure whether the place was as good as the staff tried to convince him it was.

Once more, Marko asked Mitra if she was sure that she wanted to move away from home. Her firm answer was, "Yes, I'd like to. I think I'm going to be all right." The family had no choice but to accept her decision.

They made arrangements with Baba for what she wanted for her new place and how she would like to furnish her new room.

Marko believed that she would not last very long there; he thought she would soon ask to move back home because Mitra had never lived away from her family. Because of this, he suggested she only move her most essential things at first.

When the day came for Mitra to move to Maple Retirement Place, the weather added to her sadness. Heavy, dark clouds hung close to the ground, dripping slow spits of rain.

Chapter 2

Mitra could not sleep the whole night. She tossed and turned every which way but found no comfort after each turn. After tiring herself out, she closed her eyes and dozed off an hour before she needed to get up.

She dreamt she was in a very thick forest, trying to find her way out. Suddenly, she heard a loud thump coming from somewhere. Mitra opened her eyes and looked around. Everything looked so strange, until she realized this was not her home but the Maple Retirement Place. This was her new spider web environment.

This was her new home now, away from her real home and the family she'd enjoyed for 70 years.

After realizing where she was, she remembered the nurse telling her the meal times: breakfast at 8:45 am, lunch at 1:00 pm, dinner at 5:30 pm.

Mitra was told to be downstairs at 8:30 am to wait in line to pick up her breakfast at 8:45.

"Lunch and dinner will be brought to your table," the nurse warned her. "Be on time for meals; otherwise you may go hungry."

Mitra was wondering whether to go for her regimented breakfast; she decided not to make waves and follow the rules.

She had never thought separation from her family and the comfort of her home would be so traumatic, sad, and painful, but how could anybody imagine such an enormous change, unless one actually experienced it?

Mitra slowly got up and stepped into her private washroom to do her morning needs before heading downstairs. In the washroom, she lifted her head and looked straight in the mirror.

She looked strange; her skin was sagging, wrinkled and covered by age spots. Her eyes were still full of tears, swollen from crying all night, two sand dunes underneath them. She held tight with both hands to the edge of the sink, because her balance wasn't strong.

She looked at her hands and saw thick blue veins meandering under her skin, as if they were worms trying to suck the remaining life out of her.

She eased her tight grip and noticed that her veins receded somewhat, but her loosened skin became more prominent. It looked like all the muscles under her skin were melted away, revealing bones, moles and age spots.

Mitra never noticed before how much her body had changed since she'd fallen a couple of months earlier. She felt she'd aged 10 years. She looked once more to the mirror, shook her head and exclaimed, "So this is me at 90."

She nodded her head again.

"No, I don't recognize this face anymore."

With a painful grin, she wondered whether her life was worth anything, either to herself or anybody else, since her vitality seemed drained.

"There's no more purpose in my life to go on living. Now, I am vulnerable and depend on someone else to help me get on, but since my death is so inevitable and not far away, I wish it would come sooner rather than later.

"I regret very much that I'm no longer in my family circle and I don't see young people around me anymore. Instead, all around me I see old, unhealthy people, walking around in circles like zombies, pushing their walkers or their canes just like me. The smell of human excrement, the sight of stained garments and mouth drool, the sound of whimpers, is ever-present in the establishment.

"It feels we are serving a prison sentence here for the crime of living too long."

Mitra still believed in village culture that said the old should live and die among their family; her grandmother was a very lucky woman to die in such a way.

"Yes, I have had a much better life than my grandmother; still my end is scary and regrettable because I will die alone with nobody in my family to hold my hands, so I can have a smile on my face because my dear ones are around me. That's the kind of death I always dreamt of and wish for as my ending."

Mitra shook her head as if being angry with herself. Why was she so bitter and melancholic? It is not all that bad!

"What is the matter with me? I have a wonderful family that loves me. If anything, I should be very happy with my family because they were always the most important part of my life. They have been always good to me, and I don't think they are going to abandon me. I should have faith in them—especially my three children. As for not ending my life in my family circle as my grandmother had, it is not surprising. Family life has changed so much. And now there are institutions provided for older people."

Her fall had changed her mental attitude also. She was now more afraid of walking places. She didn't have the same appetite and had lost quite a few pounds. She knew her memory was still pretty good, although sometimes it blanked out, daring her to remember things.

"I have to calm down, accept the situation, and go on living. Everything will be better than I think. God will see to that. He won't abandon me."

She said a short prayer asking God to soothe her nerves and take away her fear. She felt a lot better, enough to finish her immediate needs in the washroom. Just as she was done, there was a knock on her door.

"Come in," Mitra said.

A nurse appeared at the half-open door, greeting Mitra with a cheerful, "Good morning, Mrs. Milutinovic."

"Good morning, nurse," Mitra answered.

"I'm just checking to see if you need some help with anything."

Mitra quickly thanked the nurse saying, "I'm good, thank you. I don't need any help for now."

Mitra could not stand the thought of someone touching her private parts. She told the nurse again that she still took care of her private needs without any problems, even though it was not completely true. She was not capable of doing a good wash even with her greatest effort. The nurse knew why Mitra refused her help. She could not bear for someone else exploring her body, but the nurse also knew that Mitra would give in soon. For that reason, she did not want to insist.

The nurse said, "That's fine, Mrs. Milutinovic. I'm glad you are able to help yourself. Please let us know in the future when you need us to help you. That's our job."

The nurse saw on Mitra's face that she had not slept very well, which was not surprising, since many people didn't for the first few nights.

"Did you sleep well, Mrs. Milutinovic?"

Mitra did not want the nurse to know that she hadn't, in fact she'd had a horrible night so instead she said, "Not very good, but I hope it will be better."

"I'm sure it will. See you downstairs," the nurse said.

"Yes, of course."

Mitra was surprised how quickly she got ready. While she was waiting for Evica to knock at her door, she sat down in her comfortable chair, which became a bed when the button on the monitor was pushed. Her children bought it for her after her fall. They'd brought it to her new room and put it in front of the window, which was open towards Lake Ontario. Her room was on the fourth floor and since the weather was clear that morning, she could clearly see Toronto and its famous CN Tower, strutting straight into the air with its 500-metre-high peak. She remembered whenever they had company from anywhere outside Canada, especially their old country, Yugoslavia, they'd take their guests to see Niagara Falls and the CN Tower. These were the biggest attractions for visitors.

She heard the knock at the door; Evica was there asking if Mitra was ready to go. Mitra quickly got up and went out to meet her. They went downstairs to line up for breakfast.

Evica told Mitra she was sitting by the window on the east side of the building. Mitra looked outside the window and saw a very nicely kept lawn. To the left of the window was a white lilac bush. It was all in bloom.

The window was partially closed because it was a hot May day. Soon it would be June. Mitra thought that she would like to take a walk around the garden to smell the grass and flowers and breathe some fresh air.

Just as she was looking outside through the window, the same nurse who'd asked Mitra if she needed help, said, "Can I have your attention, please?"

Everybody went silent. Mitra looked around to see what was going on. The nurse said, "We have a new member in our group."

She pointed a finger at Mitra.

"It's my pleasure to introduce to you a very fine lady, Mrs. Mitra Milutinovic. I hope she's going to like it here among all of us. Please give her a warm welcome."

Everyone clapped and Mitra heard some voices saying, "Welcome, Mrs. Milutinovic," and "Nice to meet you, Mrs Milutinovic." Still, some residents neither moved nor said anything. Their companion at the table was a very petite and polite Dutch lady. She had small, skinny hands, like a child's. She extended her hand to Mitra to welcome her, even before Evica had a chance to introduce them. Her name was Mrs. Decock. She told Mitra that she'd been living there for over a year, and she liked it.

"The staff is very attentive and polite. I hope you'll like it here too."

"I hope so," Mitra replied. "Thank you for your welcome Mrs. Decock." Evica offered to bring Mitra's food to her table if she was too tired to fetch it.

"No, no, thank you for offering, Evica, but I would like to stretch my legs and choose my own food."

"Good, let's go," Evica said.

Mrs. Decock had a hard time getting around, so somebody always brought her food over to her.

It was a normal breakfast, very traditional; toast, brown or white, bagels, English muffins, scrambled eggs, and little squares of roasted potatoes and tomatoes. There was orange juice, coffee, tea, but no fruit, which Mitra had always had at home.

Everything went normally. People were talking; some were even laughing rather loudly. For a moment, Mitra felt as if she was in a restaurant, not in an institution.

She started to relax a little, but she felt really tired. Evica noticed this and said to Mitra that she looked rather tired.

"A bit," Mitra admitted.

"It's a big change coming here from your home," said Mrs. Decock. "I felt the same way the first few days after I came, but things get better after a while. Things will get better for you too with time, Mrs. Milutinovic."

"I hope so," Mitra replied. "Thank you very much for your encouragement and your kind words, Mrs Decock."

"You're very welcome."

Mitra was surprised that she ate so much. She must have been hungry because she hadn't come down for dinner the previous night. Evica had brought her a couple of cookies, a glass of juice, and a banana.

After breakfast was done, Mitra cordially parted with the Dutch lady. Mitra asked Evica if she wouldn't mind going out into the yard to get some fresh air.

"No, no, I don't mind—let's go," Evica pointed at the back door to the garden.

Fresh morning air was like medicine for Mitra. They looked around admiring the bushes, daffodils, tulips, and the nicely-trimmed and groomed grass. There was a green-hedged fence that encircled flowers in the middle and a nice path of fine gravel around them. A couple of benches were also there. Evica and Mitra sat on one of them. It felt really nice and relaxing. It was nearly 10:00 am and getting too hot to be outside in the sun.

They went back into the building because Mitra felt tired. She told Evica she would go and lie down for a bit. Evica did not say anything, but it was obvious she wasn't pleased. Mitra was too tired to do anything else but rest. She did not ask Evica what she wanted to do.

When Mitra came to her room she found a message on her voicemail from her dear Sofija that she was coming to visit her after lunch. Mitra felt happy that Sofija was coming. She was Mitra's favourite great-grandchild. She was eighteen years old. She had a part-time job during the school holiday and she also took extra courses. Despite her busy schedule, she always found time for her baba.

Sofija was fascinated with space and had said many times that she would like to become an astronomer one day. Mitra would look at her, not knowing what to say. Her great-granddaughter did not believe in the biblical story of Adam and Eve or in Darwin's Theory of Evolution.

When Mitra asked her what kind of evolution she believed in, Sofija replied, "I think we came from another planet, still undiscovered. I believe that we will leave our planet Earth one day and emigrate to another planet. Baba, I believe everything has its lifespan, even the planets."

"Who told you that?"

"Nobody, it's my theory."

When Mitra heard her talking about this, she looked at Sofija, wondering and questioning where the young girl's thoughts were coming from, or whether she was well. Mitra would only shrug, saying that she herself was not thinking about such scientific thoughts, and wouldn't burden her brain with it.

"It is for you and astronomers to find out. For now, I am good with this world as I know it," Mitra would say to Sofija, "My dear great-granddaughter, when you find what you are looking for, please send me a letter so I can know about it too."

They would both laugh.

She knew that her darling great-granddaughter had a very sharp mind and good imagination. But Mitra was afraid for Sofija to go too far with those thoughts. She was the daughter of her grandson John and his wife, Julia. John was the son of Mitra's son Marko and his wife, Doris. Mitra practically raised her grandson John and his sister, Dana, because Marko and Doris worked full time as teachers.

When Mitra's daughter, Sava, and her son Stefan got married and moved out of her house, Mitra's son Marko and his wife, Doris, convinced her to sell her house to their son, John, and to move in with them.

Mitra babysat Sofija so much; she spent more time with the girl than her own parents did. Sofija became very attached to her baba. The two of them always had a very close relationship. When Sofija grew up, she no longer needed a babysitter, yet she would always visit grandpa Marko's house in order to see her baba.

As she would be entering the house she would yell, "Baba, I still need a babysitter."

Mitra lay down on her bed to get some badly needed rest before Sofija arrived. She was surprised she felt so differently than she had in the morning. She felt more relaxed as if many dark clouds were moving away from her—just enough to make her more optimistic about her new place. Mitra dozed off for a while and didn't remember anything until a knock on her door woke her up. Evica asked her if she would be going for lunch. She told Evica to come in and wait until she got ready.

Mitra washed her face and changed her clothes, because the ones she wore for breakfast were all wrinkled. Evica asked her if she felt better, "Yes, yes much better. Thank you for asking."

They went downstairs, sat at the same table, and waited to be served. Mrs. Decock wasn't there yet when they came, but she appeared soon.

She asked Mitra if she rested a bit.

"Yes, I did," Mitra admitted.

There was mushroom soup, a couple of small pieces of chicken breasts with some vegetables, and fresh strawberries for dessert.

Mitra didn't finish all the meat and vegetables, but she ate strawberries. She told Evica that her great-granddaughter was coming after lunch, and she had to go back to her room to wait for her.

Evica didn't look pleased when she heard that. Mitra didn't say anything because she loved to be with her great-granddaughter Sofija. Mitra felt that Evica was a controlling person, but hoped she was wrong.

Sofija called again to ask if her great-grandma wanted Tim Horton's coffee and something else with it. "Coffee would be fine, nothing else, please," Mitra said.

Chapter 3

Sofija rushed through the door without even knocking. She put the coffees down and ran to her baba. She instantly hugged her tightly, holding her as if she was afraid her great-grandmother would pull way. The memory of the horrible day her baba fell was still fresh.

Finally, Sofija let go of her baba, saying, "Let's have a coffee and talk."

"What do you mean by talk, Sofija? What are we going to talk about? Is everything all right at home?"

"Yes, Baba, everything is all right at home," Sofija answered, "I didn't mean let's talk about something important. I just want us to have a small, usual talk."

"All right, Sofija, sorry about that," Mitra said.

"I can see, Baba, that you've changed already since you moved in here."

"The new environment changes a person," Mitra said.

"That's true in a way. One has to change according to the situation."

Sofija sensed sadness on her baba's face. Mitra couldn't hide it, even though she tried very hard by taking an optimistic view of the situation in front of Sofija.

Sofija excused herself and went into the bathroom. She started to cry as she opened the tap full force in order to cover the sound of her sobs. Tears were running down her face, and her heart was breaking for her baba. She was in the bathroom a little too long regaining her composure. She didn't want her baba to see her like that.

Mitra called her.

"Sofija, are you all right?"

"Yes Baba, I'm looking around the toilet to see how best we can arrange things and what else you need us to bring you."

"What are you talking about, Sofija? I have everything I need. Please don't bring me anything. You know I don't like clutter."

Sofija came out.

"So, Baba, you're determined to live with the smallest number of things?"

"Yes, Sofija, that is true, and that is what I learned in my life, to be modest and not to waste unnecessarily. If I need anything, I will let you know, but for now everything is all right."

Baba noticed that Sofija's skin was red underneath her eyes.

"Is that why you went to the washroom—to cry?"

"I didn't, Baba."

"Don't tell me that. I know you did."

"So, what if I did? Am I not allowed to cry?"

"Yes, you have that right, but for a good reason. Now you don't have any reason to cry because I am fine."

"Baba, we all have our own reasons and our own feelings for how we react in certain situations."

"So, you are telling me that you don't like me being here."

"Not particularly."

"Let's leave that alone. Let us have a good time as we always do," Mitra said. They usually threw silly looks at each other and laughed.

Sofija agreed.

"So, my dear, is there a special young man in your life?" Mitra asked.

"Nope, Baba, not really. Aunt Sava warned me the other day when I talked to her to be careful and have my eyes wide open going into a relationship with a man. I didn't know what she meant by that, but I am sure she knows what she is talking about."

"Yes, she does, child, yes, she does," Mitra said, not wanting to talk about that anymore, even though she sensed Sofija was expecting her to do so.

"Don't worry, Baba, I don't need to rush. There is lot of time for me. I'm only 18."

"Wise girl," Mitra added.

"What about you, Baba? Have you found somebody nice to pass the time with in here?"

"Of course I'm trying, but they are all too busy constantly looking down at the ground as if they have lost something."

Sofija started to laugh.

"They are probably trying to look for their lost youth."

"You are right in that, just as I do. That seems to be what occupies our time. What can you do, there is a time for everything in our life?"

"Yes, Baba, I believe you are right as always."

Suddenly, there was a knock on the door; it was Evica.

"Are you ready to go?"

"Come in," Mitra said.

"Oh, sorry, I didn't know your great-granddaughter was still here," Evica said.

"That's all right. Where am I supposed to go?" Mitra asked.

"Have you forgotten that we have a meeting at three o'clock?"

"Oh my God, I forgot all about it," Mitra said.

"Do you still want to go since your great-granddaughter is here?"

Sofija jumped up off her seat when she heard that, telling Mitra to go.

"I have to leave anyway," she said.

"It looks like I have to do what you tell me to do," Mitra joked.

"Yes, that's right, Baba. We know better what's good for you than you do."

As Mitra and Sofija laughed, Evica was seriously wondering what was so funny.

She even felt offended by Mitra's statement. She almost turned around to leave when Mitra stopped her.

"Evica, don't take it that way. My great-granddaughter and I always joke around. I didn't mean anything offensive towards you."

Evica's discomfort eased but she still could not figure out how Mitra and Sofija could speak to each other that way.

Sofija came over, exchanged hugs and kisses with her baba and hugged Evica telling her, "Thank you for being my great-grandma's friend."

"You're welcome," Evica said.

After Sofija left, Mitra quickly got ready and she and Evica went to the residents' meeting. Even though the residence had about 60 people, only a little more than half attended the meeting.

New residents—Mr. and Mrs. Simpson—were introduced. Everybody clapped. Mitra was envious thinking how it would have been nice if she and Petar had had the same chance to grow old together and keep each other company. Although she tried to hide her feelings, her eyes filled with tears. Evica asked Mitra if she was all right.

Mitra didn't want to reveal her feelings to Evica; instead she said that something got stuck in her throat and she refrained from coughing, so her eyes became tearful.

"That's fine as long as you are all right."

"Yes, I am. Thank you for your concern."

"You're welcome," Evica answered.

The residence manager introduced herself, saying that most residents knew who she was, but there were some new ones who didn't.

"My name is Margaret Watson. I have been managing this place for the last 10 years. We usually don't have general meetings with all the residents but I decided to try something new; once in a while we'll have these general meetings for all of those who are interested in attending. I'd like to hear your comments about our residence and how we can make you more comfortable."

A loud voice complained, "How about better food? That would make me more comfortable."

There were different sounds of approval for what was said but also disappointment. Mrs. Watson smiled and dismissed the statement as a joke.

A man sitting close to Mitra and Evica said, "I bet Mrs. Watson regrets that she called the meeting at all. She didn't anticipate such instant, negative reaction."

Hoping to hear some compliments for the way residence was run, Mrs Watson asked, "I'd like to hear some more opinions."

Another guy got up and said, "I wish we would have some more outings."

"What do you mean by that, sir?"

"I mean for us to visit some interesting places, instead of constantly being cooped up inside like chickens."

People laughed at first but then seemed to approve of the man's suggestion.

"May I have your name, sir?" Mrs. Watson asked.

"Gerry," he answered.

"The centre doesn't have any obligation to organize outings, but it can be done. The centre can cover some expenses, but it would have to come mostly from the residents' pockets."

The discussion was going contrary to what Mrs. Watson had been expecting to hear. She decided to end the meeting.

"I will think about your proposal. For now, that will be all. We will talk about it the next time."

It was obvious that Mrs. Watson had enough of hearing only negative things.

"Thank you all for coming. I'm not sure when we will have another meeting."

"Fix things first, and then we'll have a meeting," somebody shouted.

"I will look into your concerns and see what we can do to improve," Mrs. Watson said, before she took her briefcase and left.

When the meeting was over, Mitra and Evica went to the elevator to go back to their rooms and rest a bit before dinner. Two gentlemen, Gerry and Adam, entered the elevator.

Gerry said to Adam, "What did Mrs. Watson think she was going to hear? How we are all very happy in here? Let her bring her own parents and see what they would say."

"That would have been the right thing to say to her," Adam said. "Mrs. Watson's parents would say the same."

"But what choice do we have in our modern age? Sometimes, we are looked at as robots whose batteries have run out of juice," Gerry said.

"I'm not going to allow anybody to treat me as a robot," said Adam.

"Nobody will ask you what you think," said Gerry.

When Mitra and Evica exited the elevator they looked at each other. Mitra asked, "Did you hear those two men?"

"Of course," Evica said.

"I don't think it's all that bad in here," Mitra said.

"Not so much now, but a while ago before you arrived, there were a lot of complaints. I heard that a government inspector came here to check out the complaints. Things have improved since then, but I know the same men complained before. Some people were quiet about it but there were a lot who complained."

"Why didn't you tell me about that before I came in?" Mitra asked.

"What good would it do? If you went somewhere else, it would be the same."

Mitra guessed Evica's motive, she wanted Mitra's company rather than tell her the truth. Mitra wasn't pleased about that. That was the first time she began to doubt whether Evica was always telling her the truth.

They had an hour to rest before dinner. Mitra lay on the bed instead of the chair because she could rest better. After she lay down, her son Marko called.

"How is everything?"

"Not too bad."

"How was your meeting?"

"Who told you about our meeting?"

"Sofija told me you almost forgot, and Evica came to pick you up."

Mitra told Marko everything, even the two gentlemen's conversation in the elevator.

"I didn't know it was that bad, mom."

"The way Evica was praising it so much, I thought it was the best place."

Mitra didn't want to tell Marko that she was concerned about Evica's honesty.

"Mom, please don't worry. If it gets that bad you can come home."

"I know, son, I know. I don't think it will be that bad. Don't worry, I'll be fine. How is everybody at home? Is Doris busy?"

"Yes, she is. You know my wife; she always finds things to do just like you did."

"Have you seen your brother, Stefan, lately?"

"Yes, I saw him yesterday. He came by."

"Did Suzan come too?"

"No, she didn't. He said she went shopping with her daughter, Marianna. You know Suzan, she loves to shop. Sometimes Stefan complains that she shops too much and buys things that are not needed."

"Oh well, we all like something different."

"Mom, you'll be going for your dinner soon. I hope they made good dinner for you guys."

"It will be fine. It's really not as bad as the people were saying today."

"Mom, you're always an optimist."

"One has to be at my age."

"Hopefully, Doris and I will visit you soon."

"That will be nice. Come whenever you have free time."

Right after Mitra put the phone down, Evica was at the door. Mitra came out and they went for dinner. Dinner was good: roast beef, mash potatoes, and some steamed vegetables. Dessert was a piece of apple square and tea or coffee.

Evica said, "What do the people want? The food is pretty good here."

Mitra agreed.

After dinner Mitra felt really tired again. Not realizing this, Evica asked her to go for a walk. Mitra agreed that it would be a good idea, but she was not sure about her legs moving forward. She admitted she was still very tired because she still hadn't had a good sleep to regain her strength.

Mitra suggested to Evica they play cards or watch television or just simply talk. It was obvious Evica wasn't pleased with Mitra's answers.

"You go ahead and do what you want; I will go for a walk by myself," she said, turning around and leaving Mitra standing there.

Mitra went to her room to rest for a while. There was a knock on the door.

Outside the door was a big bouquet of flowers sent by her family. Mitra's family knew that more than anything, their mother wanted her children to have good relationships with each other, and that they do something nice for her together rather than separately. She'd also received some greeting cards from relatives and friends, wishing her a pleasant stay in the new environment.

The flowers and cards gave Mitra funny feelings. They gave her more sadness than happiness. It felt odd that somebody would even think of wishing her comfort and well-being in a seniors' residence. Evica's behaviour wasn't really helping Mitra to adapt more positively to the place.

Mitra felt sad about the whole situation, even that she was still alive. The next few days were as usual. Evica was always the same. Mitra didn't want to make things worse so she kept trying to move forward as smoothly as possible.

Chapter 4

Mitra, Evica, and a Dutch woman sat at the same table. Another lady, with jet-black hair, neatly styled and short, joined them. She wore dark pants and a sweater with two tones: grey and white. Her complexion was very clear without age spots.

The woman, who looked southern European, was quite short and well rounded. The nurse came over to their table and introduced them to their new companion: Mrs. Kachatory. She'd arrived last night. All three greeted her.

"Good morning, Mrs. Kachatory."

Mrs. Kachatory looked at them without saying a word.

They all said again with one voice, "Welcome, Mrs. Kachatory."

The woman never said anything, only slightly adjusted her position on the chair. After a while she started to say a few words. Her English was very poor and often she used the wrong words when trying to explain something.

Today, on the menu was mushroom soup and a nicely sized tenderloin with cauliflower and broccoli. The new resident looked at the soup, and asked the serving lady, "What's this?"

The waitress said, "This is mushroom soup; it is very good soup, Mrs. Kachatory."

She pushed the soup away with such force that some of it spilled over the table.

"No like that. That's pig food. No people eat that. No, no, me no eat that."

We all kept quiet not knowing what to say. Evica said in a low voice, "So we are all pigs, eh?"

When they brought her the main course, she looked at it with wide-open brown eyes.

"What this?"

The waitress had enough of her and responded, "Food, Mrs. Kachatory, food."

"No, me no like, no eat that. No food good."

She took a bun and coffee. That was her dinner.

The Dutch woman was very quiet. She had proper table manners. Mitra and Evica kept quiet too.

Mrs. Kachatory teared at her bun while looking at the Dutch woman in total disgust over her fine manners.

Evica took a quick glance at Mrs. Kachatory. When she noticed Evica looking at her, she said, "You look me for what, you look me. You like here? No problem for you. Me no like here. You crazy? You here like. Me no crazy, me no like here, Crazy people like here."

Evica understood that she could not have a casual conversation with Mrs. Kachatory. She turned her head in a different direction. In the meantime, the serving woman came by the table asking if everything was okay. Mrs. Kachatory was quick in giving her opinion, pointing her finger at Evica.

"She like o-o-o-everything much."

The waitress turned to Mrs. Kachatory to tell her that somebody had asked to see her.

Mrs. Kachatory jumped quickly off her seat.

"Yes, yes, that my friend, she say she come me see. Me go, me go. No like your food, me go look my friend."

She looked at the three other women in disgust and left.

Mitra asked the waitress, "Is that a normal way for people to behave when they come in?"

"For some people, yes. But usually after a few days they settle down and behave normally. It takes a little time to get adapted to the new place after being in your own home so long with your own routine."

Mitra thought, "That's so true. It does take time to get used to the new place and the new family while dealing with your stiff and old body at the same time." Again, she wondered whether she would ever get used to it. She could have cried right then and there, but she had to suppress her tears until she was alone.

Dinner was done and Evica and Mitra headed to their floor. When the elevator opened up, Evica's daughter happened to be inside.

"Where were you, mom? I was looking for you upstairs," Evica's daughter said.

"We were having dinner, dear. Dinner was a little longer than usual because of a little incident with the new resident. When did you come?"

"I got here a few minutes ago. I didn't go home after work but came straight here to see you."

"Thank you, dear," Evica replied.

Evica's daughter turned her attention to Mitra asking her mother if Mitra was her new friend.

"Yes, this is my new friend, Mrs. Milutinovic. She is a new resident."

Evica's daughter asked Mitra how she liked it there.

"It is not too bad; hopefully, I will get used to it."

"I hope so," Evica's daughter said.

"I am grateful for your mother's company, that helps me a lot," Mitra said touching Evica's shoulder.

"I am glad you appreciate my mother's company because I know she appreciates yours."

"Evica, I will see you later. Enjoy your daughter's company. I am going to call my daughter as soon as I get into my room," Mitra said.

Mitra went into her room but she didn't feel like calling anybody. The incident with Mrs. Kachatory made her sad realizing how the woman was suffering; not knowing the language was a double whammy. She wanted to be alone for a while and shed a few tears of her own. Whenever she felt melancholic, she always thought of her husband, Petar, longing for his presence.

"Oh my God, what am I thinking? Am I losing my mind or what? Why think of something illogical? But what has logic to do with anything when your heart is breaking and longing for something you would like to have? The heart wants what it desires, even though it cannot get it."

As usual, Mitra changed her thinking to a realistic understanding of the situation and said again, "Oh, what is the use of thinking about that? Nothing can be changed. It is what it is, and I have to live with it."

She lay down to rest a little, trying not to think too much about impossible things. The more she tried to push it out of her mind the more persistent sadness pressed on her emotions.

Mitra's moment was saved by her daughter Sava's call. She answered the phone reluctantly, but when she heard Sava's voice saying happily, "Hello, mom," Mitra's voice changed instantly to a happy and mellow one.

"Hi honey, is that you?"

"Yes, it is me, mom," Sava answered.

After they exchanged hellos, somebody came to Sava's office and the conversation ended. Sava was calling from British Columbia. She was sent there to correct some issues that pertained to government matters. Mitra was told that her daughter, Sava, was an exceptional lawyer. She was very good at solving problems.

Sava was a strong student and a good orator. She competed in public speaking at school and often won first place. Ever since, she volunteered for any debate. Mitra and Petar were always Liberal Party supporters, and she too became one, as soon as she was allowed to vote.

When she turned 19, there was a federal election. She volunteered to canvass for the Liberal candidate. Mitra and Petar were worried for her. They always warned her not to trust people easily. Petar used to say, "You're a beautiful girl; that makes you desirable to men. Please be careful."

She was extremely excited about what she was doing. Her candidate didn't win, but she decided to pursue a career with the government working for the public. They were so surprised—actually shocked—when she told them she wanted to be a lawyer.

Can one imagine Mitra and Petar's thinking? The two of them could barely read and write in their own language, let alone in English. Their daughter, a girl, wanted to become a lawyer! When the Liberal candidate Sava was helping in the election came to talk to them, urging them to support their daughter going to law school, they were very surprised.

They also heard from Sava's teacher about what a strong and ambitious student she was. Petar and Mitra stopped opposing her pursuit.

Most of Petar and Mitra's friends were surprised when they heard what Sava wanted to do. Some said, "Who does she thinks she is? She should prepare to get married and have a family, not run around with different men, jumping in bed with them and ruining her life."

Petar and Mitra had to drop some of their long-time friends for talking like that about Sava. They would also have rather seen Sava's life turn out the same as their friends' daughters' lives. Sava didn't want to hear about it.

From that time on, she became very serious about making her dreams come true. When she graduated from grade 13, she received the top student award and a leadership award for helping the teachers and fellow students. When Petar and Mitra heard all this on her graduation night they were flabbergasted. They didn't know what to think. When they heard that Sava Milutinovic won a full scholarship to Queen's University, they almost fell on the floor. The school principal and some teachers afterwards came over to congratulate Sava and her parents. Petar and Mitra looked at each other in wonderment.

From then on, there was no stopping Sava. Neither did they try; instead they completely supported her. But even the best things in life don't always go smoothly, something often happens to spoil it.

Mitra's children were very polite and smart. She and her husband, Petar, had spent a lot of time talking to them, playing with them, and teaching them how to behave properly. She remembered how her husband, Petar, used to tell them every day to study and be good students.

"Education will give you a good income and respect in society. That is why you have to get the best education you can. I know what it means to work hard for little money, and have people looking down on you."

Even before the children were born, Petar used to say he would work hard and save every penny for their education, but they had to be educated.

Mitra thought how her husband used to have so many wonderful ideas. He was a truly wonderful man and a very caring husband and father. She had wonderful memories of their lives together. She took a deep sigh.

"God please be kind to him because he never complained or carried hatred towards anybody."

As Mitra eyes filled with tears, there was a knock at the door.

"One moment, please."

She wiped away her tears and asked the person to come in. The housekeeper came to collect dirty clothes, promising to bring them back clean tomorrow.

Mitra gathered a few pieces of her underwear. One was stained from a bowel movement, because she was not able to reach back far enough. A memory of her grandmother came to her, how she used to say that her arms got shorter. Now Mitra understood what she meant.

She was contemplating whether to allow the housekeeper to take that piece, when the housekeeper took it from her. She asked her very politely not to keep her dirty clothes hidden.

"I am sorry, but I have to remind you of that, Mrs. Milutinovic."

Mitra blushed knowing full well that the housekeeper was right. She tried to tell herself that she really had to change and not feel ashamed about the things she could not do. Then again, she thought it was one thing to keep saying to yourself you have to change, but totally the other to actually change. Mitra still had that old-fashioned feeling of shame when revealing her personal things.

Her children would often remind her of that, especially her daughter, Sava. She was glad for Sava's sake that she was not like her mother in that area.

Mitra knew that every day she was less able to do things for herself; she knew that her needs would eventually overtake her shame.

She stretched on her bed, finding comfort for her entire body.

Mitra felt rested, so she got up to attend to her needs. When she came out of the washroom, she looked outside. The day was not too hot for that time of year. It had rained a lot recently, and everything looked so nice and green. There was a farm nearby with strawberry patches. Lots of people were picking strawberries, which they would preserve for winter because some people were carrying more than one flat in their hands.

Mitra heard a loud knock on her door. Before she opened her mouth, Sofija burst through the door. She grabbed her baba and hugged and kissed her many times.

This was Sofija's second visit in Baba's new place.

Sofija asked her about many things. She also asked her if she'd slept well. "Yes, I slept a lot better in the past few days," Mitra said. She had a lot of time to sleep so she would catch up—reassuring Sofija not to worry.

Sofija asked again, "Are you telling me the truth, Baba?"

"Yes, of course I am telling you the truth."

Sofija was shocked at how Baba had changed. She realized that Baba wouldn't be around too long. Even if she lived another 10 years, it was not very long.

She imagined how dreadful parting forever with her baba would be. She panicked as she thought about that. Mitra noticed sadness on her face. She asked Sofija if she was all right.

"Yes, I am fine, but I'd like to ask you something."

"What would you like to ask me?"

"I would like to write your biography."

"Why would you do that?"

"Because I want to know details of your life," Sofija said.

"What is it that you want to know, my dear child? You already know everything about me. We talk so much," Mitra said.

"This time, I am going to write your life story in my notebook. Please, Baba, tell me everything you can remember, starting from when you were a small child, and then growing up in Yugoslavia, coming to Canada, living here—everything you can remember to the present day."

Mitra took a deep breath. A little smile appeared on her face.

"Oh, my child! My days, weeks, months, and years are like a big pot full of fine sand mixed with some gravel. Memory is like a sieve; it gets twisted, shaken, swirled, and all the fine sand falls through, and disappears. Only some bigger pieces remain. So, I will try to answer all your questions as much as I can remember."

"Never mind, Baba. I am sure your memory is far better than any sieve," Sofija said. She grabbed some writing paper off Mitra's table so as not to miss one moment. "Let us begin. Here is my first question: what was it like growing up? Try to remember as far back as you can. How did you spend your time?"

"Mmm mmm," Mitra seriously tried to remember things that were more than 80 years old. "I can't remember very much but I can still vaguely remember some things when I was maybe seven or even nine. I remember how we used to sit together inside our small kitchen. We had a long table and benches on each side that could seat 8 to 10 people. Most families had at least that many children, if not more. In our family we were mom, dad, grandma, grandpa, and four children. We did not have electricity or running water in the house. We had to burn wood in the stove. Only a few families in our village had a wood stove; most others had a hearth. For light we used candles. We used water from our well.

"Let me first explain about houses in our village so you can better understand our way of life in the '40s, when I was around 10 years old. Try to understand how simple and frugal our lives were. The houses in our village were very small, one level, about 400–500 square feet in size, with stone walls, and rough wooden floors. The houses were no more than five metres tall including the chimney. The hearth was placed close to one wall, about three to five feet away from the wall. There was a wall called *Perda* several feet long and the height of a person, built by the main door entrance on the side of the hearth, to prevent cold from coming directly in contact with the people sitting around the hearth.

"People sat around the hearth on small, low wooden stools supported by three wooden legs. One or two large chairs, which had arms and a back rest, were used by the oldest person in the family. These chairs were called *katriga*.

"There was a strong steel bar attached to the inside wall of the house, stretching out and above the centre of the hearth. A strong chain was attached to the bar to hold a heavy cooking pot. The chain swung back to the wall when not in use.

"There was a round wooden table similar to a large coffee table, used as the main table for family meals. A big wooden bowl held food for the whole family. Each person had their own wooden spoon with long handles. Everybody sat around the table and ate from the same bowl, grabbing food from the bowl with their wooden spoons.

"Bread was baked in the middle of the hearth. The cinder was cleared to the sides and bread would be put on the clean brick floor. It would be capped with a round steel dome, called a *peka*, with the cinder mounded all over it. Goat meat, mutton, and pork were smoked above the hearth, usually in winter time.

"These houses had one, two, or even three cubicles for some privacy where people slept, especially married couples.

In larger families of 10 to 15 children, many would sleep either in the barn on the hay, or among small animals, which was the warmest place in the winter. Beds were very simple, if they could be called beds. They were made of four wooden poles, with a platform on top of that, and another wooden board to prevent the person from rolling out of bed. The mattress was a sack filled with some hay; the same for pillow cases. The cover was made from coarse domestic wool called *biljac*. It was rough and warm. This was the way we lived in the early '40s.

"Village life provided very simple and basic comfort; it did not contain any luxury. When strong winds were swirling, they pushed smoke back into the house. Men knew how to prevent that from happening by building smart chimneys."

Mitra looked up at Sofija, thinking she was hungry because her expression seemed sad. But Sofija was sad thinking about her baba's poor childhood.

Mitra asked her if she'd gone home for dinner.

"No, Baba, I didn't. I came straight from my class here."

"Are you hungry, dear?"

"Yes, I am."

"Why don't you go to get something to eat while I take a little walk."

Sofija welcomed Baba's suggestion, because although her story was interesting it was also upsetting to Sofija. She nodded.

"That's a good idea. We'll continue with your life story after. Do you want me to bring you something, Baba?"

"A small coffee, please," Mitra said.

When Sofija left, Mitra got up and started walking around. She felt more stiff than usual. She could not figure out why one day she felt pretty good, and could walk well, but the next day, she was uncomfortable and stiff.

"Oh, what can I do about that?" Mitra exclaimed, "I have not been old before, so these feelings are new for me."

Old age came with new experiences that made her unhappy. Mitra shook her head, saying to herself, "What is the matter with me? I have much better things to think about."

Chapter 5

As Mitra walked around, her cane slipped from her hand and fell on the floor beside the door. She was not able to bend down and lift it up. Sofija quickly entered the room and not seeing the cane, she tripped on it and fell forward on her face. One coffee spilled everywhere. Sofija quickly picked up the other coffee. A sandwich went under Baba's bed and a donut fell into the spilled coffee.

Sofija quickly cleaned up.

"Sorry about the accident. I'm all right. I'll clean up everything."

The nurse downstairs had heard the big thump. She quickly came up to see what had happened. The nurse thought that Mitra had fallen. Since the door was still open, the nurse walked in.

"Are you all right, Mrs. Milutinovic?"

Sofija smiled.

"Great-grandma is all right; I fell, not Baba."

"You—a young agile person—fell?" the nurse wondered out loud.

They explained to the nurse what had happened. The nurse asked Sofija if she was hurt.

"No, no, I am not hurt, but our coffee spilled. Sorry about that."

Sofija wanted to call the nurse by her name, but at that moment she could not remember it. The nurse said to Sofija not to worry about cleaning up. She would ask the housekeeper to do it.

"You two ladies go to the community sitting room for a few minutes. All will be cleaned up."

Sofija offered to help again.

"No, please, go with your great-grandmother and keep her company. I will let you know after everything gets cleaned up."

"That's fine," Sofija said. "Thank you very much."

"You're welcome."

They went to the common sitting room. They were lucky no one was there so they enjoyed their privacy.

All of a sudden Baba started laughing. She was happy Sofija wasn't hurt and her granddaughter's fall reminded her of a funny anecdote her father had told her when she was about Sofija's age. Sofija asked Baba why she was laughing.

"I am laughing because your incident reminds me of a story. A man was felling a large tree, which was on the side of a small hill. The man wanted the tree to fall towards the top of the hill. To ensure that happened, he tied his donkey to the tree hoping the donkey would pull the tree in the desired direction. But gravity pulled the tree down to lower ground. The force of the falling tree flipped the donkey over and down the hill. The poor man looked at his donkey and said, 'small animal, but a real big jump.' When I saw how you fell, I thought the same when you appeared at the door and quickly ended up on the other side by the window."

"So, Baba, you think I'm a donkey?"

"No, no, I don't. Your fall made me remember that story. My father told us a lot of fairy tales. We kids were curious about how the donkey jumped and if he was hurt. Sometimes in the winter, we would spend hours listening to our father's fairy tales. I loved these times because there was a lot of laughter. As we get older, more and more we think of our childhood—the best time in life," Mitra said.

"Baba, are you sad being here? Is that why you are thinking so much about your childhood?"

"No, no, I am not sad because I am here. This is the best place for me in my situation. Thank God for my good friend, Evica. She makes me laugh a lot."

Baba told Sofija about the Italian and Dutch ladies at the dinner table. When Sofija heard the story, she felt sorry for the Italian woman because she couldn't converse with people.

"So, Baba, it's not altogether bad here."

"Right, right," Mitra confirmed.

Just as they were laughing, the nurse came by to tell them that everything was spotlessly clean now. They could go back to Mitra's room. Sofija thanked the nurse and the nurse left.

The room was all nice and clean as if nothing had happened. Sofija asked her baba if she should go and get them fresh coffees.

"Never mind about the coffee," Mitra answered, "Sit down, we can have nice talk without coffee."

When they sat down, Mitra asked Sofija again whether she was sore anywhere from the fall.

"No, Baba, I'm not sore at all. I told you that already. Please do not worry about me all the time. I'm a big girl and can take care of myself."

When both of them settled down, Sofija asked Mitra if she felt comfortable enough to start their new project. She'd forgotten already about the project and asked, "What project are you talking about?"

"Baba, you forgot we started your life story. Did you already forget about that?"

"Fine, go ahead and ask me questions that interest you," Mitra said.

"Baba, how far was the nearest city from your village?"

"About 16 kilometres."

"Oh, that was not too far," Sofija exclaimed.

"Sure, it wasn't according to today's transportation, but at that time walking that distance on a rough and dusty road was very far."

"Oh, sorry, Baba, I must be stupid to suggest that."

"Oh, no, no, you are not stupid, but only a little too slow to calculate the difference in two very different situations."

"Yes, that's right, Baba. How often did you go to the city?"

"Maybe, I was there only two to three times. Once, I was sick and an ambulance took me to the hospital to see the doctor."

"How did you feel that first time in a hospital?"

"I was too sick to think of anything else but my pain."

"Were you that sick, Baba?"

"Yes, I was very sick."

"What was wrong with you?"

"I don't really know. Doctors did not tell their patients what was making them sick," Mitra said.

Sofija's eyes opened wide.

"Oh my God! How could a doctor be so insensitive?"

"Even if a doctor would mention some technical name of an illness, who at that time would know what it was? There was no literature or cell phones to find out what the symptoms were. You would be very lucky if some remedy the doctor prescribed helped you. If a patient died, people would usually say, that was his time to die."

"Baba, did your way of life gradually improve, or was it always the same?" Sofija asked.

"Our lives were significantly improved after my father bought a wood stove. It was one of the few wood stoves in the village. Most other people couldn't afford to purchase one. As I already mentioned, we sat in the kitchen because it was the warmest place in the house and also the brightest area. It felt comfortable and warm. You could smell the wood. Often times we would bake some potatoes on the top of the stove. There was enough light from the lamp, which was filled with oil and closed at the top with a wide cut for a good-sized wick. On the neck of the wide container was a glass cylinder about 10 inches high, which was wide at the bottom and narrow at the top. That was the only light we had in the house."

"It's like a camping lantern," Sofija guessed.

"Yes, yes, but different in shape," Mitra said.

"So, you sat around the stove and played," Sofija asked.

"We had plenty of time in winter to be lazy. We were more relaxed compared to summer when there was a need to get things done on time and prepare enough food for the family and the livestock."

"Baba, how did you feel being cramped up in such a small place?"

"Generally, it was all right except some winters were very cold, especially when the north wind carried a stream of cold air called *bura*. It was particularly hard for old people and children. They fought to survive, but often lost the battle.

"We felt very good. Nobody complained about space. We never had any luxury, but at the same time we never knew anything better existed. That is why we were satisfied and even happy with our way of life. We played our old-fashioned games that our predecessors played and taught to us."

"What kind of games did you play?"

"In the wintertime, we played, 'prstenkanje.' The game required two or more people and usually no more than six, three on each team. The main point was to find a small object, usually a ring, in a team member's enclosed fist. An agreement was made between the teams who would start first. The team that started first had the object in their possession.

"They hid their hands underneath a table or some other cover so that their opponents could not see what they were doing. They placed the object into one of their player's closed fists.

"The other team tried to locate the object. They did some calculations among themselves in order to get some vibes from the team who had the object. They studied body movements—twitching fists, eyes, changes in their facial expressions and so on.

"Once the team agreed which fist held the object, then one of them asked the question as he pointed his finger at the fist, 'Give me, us, this fist.' If the object was found in that fist, they had to give it to the searching team. If the object was not in that fist then the hiding team kept the object, scored a point and continued to play.

"The searching team could also use the system of elimination by using a different phrase asking, 'Let go of this fist,' and pointing a finger at the fist. The player opened up that fist. If the object was in that fist then the entire hiding team opened up their fists, kept the object, scored a point and kept playing.

"If the object was not in that fist, the elimination process kept going forward. The only way they could get the object was by asking the right question: 'Give me, us, this fist,' and actually finding the object in that fist. The funniest times were when some small children were on the team. They would usually insist the object should be in their fist, but they would be very easily discovered. We always used to tell kids, 'Look down, don't look straight at the person looking for an object.' The losing team were given some kind of penalty."

"That was nice, Baba. Did you also play with other kids from the village?"

"Of course we did," Mitra said. "We all interacted with one another all the time, especially during winter. Older men would sometimes gather in one of the homes. Most of the times they discussed the previous year's crop, how they could have improved yield, and how the weather played a part in it. They learned a lot from each other's experience. They would talk about making some changes to improve the yield. But this was only talk. I never saw them changing much of anything. They always did the same thing.

"To experiment with the crop was a dangerous game, because it could be damaged and lost. In that case, starvation was at the family's doorstep.

"Many times, if something was happening in the village, they talked a lot about that. For example, if somebody behaved badly and hurt somebody else. They would usually approach the person and ask them not to do that, even warning them of the consequences they could suffer for doing a bad thing. I remember, I heard my grandfather and his companions talking about our neighbour, Luka, who had just died.

"One of the older men from the group said, 'He died like an animal and he lived like one. Nobody is going to miss him, not even his family.'

"My grandfather said to him, 'Mile, how can you talk like that about a dead person? Talking like that is a sin.'

"Mile answered, 'How can it be a sin, if it's the truth?'

"'But you don't have to talk about him in that way. It is for God to decide what to do with him, not for us,' my grandpa said.

"'I'm only helping God to make a good decision, that's all,' Mile answered.

"When they had enough talk for that night, they would play a game called *sije*, an Italian game between two men. Each man closes one fist. As the players straighten out one or more of their fingers, each says a number at the same time. Whoever guessed the correct number of the outstretched fingers combined from both players' hands, wins.

"Women and older girls were always busy with their handiwork. They did a lot of knitting, darning, crocheting, making yarn, and mending in order to make garments last as long as possible. It was costly to buy new garments, or it required a lot of work to make something from our own domestic wool. Our wool was very coarse because of the kind of sheep that was suitable for our climate. Some women were very professional in mending.

"It was a shame to see a woman sitting in one place for too long a time and not doing women's handiwork. It also reflected badly on her daughters of marrying age."

"It seems that men mostly relaxed and let you women work, which wasn't really fair," Sofija said.

"Oh, no, no, men had their own chores. They looked after the livestock and sometimes minded the sheep but usually sheep minding during winter was women's, or young people's, duty."

"What was cooked for your main meal? When did you eat it?" Sofija asked.

"The main meal was always between one and two in the afternoon. There were usually three different types of food for the main meal: first, sauerkraut with smoked pork; secondly, a thick broth-like soup made of beans, barley, and potatoes; and third, corn meal eaten with milk, sour milk or melted cheese. In the morning we would have a glass of milk, a piece of cheese and bread. We had a similar meal in the evening."

"Did you have any snacks between meals, like cakes and pastries?" Sofija asked.

"Of course we did. We even had chips and cookies," Mitra joked, laughing. "No such thing. Our special treat was when our mother would make us pastry similar to what they call beaver's tail here. Boy, were we happy with that special treat!"

"Is that all the games you played?" Sofija asked.

"Oh, no, no, we played a lot of different games but a very popular one in the winter time was 'tovar gre.'"

"How was that played, Baba?"

"Easy. We would mark initials on the floor with a stick or a finger. Paper was expensive and hard to get. The player who went first was blindfolded with a kerchief. Another player with the stick points at the initials and says, 'Tovar gre?' The blindfolded player can give two answers, 'go on,' or 'stop.' On whoever's initial he stops, that person is given a penalty by the blindfolded person.

"Sometimes, to make the game more interesting, the person who points at the initials stays mostly on the blindfolded player's initial, but since the blindfolded player does not know on whose initial it is, he says stop. If it is his initial, he has to carry out a penalty and again be blindfolded. Most of the time it was funny, but sometimes the person would be angry because, he or she would complain of cheating.

"Other times we would play the 'silence' game. This would mostly be initiated by our parents because they would have had enough of our loud laughter, talking, and arguments. Usually, parents would give something small as a reward to the person who kept silent for the longest time. Sometimes we would last half an hour or longer even though we teased each other with some gestures or tricks. Our parents had the ultimate reward, enjoying a few peaceful moments."

"That was really nice, Baba. You invented your own ways of entertainment, which were simple and involved the whole family."

"Yes, my dear, we had to, and we truly enjoyed it."

Sofija waited for a moment for Baba to keep on telling her the next story, but Baba kept silent for a bit, remembering things they used to do as children.

"What other things did you do or play?"

"We were always occupied by something. Often times we were entertained by our brother who had a beautiful voice. He sang to us from the book of old ballads and fairy tales."

"Was that your special play night?" Sofija asked.

"Yes, it was," Mitra replied. "And a pleasant one, without any cost involved."

"You were really lucky, Baba."

"Yes, we were lucky and very happy," Mitra confirmed. "Two ballads were my favourite; one was about the marriage of a handsome prince, and the other was about Marko Kraljevic."

"If they were your favourites, I really would like to hear about them."

"The handsome prince decided to get married. He was looking for his future bride throughout his kingdom and outside. He finally found the girl who fulfilled all his dreams. The girl was stunningly beautiful. When the prince saw her, he was smitten by her beauty. The prince asked the girl's mother how her daughter became so beautiful, 'Did you sneak her from the sun? Or did you mould her from the gold or silver? Or did God give her to you from your heart?'

"The girl's mother answered to the prince, 'I did not sneak her from the sun; I did not mould her from gold. I did not mould her from silver, but God gave her to me from my own heart.'"

"Oh, that is beautiful fairy tale," Sofija said.

"But wait, wait, the story isn't finished yet," Mitra said.

"I'm glad there is more to that beautiful story. Please go on, Baba."

"The wedding party's road home went through a thick forest where a fairy lived. Old ballads claimed that there was never a living entity more beautiful than the fairy who lived in those woods. When a fairy saw how beautiful the bride was, she became very jealous. She killed the bride with her bow and arrow. The prince was devastated at losing his beautiful bride. He ordered his wedding party to find a river and dig the grave beside it, plant some roses, and make a nice sitting bench.

"When all was done the prince spoke, 'Whoever is thirsty let them have a drink, whoever is tired let them have a rest, whoever is young let them pick a flower, and whoever has died, let them rest.'"

"Is that all there is to the story?"

"Yes, it is the end of the story."

"Poor prince; how devastated he must have been to lose his perfect love," Sofija said.

"But that is why the story is so meaningful: it deals with the two opposing feelings: love and sorrow," Mitra said.

"I agree with you, it is a beautiful story. Are you going to tell me now about Marko Kraljevic?"

"Marko Kraljevic was a descendent of a royal family. He always fought for justice and stood for vulnerable people."

"How does that story go and why did you like it so much?"

"I like it because it deals with justice and heroism. It reveals the character of his mother and how strong and just she was. We can describe Marko's life, and what he stood for, in a couple of sentences so you can understand a little better about him.

"Marko Kraljevic was a mythical character. He was the only child of his parents. Marko had never married. He was very brave, and always spoke openly and truthfully. He rode his dappled horse. In this story he deals with four powerful figures who strive to inherit the kingdom from the king who passed away quite young, leaving behind a very young son.

"Because of the dead king's underaged son, an opportunity arose for powerful men to contest the young prince's inheritance. Marko's father and his two brothers were contesting the dead king's son's, the young Uros's, right to the throne.

"They first sought out the priest who had given the king his last rites to find out who'd inherited the kingdom. The priest hesitated to talk about the late king's last will, because he was afraid the angry contestants might kill him. He told them he didn't ask the king to whom he was leaving his kingdom; instead they talked only about the king's sins. The priest told them that Marko Kraljevic wrote in a book all the things the king told him.

"'Marko is the only one who can tell you to whom the king left his kingdom,' he said.

"Marko was not afraid to speak the truth. He feared only God, not any man. The contestants sent the messenger to ask Marko to come over to resolve the issue about the kingdom. Before Marko set out on the road, his mother, Jevrosima, begged her son not to lie. This part to me was emotional. Jevrosima tells her son, Marko, 'My son and my only child and the love of my life, I beg you not to say a lie. Do not allow your mother's milk you sucked curse you for telling lies, but tell the truth, God given truth. It is better for you to lose your life than to lose your soul lying. Disregard what your father and your uncles mean to you in the face of the truth.'

"Marko understood his mother. When he arrived near the church where the contestants were waiting for him in their tents, every one of them except the young Uros raised their voices to flatter Marko.

"Marko's father, who already had his own kingdom, said to Marko, 'If you say the kingdom belongs to me, it will be yours after me.'

"His one uncle said, 'If you say that the kingdom is mine, I will share it with you.'

"Another uncle started to tell Marko how good he was to him when he was a baby. For that reason, Marko should say the kingdom belonged to him.

"Marko didn't pay attention to their flattering words as he was passing each of their tents, but went straight to the young Uros. Marko opened the book and read the late king's last will, showing who was going to inherit his kingdom. First, he cursed his own father, telling him, 'May your own kingdom be reduced to nothing, because you wanted to seize what rightfully doesn't belong to you.'

"He also cursed both of his uncles for lying in order to steal someone else's kingdom.

"He turned to young Uros, telling him that the book said the kingdom belonged to him.

"'Don't you see? God has shown that the kingdom should belong to him; the father left it to his son.'

"When Marko's father heard this, he started cursing his son, Marko, and chasing him around the church with his sabre. Marko didn't want to raise his hand to his father, so they ran around the church three times. He almost caught Marko. Suddenly, a voice from inside the church told Marko to escape into the church.

"The church door opened, and Marko ran inside. His father swung his sabre wanting to slay Marko. Instead of hitting Marko, he struck the church's closed door. Blood began to flow from the door. That was testament that God had intervened in their lies and greed. That was the end of the story. Young Uros inherited his father's kingdom."

"I like this one, but I like the first one much better," Sofija said.

"I am not at all surprised, dear. The other one is closer to your heart."

"What else did you do during winter, Baba?"

To be funny, Mitra said, "We went to McDonald's."

"Oh, Baba, don't be so funny. There was no such thing when you were a child."

"You are right, dear, and if there was McDonald's, I would never see Canada."

They both laughed.

"When the weather wasn't good outside, we spent a lot of time in our barns where we kept hay for the animals' winter feed. We would go to the barn and jump down into hay, sit and talk about different things like which kid got punished and which one escaped the punishment. At about age 10, we girls started talking about the boys.

"We didn't get much snow and within a day, the snow would melt. Certainly, we fought in the snow; we loved it. But there was one problem; nobody had boots, so our feet became wet quickly. We had a lot of colds."

"I bet you did, poor you. And yet you were happy," Sofija said.

"Yes, we were happy because we didn't know any better. As we got to around 15 years of age, boys and girls were separated. Boys were looking out to see a beautiful girl, and if they were from a good family that was a big bonus. They cruised around through our village and also the neighbouring ones. They used to sing songs through the evening as they travelled from place to place.

"Girls didn't go far from their homes. Sometimes they gathered in one of their homes to have some fun, do some handiwork, and talk about boys."

Sofija got irritated; she felt sorry for the girls and what they had to go through when they were still children themselves.

"How can any mother feel good about putting their daughters through such ordeals and at the same time watch them suffer at the hand of male dominance?"

"What is the matter with you Sofija? We're not talking about the present-day system, but 80 years ago."

Sofija raised her brows thinking, "Maybe Baba is right in one way. But why should women be subservient to men? They should have the same rights as men."

Mitra looked at Sofija questioningly.

"So, you think it is the right approach in marriage—if you don't approve of whatever your husband does, wave a finger at him and start threatening him because you demand equal rights. You think it is the most important thing to be liberated. If you want your liberation, then you should not get married.

"I suggest, Sofija, don't get married if you want to be totally liberated. Remember, both husband and wife carried responsibility for their family based on the system that was centuries old. Is it possible to turn that around in a short span of time? I don't think so," Mitra argued.

"That is why we have social crises today," Mitra continued, "because of broken families; when spouses consider themselves just partners instead of husbands and wives. The worst thing about broken marriages is when children are tossed around from one side to the other, from one parent's new companion to the other parent's new companion. What kind of security or stability do children have growing up in such situations?

"How can you expect these children to have their own solid marriages, when they were raised in broken ones? I say again, Sofija, if you want total freedom and total independence—stay single. In marriage, both sides have to compromise; don't expect everything to be perfect. Expect some rough moments. It's worth it if you have children. Do it for their sake. You will be happy about it, seeing your children successful and happy."

"What about us women being happy and having freedom even when we are married?" Sofija asked.

"I don't understand you, Sofija. Our opinion on this subject is so far apart. We better leave this subject alone. I don't want to create a rift between us," Mitra said.

"That would never happen," said Sofija. She jumped up and hugged and kissed Mitra to reassure her that nothing could tarnish their relationship.

"This is a perfect example of how rifts start in families—differences of opinion. When those opinions become more important than anything else, the clash and breaks will happen," Mitra said.

"Baba, you are right. We should leave this subject and talk about something else we agree on."

"Nothing is wrong with different sensible points of view, but I don't find much sense in today's society because the basic structure is lost. In my time, life was far simpler than yours today. Children were taught early in life to help however they could. Smaller children were given simpler and lighter duties around the house; when they grew older, they were given more responsible chores."

Chapter 6

"What about boys, Baba? They sat, and girls waited on them like some kind of kings. You said that girls had to do everything?"

Mitra got mad.

"Please, stop with that or everything will be stopped. You are so stuck on your equality, it makes me sick."

"Please, Baba, don't get mad, please continue," Sofija said.

"Boys didn't stay idle either; they were getting instructions from their grandfathers and father. As soon as they were strong enough, they were working the fields learning how to plow and sow wheat and corn. They were taught all the responsibilities very early in life in order to be good family providers.

"People depended on the crop for their livelihood. Summertime was always busy. The livestock had to be watched because there were no fenced-in properties where livestock could graze without being watched.

"Our small plots of land were scattered due to a generational divide between siblings. Animals grazed away from the crops—usually somewhere in the bush or on pastures. In the summer, after the crop was harvested, gathered, and taken away—livestock would be grazing in that area. That was the easiest time for shepherds to watch their livestock.

"We used to have so much fun roasting corn, playing different games, or simply goofing around."

"Baba, from what you have told me, I don't know what to think of your lives at that time. It seems very harsh even though you claim that you had a lot of fun."

"Yes, of course it was tough but even here in Canada in the '40s and '50s, life was not as good and easy as it is today. Situations have changed everywhere. Life in my village has changed big time. Even if they live in the village, people now also work somewhere in the city. I was very surprised by how much life has changed there. Now, they have farm equipment to use, cars to drive around."

Just when Sofija wanted to ask more questions, Mitra's friend Evica came in.

"Oh, your granddaughter is here. That's very nice that she visits you quite often—good girl."

"Yes, I'm a very lucky grandmother," Mitra said.

"I can see you're busy with your granddaughter so I'm going now to bingo. See you later on."

Knowing how much her baba liked bingo and how long the two of them had been sitting, Sofija said, "It would be better if you go and play bingo with Evica. We have had enough talk for today. We will catch up next time. I have to go and study for my test, which is coming up in a couple of days."

"You always have tests, or do you use them as an excuse, so you don't have to spend too much time with me. Are you sure, my sweetie?" Mitra teased.

"Yes, Baba, I'm very sure, that's exactly what I will do," Sofija said.

Mitra asked Evica to wait for her. Sofija kissed her great-grandma, telling her she would come back in a couple of days.

As Sofija was leaving the centre, she began to analyze what her baba had talked about, and how different her life was from

Sofija's own. She thought about how Baba had reasoned that such a life had been normal and quite happy. Sofija still could not fathom that this could be true.

Is it possible that one could feel pretty good about such a state of life? Mitra had talked before about her young life and her growing up in the village, but Sofija only brushed it off as something mentioned in passing or as not being true. Sofija was very happy she started this conversation with Baba, writing it down in her notes to keep a record of Baba's life.

A couple of days later, Sofija came back to see Baba. She brought her a bunch of yellow daisies to cheer her up, but very seldom did Baba need cheering up. Most of the time she seemed to be in a good mood; she hid her negative feelings from Sofija and convinced herself that everything was all right. Once Sofija asked her how she could always be in a good mood even when she should not be.

Mitra would look straight at her.

"And what would I get in being miserable—nothing, really nothing. Life cannot be smooth all the time; we need to experience some bumps to remind us that real life constitutes a mixture of everything."

Sofija looked at her baba with pleasure and admiration.

"So how are you feeling today, Baba? Are you ready to tell me some more stories about your life?"

Mitra smiled, saying, "I thought you might have enough information about my youth already, but it seems you want to squeeze out all my memories before I forget them completely."

"Not a chance, Baba. Your brain is that of a young person. You should be very proud of your cognitive ability."

"Now, I would like to know what cognitive means. I know I've heard it somewhere, but since I don't use it often when I converse, I have forgotten."

"Cognitive means your intellectual understanding of life's realities."

"Oh, my dear, I don't know if you should go that far because I am starting to forget things and pretty soon my cognitive ability will vanish."

"Not a chance of that, unless you double your age, Baba. Tell me more about your life; I'm sure you've got more things to tell me," Sofija said.

"Us kids liked summer. It was more comfortable and easier to do everything, either work or play. We were not inside the house much in summer except for meals and sleep. Winter and summer each had their special meaning and fun," Mitra said.

"Was it very hot in summer, Baba?"

"Yes, it was. There were days when it was pleasant, but other times it would be awful, especially during the night. One could not sleep in such heat."

"What did you do? Did you put on the air conditioner?" Sofija was laughing as she said this.

"Of course we did, by waiting for the weather to cool down," Mitra answered with laughter.

"So, Baba, you had a very smart air conditioner." Sofija laughed again as she said this.

"Of course," Mitra answered, laughing. "Everything around us was smart. We did not interfere in the natural cycles we experienced."

"I believe it was a very hard life," Sofija said.

"Yes, it was, but as I said before, we did not know any better and we always found ways to survive and have fun too."

"What did you do during the summer?"

Mitra took another deep breath.

"Oh, my dear, you want me to go through that now?"

"Of course I do, Baba. Please tell me everything you remember."

"In summertime, we kids liked to play in the grass barefoot, especially after the rain. We used to splash in puddles and sometimes we pushed each other into the puddles and mud. We were punished for that by our parents because there weren't any other garments for us to put on. We only had two sets of clothes. Washing was expensive because we had to buy soap."

"How were you punished, Baba?"

"A slap on the bottom, or a twig or more across the palms."

"Oh, Baba, you children had it very hard."

"We also played a lot of hide and seek. It was perfect terrain for such a thing. We could easily hide in low bushes and would not be found easily. That was a lot of fun. Sometimes we girls would get pinched by the boys but that was normal and accepted. Rarely was there sexual intercourse between a girl and boy because that would be severely punished. We would get angry at each other, but that would not last too long."

"How can such behaviour by the boys be normal?" asked Sofija.

"In our eyes it was considered that males were a little mischievous towards females."

"Is there still such a thing over there?"

"Perhaps there is. But now that is restricted. They are all being Americanized," said Mitra.

"Baba, from what you are telling me kids were punished too much and severely, for no good reason."

"Spanking was our parents' way of teaching kids not to do the same bad thing again."

"Did it work?"

"You bet it did, because the second punishment for the same wrong was much harsher. The best time to teach kids hard lessons is at an early age, rather than wait when they were grown up—too late then!!!"

Sofija again said, "It was awful and cruel, Baba."

"No, no, we did not think so; we accepted it and considered that it had to be done that way. We did not beat kids to harm them. Once, I was playing 'buttons' with several of my girlfriends. I was the youngest in the bunch. The older kids had an advantage over me because they could play better or at least they could manipulate me more.

"They coaxed me to tear two buttons off my garment in order to be able to play. At the end of the game, they won both of my buttons. When I came home, I was punished for doing such a stupid thing. Two buttons were very expensive to buy at that time. That was an extremely good lesson for me not to do that again. I never did."

"How old were you, Baba, at that time?"

"I am not sure, but maybe seven to nine years old."

"Did you know you were going to be punished on account of your lost buttons?"

"Of course I knew. I was punished one more time. It happened during winter. I got it really good that time, so much so I have never forgotten it. I was about 12 or 13 years old. One morning, my father had to go somewhere, but before he left, he told me to look after the cattle, to feed them and give them water to drink. Usually cattle didn't go out of the barn if it was cold outside. As I mentioned before, it was usually the boys' chore to look after animals during the winter. My father always did that.

"My grandma always liked to remind us kids to do our chores. I was angry because she always had something to remind us children about. I didn't know that my father had already returned. She asked me several times if I had fed the cattle, which I had, but she asked me again and again. I got a little mad at her, and raised my voice, and told her angrily to stop asking me the same thing over and over again.

"As I was saying this to grandma, my father stepped in front of us. He asked me angrily what was going on between the two of us. 'I heard it all,' he said. I knew right away I was in trouble. He called me to come and stand in front of him. He asked me why I talked to my grandmother the way I did. I tried to explain, but he said, 'No matter what Baba says to you, she is older, and you don't raise your voice to elders, especially your grandparents or parents. I will not allow you to do that ever. You understand me?'

"'Yes, dad,' I said.

"He gave me a few twigs on my hand and warned me to remember not to do it again.

"'If you ever repeat the same thing your punishment won't be as light as this one.'"

"Did it hurt, Baba?"

"Yes, it did. I was bleeding from a couple of places because the twig was rough but, believe me, the punishment was nothing in comparison to my emotional suffering. I felt very bad for what I did to grandma, and for making my father angry at me."

"Grandma, these were terrible punishments for such small things."

"No, you're wrong, Sofija, it was the right punishment and I agreed with it then and even now."

"Baba, how could you agree with corporal punishment when kids get hurt?" Sofija asked.

"They get hurt a little, but it surely helps to keep them in line. I did the same with my children," Mitra admitted. "It didn't hurt them that much, but they learned a lifelong lesson not to do bad things. I did it to you a couple of times Sofija when I was babysitting you—look at what a smart and wonderful person you have become."

"No, you didn't do that to me, Baba."

"Yes, I did," Mitra confirmed. They both laughed on account of that.

"What other punishment was used on the kids?" Sofija asked.

"That was the punishment used for bigger offences. For smaller ones, you were told with raised and angry voices to stop doing whatever it was your parents or grandparents did not approve of. It was usually fathers who disciplined children with the bigger punishment. Mothers' punishments were usually lighter—a smack on the behind or a little whack here and there, but nothing like what fathers did."

"Did you punish kids by putting them in the corner or taking privileges away from them?"

"No, we didn't do anything like that. That would have been a waste of time."

"No, Baba, it would not have. That's the way kids are disciplined today. It works pretty well on the kid's behaviour. Why should little children be punished physically? That's very wrong, Baba."

"You are a stubborn young person, looking at life from today's standards, which are different. I should have given you a little more whacking when you were small to teach you good manners."

Sofija knew that her Baba was joking; they both broke into laughter.

"Let's leave the past where it belongs. Believe me we were always afraid of making our parents angry. Losing a parent's confidence and love was the greatest fear and punishment. Elders were respected as if they were gods walking on earth," Mitra said.

"Oh my God, that is so different from the way society thinks today. You were punished too much as kids. It didn't teach you very much; only made you harsher," Sofija said.

"Not really," Mitra answered. "Why would it be so cruel? I was brought up under these rules and I also brought my children up that way. Are we so terrible in your opinion?"

"No, Baba, when I was saying that I didn't think of you, but of the people over there in your old country."

"What are you talking about, Sofija? I am one of those people; so are many of us."

Sofija realized that she had made a mistake for saying what she did. She apologized.

"You are right, Baba; grandfather Marko, uncle Stefan and aunt Sava are very good people. I only wish to be like them. What I said was wrong. Please forgive me, Baba."

"You are good, Sofija, I forgive you, but your judgements are too far from mine. Please, do not underestimate old people's experience. It is worth something, believe me. You will understand it when you reach my age. My dear Sofija, I am very proud of what a good and smart person you have become."

"Thank you, Baba. Coming from you, that's really a compliment."

"You are welcome."

"Baba, can you give me some insight on how the situation changed so much?"

Mitra got irritated by this question and said, "I am not a psychiatrist. My way of thinking is based on what I observe in everyday life. The changes in lifestyle, compared to when I was growing up, are unbelievable, especially technological changes. But people have also changed along with it. The basic, fundamental social values declined, especially in the family because material values took precedence—the family fell behind.

"Children's feelings are natural and the same now as before. They desire continuous physical closeness with their parents, but instead of getting that, they get lots of toys, comfortable homes, cars, furniture, wardrobes, electronic gadgets. For that reason, children have to be raised in daycare or by babysitters. Everything has its price, my dear girl."

"How true, Baba, how true," Sofija confirmed. "How did kids behave with each other?"

"What do you mean how did we behave? Normally. Like kids always behave. We played a lot. Sometimes we fought. Sometimes we swore at each other. Something was going on all the time, but nobody took it too seriously."

Sofija first smiled and then asked, "Was there lot of harassment among children?"

Mitra smiled back, "Of course, we even hired lawyers to establish whose fault it was. What are you talking about, dear girl? Nobody paid much attention to such things unless something really bad happened. In that case, the parents of the offender would deal with it. Parents had the freedom to discipline their children how they wanted or needed. The law did not interfere with that unless the child was physically or mentally harmed. Kids were afraid of doing bad things because of the punishment they would receive.

"You need to know and remember one thing: people or families were shunned for doing bad things. This was considered a very big punishment. For that reason, everybody avoided doing bad things and tried to uphold social standards and morality. There were no lawyers. People did not have money to sue other people. It was even shameful to consider that."

Sofija excused herself, telling Mitra she had to be at her hairdresser's home for seven. She'd forgotten all about that appointment. She promised Baba she would be back soon and continue with their project.

When Sofija came back the next day, after she hugged and kissed her baba, she sat down across from her, looked into her eyes, and began with the question that was bugging her.

"Baba, you told me you deserved punishment for pulling off your buttons. You thought it was right to be punished?"

"Yes, of course it was right. I already told you that."

"Do you still think the same with your present-day point of view?"

"Probably not. My present situation and living standard have changed so much. How much does it cost today to buy a set of five to 10 buttons? But then as I told you, it was a very big deal. You cannot compare that time with now. My punishment was a warning not to repeat the same thing. I remember a short story I was told; a father sent his little son to bring him a bottle of wine. Before the boy was sent off, his father spanked him. A neighbour saw this and asked the man why he spanked his son who hadn't done anything wrong. 'This was to make sure he would be careful and not spill the wine,' said the father."

"Baba, please continue with your life story," Sofija asked.

"We played mostly in our village. During summer or in fall we used to fight with kids from another village. It was mostly verbal. We didn't like each other, and sometimes fought, throwing rocks at each other across the river. I remember one day my friend was hit by one of these rocks just above her left eye. She was lucky; if the stone hit her a little lower, she could have lost her eye. The blood was gushing all over her face. She was crying so much, afraid she was going to die. I tried to comfort her by reassuring her that the wound wasn't that big or deep. She continued crying and sobbing."

"What did you do for the girl?"

"I kept wiping her blood off with water and my bare hands. I didn't have any napkins like we have today. I took the girl to her house and told her mother what had happened."

"What happened then?"

"Her mother washed her wound and poured some domestic brandy over it to prevent infection. The brandy application was painful, like a needle. The girl screamed. Her mother kept saying to her, 'I told you not to go to the river and fight with bad children. See what happened to you! Thank God that rock missed your eye.' When you are a small child, you forget about fear because your desire pulls you to do things other children do."

"Poor girl," Sofija exclaimed. "Did her mother take her to see a doctor?"

Mitra smiled saying, "She jumped into a car and drove off to see a doctor. The nearest doctor was 20 kilometres away. The only way to get to the doctor was on foot or riding a donkey or riding in a cart pulled by horses. We used to have a lot of donkeys. Nearly every family had one or two. The terrain was rough to travel on. Donkeys were cheap to own, and they were able to carry a good-sized load over the rough terrain.

"It would have taken a few days to get to the doctor and back home. In severe situations an ambulance would come to pick up an ailing person. It was not easy to convey the emergency message. The nearest post office was five kilometres away. There was one ambulance. Lots of people died waiting to be helped by doctors. Many small children died from something that today would be easy to take care of, mostly because of infection, colds that would turn into pneumonia and fever. During summer, because we would go barefoot, we would be pricked by thorns and the wounds would get infected. My mother would take a leaf of Swiss chard from our garden. She would make it limp, then put a couple of drops of olive oil on it and apply it to the wound. She would tie it down with a piece of cloth. By the next morning, all the pus from the wound would be gone."

While Mitra was talking about different things, Sofija's mind was fixed on the young people's lives. She still could not comprehend how those aged 15 to 20 were thrown into full family responsibility and had families of their own. Sofija said to her, "Oh my God, Baba, how can they be thinking about such important things at that age? They should have fun and enjoy their youth."

"You have a one-track mind my dear. Remember, we are talking about different times and different situations. I know you cannot grasp that because you only know the system in which you live. Now, you go to school for a very long time, especially if you want to be a career woman. After school, you have to to work long and hard to establish your career. By that time, you are 25 to thirty years old. In my village girls or boys didn't even think of those things because it never existed for them. The only true existence for them was to get married and start a family.

"Married couples were very lucky if they were provided with some kind of dwelling and some land. Sometimes two to three families lived in one dwelling and shared everything. Everything was limited and if you could survive on what you had, you were lucky. I tell you again; you can't imagine how different my way of life was from yours. Things have changed rapidly everywhere in the last 70 years of my life."

Sofija was afraid she was going to make Baba mad and said, "I am sorry, very sorry, Baba. You are right; I cannot understand the difference between your life in the village and my life."

Mitra apologized to Sofija for being hard on her.

"Let's leave it for now. I'm not in the mood right now to rehash that time of my life."

Mitra took a rest while Sofija went to get coffee. Mitra thought, "How can Sofija comprehend such a life and such poverty with the comfortable life she is living now? I was hard on the girl. What is the matter with me that I cannot comprehend her inability to understand my life in the village? If I were in her shoes, I wouldn't do better. Now, it's even hard for me to comprehend that harsh life after experiencing a better life in Canada."

Sofija came back with two coffees, a different mood, and a question. "Baba, please tell me if life for people in your village ever improved?"

"Of course it did. I already told you that several times before. After the Second World War, things started to change. There was more interaction with people who were knowledgeable about how to improve our lives. People in villages became smarter. The Communist government was really helping the poor, especially orphaned children whose parents died in the war fighting for the Communists. They gave some of them free education. Many young men went into the cities to go to school or simply get a job. People who stayed in the village also found some ways to make more money, either going to the closest city for some work or raising and selling more animals. Life improved every day. Lots of houses now had wood stoves to cook on and keep the place warm in the winter.

"There was a woman in the village who started making very good mattresses stuffed with domestic wool. Soon people started having comfortable beds, nice wooden tables and chairs. No more wooden bowls, 'zdjela.' Nearly everybody had their own metal spoons, knives, and forks.

"Later, people began to build better and bigger houses, partitioned into several rooms. Things were changing rapidly. There was also a lot of help for families from the young men who went into exile after the war. They were able to send food and clothing using the Red Cross, but not money, because the Communist government didn't allow it at first.

"I remember how my grandma used to make woolen materials for blankets and garments and warm clothing for winter. This was a very skilled job. Only a few women knew how to lay down all the threads in two separate horizontal lines without breaks in them, which was called *snovanje*. When she took off all the threads of the stick, she would put them on the foot-loom, called *tara*. When the foot pressed down on the pedal, the lower and upper threads separated enough to put a spool with thread on it through them. Granny would pull the board towards her, press down with the foot again for threads to be locked together, and eventually the cloth would be born.

"Granny used to weave tapestry, costumes for men and women. They were very fancy and beautiful. This was the way life was lived 80 years ago when I was a very young girl.

"I remember my son Marko and daughter, Sava, used to complain once they started going to school that they were poor compared to some other kids in school, who were bragging about their expensive clothes. When I heard my children using the word 'poor' I was very upset, thinking about how they were talking. They didn't know what it meant to be poor. We never thought of ourselves as poor even during our worst times. Yet, my children, who had everything they needed and more, still considered themselves poor."

Chapter 7

After Sofija left, the next few days were without any special incidents. Mitra liked that. She talked to her family and her friends regularly. Everything was normal. When Sofija went back again, she continued with her questioning.

"Everything is very interesting, how you lived and worked to survive. Thank you, Baba, for all of that; if I make you mad sometimes with my questions and reactions, please forgive me. Who tended the sheep during the summer?" Sofija asked.

"Sheep tending was the younger children's or teenagers' job because the older ones had to work with the parents and learn to secure their future. Many times, we would stay out all day with our sheep or goats. This would happen if the weather was very hot. We would not bring our livestock home; instead we would take them to a heavily shaded area near some watershed. There would be 5 to 10 shepherds and all the animals would be flocked together. We would bring our lunches and stay there all day. We used to have lots of fun: playing different games, telling jokes, splashing each other with water.

"We would spend all day long playing different games and competitions: running, jumping, and stone throwing.

"We also played a game called *piljanje*."

"How was that game played?" Sofija asked.

"*Piljanje* was usually played between two or more people. It required five small rocks, the size of a hazelnut. Four rocks were always on the ground, while one rock was constantly thrown into the air. A player threw one rock up in the air, at the same time he had to grab however many rocks were on the ground, still catch the rock falling down from the air before it hit the ground. It started with one rock, which the player placed in front of him. The second time, two rocks were spread farther from each other in front of the player. The third time, they're spread even farther and the fourth time, they're spread as far from each other as the player can spread his arm. The player who successfully completed the entire task won the game."

"Were you good at it?" Sofija asked.

"Yes, I was pretty good. There were better players than me, but I was among the better ones. Look, I'm bragging about how good I was."

"No, no, Baba, that is not bragging, but telling the truth."

"Boys went into the river to swim in their own pants, girls didn't swim with boys. Nobody owned swimming suits. When it came time to move from under the shade, the animals initiated the move. They'd stand up and separate into their herds. Not one would go with a herd that wasn't theirs. At the same time, they began to move towards their dwellings as they kept on grazing. They sensed that the night was near. We usually returned home at dusk.

"The animals had to be milked because their udders would be full of milk. We helped how ever we could. Mother would prepare something to eat after everything was done and all the animals were in their proper places, secured and locked up. We usually didn't have heavy meals at night, only some cheese, bread, and lot of milk. The heavy meals were usually around 1:00–2:00 pm in the afternoon. We would go to sleep after supper. Every morning we would get up at five o'clock. We had to take animals to graze before it became hot. Our animals were very important to us. They were our livelihood."

"It seems you looked after them well," Sofija said.

"During the winter, our livestock would move into their enclosed areas, usually in the barn below the stored hay. We didn't have very many animals, usually two milking cows, 20 to 50 sheep, 10 to 15 chickens, two to three pigs, which were always killed in November. Meat would be cut up, salted, and hung high above the hearth to dry. The smell of smoked meat was wonderful. I still enjoy smoked meat and sauerkraut."

"Baba, you taught me to eat smoked meat and sauerkraut. I too like to eat that now. When was mating season for your sheep?" Sofija asked.

"Mating was in the fall. That part was really, really funny," Mitra said, "When mating started, rams began to challenge and fight each other. They fought fiercely, running towards each other at full speed, clashing head to head. Sometimes they bled, and wool flew off them as they hit each other with their horns. You could hear the horns crush against each other as the fight went on and on.

"Eventually, one of the rams would win the contest and earn the privilege to impregnate the ewe. The others would not challenge the winner anymore. Occasionally the losers tried to mate with a sheep if they saw the winner was farther away, but if he noticed them, no matter what he was doing— even if he was mating with another sheep—he instantly charged and attacked the loser."

"I find all of your stories very interesting, occasionally sad, and even funny too," Sofija said.

"I am telling you the truth about how it was as I was growing up, even though I question myself sometimes whether I should tell you the whole truth because it is too much for you to grasp about such a life."

"I know, Baba, and I appreciate that."

"But it is not so perfect today either because of a lot of turmoil and mistrust between men and women."

"Why do you say that, Baba? Today is much better than ever before," Sofija said.

"It is true about material things but not general respect in the family," Mitra said.

"No, I don't agree with you. People are polite and behave better than before. That is the way I see it and I believe it is true," Sofija said.

"If you insist, let it be the way you say, my dear girl. But even though our way of life was poor it was blessed with morality and respect."

"How can there have been better morality before? How do you measure yesterday's morality with today's morality?" Sofija asked.

Mitra looked at Sofija wondering what was happening with her.

"You don't have a clue about that," she said.

"Why don't you try me, Baba?" Sofija challenged.

"There is nothing to try you over. I'm telling you we worked for bare survival. Today you work more for your extra comforts. To achieve that, you sacrifice your morality. Social morality is material power nowadays."

"Baba, you twist things around."

"Not at all, I'm just telling it how it was and how it is now."

Sofija sensed that Baba wouldn't budge from her position. She was afraid she'd make her angry by pushing too hard. Mitra started explaining their chores.

"We each had to do our duty and work very hard in order to survive. We started early in March to prepare the soil for seeding. First the garden: lettuce, onions, cabbage, radishes. We planted a lot of potatoes in early spring, then a short time later, all the garden vegetables would be planted, except some more tender vegetables that could be harmed by cold, such as tomatoes, and cucumbers. In March, April, and May, all the heavy work began, cultivating the land for planting corn and other stuff. Younger healthy men did most of the heavy work, cultivating the crops a couple of times during the season to keep the weeds out and the soil porous so more moisture and oxygen would allow crops to grow better. Men also cut a large field of grass. They would leave it on the ground for a couple of days to dry up properly. After it was dry enough, it was gathered and piled up to form a dome, about 6 to 10 feet high. The height of the dome depended on the amount of grass.

"These domes were piled so skilfully so that no rain water could break inside them. They could stay in the fields for a month before they were transported into the barn. The grass would still have some of its green colour and be full of nutrients for animal feed. It also would be dry enough to protect it from mould. Usually, cattle and horses were fed hay. Sheep and goats would get some if there was snow on the ground, otherwise they would be taken out to find some grass or young twigs."

"Baba, I was afraid that men were free of work and that all the labour was done by women, but what you are telling me now, it seems like men worked too. Good that they were not free of labour. Good to hear for once that men pulled their weight," Sofija said.

"What are you thinking, how can heavy jobs be done without men? Of course, men worked, and they worked very hard all summer long. Who told you men didn't work?" Mitra questioned. Sofija didn't say anything more about men's work. She was afraid of upsetting Baba.

"Women harvested the wheat by hand, using a sickle, being careful not to harm the grains. Men gathered the wheat and put it in bundles that could be scooped between two arms.

The bundles were left on the field for a couple days to dry up. The crop had to be brought home by horse and buggy. Wheat had to be thrashed. Most households had a concrete, circular space about 20 feet in diameter, called *guvno*. The centre of the circle was a strong post with strong ropes attached to the post for two horses. At the end of the rope was a soft circular rope to fit around the horses' necks. At the end of the ropes was a strong hook that held the rope around the horses' necks.

"Horses were made to go in a circle one way until they got very close to the post, then they were turned around to go the opposite way until they got close to the post again. It was usually done on a very hot and rainless day. Sometimes it would take all day to complete the task because the horses had to be rested and afterward the wheat had to be separated from the hay with the help of the wind.

"Some people were very good at it while others were not so much. That was a fun time in some way because you needed a few men to do the work. A lot of good food was prepared for the working people that day, especially if the crop was plentiful.

"The day would be so busy but also so much fun for everybody, especially us kids. Wheat would be stored in the granary. Hay was usually spread underneath the animals for two reasons, to give them warmth in the winter, and to combine with animal waste to make manure.

"There were never ending chores to do. The entire crop had to be brought home by horse and buggy, corn husks separated. By the time all was done, winter would be upon us. Late in fall, pigs had to be slaughtered, cured, and hung up to dry over the hearth fire. Cabbage had to be put into a big wooden barrel to ferment and become sauerkraut. We used lots of barley for soups. Barley had to be pearled. Manure had to be spread on the fields and rotated into the soil. Wheat, barley, and garlic had to be planted in the fall. Everything had to be prepared in time before the first snow fall.

"We didn't have any large equipment; only shovels, picks, scythes, and sickles. The family who had able-bodied men were lucky because they finished their work on time and everything was good. Some families did not have such luck and they were struggling even though neighbours would usually help them. Each of these eventful days were celebrated with good food and fun, like wheat thrashing, corn husking, pig slaughtering, and other important events."

"What was the average lifespan at that time?" Sofija asked.

"Who knows? We were not thinking about that. My grandma used to say, 'live until God calls you home.' I think an average life was not much more than 60."

"People didn't live that long, Baba, because they suffered too much, and never had a doctor to help them out when they were sick," Sofija said.

"Oh my God," Mitra jumped in her seat. "Look at the way you're thinking and comparing everything to today's way of life. I told you we didn't feel that way. We were continuously interacting with each other, women with women, men with men. Outside of their houses, married couples were not sitting together."

"That is why there weren't many divorces," Sofija said, as she giggled.

"Maybe you are right in that."

"What about money or did you also make your own money like everything else?" Sofija asked laughing.

"I didn't know you could be so sarcastic," said Mitra jokingly. "No, we didn't make our own money. In most things we were self sufficient. We needed cash to fix houses, roofs, and to buy salt, sugar, coffee, and some clothes. We earned cash by selling our animals. Our animals were very valuable to us, as I mentioned before, for many things: meat, wool, manure to fertilize our soil and also for cash. We spent a lot of times looking after our animals."

"Sorry, Baba," Sofija said. "I forgot that way of life was 80 years ago."

"You are coming to your right senses finally."

"Yes, that is right," Sofija confirms. "It's about time I did."

They both laughed.

"Were people very religious and did you go to church very often?" Sofija asked.

"In a real sense, people were more spiritual than religious. My mother always prayed in bed before she would fall asleep. I listened to her prayers, how her voice would rise and fall, before falling asleep. I didn't understand completely the meaning of the prayers. Women prayed more than men. We didn't go to church often—only during important feast days. For example, if the church was dedicated to St. John then that day everybody in the vicinity would come to church and celebrate. We celebrated Christmas, Easter, and family day saints, weddings, christenings, and mourning for somebody who died and received the last prayer at the church.

"We had three major religions: Greek Orthodox, Catholicism, and Islam. There were smaller ones too. Nobody interfered in anybody's religion and how each group worshipped. Everybody went to their church and worshipped as they preferred. Once the Second World War came, everything completely changed on all sides because war propaganda turns people against each other. Your neighbours became your worst enemy instead of being good neighbours and friends. People became jealous of each other and sought revenge on each other, because of religion. Ever since that time, hatred took root among people with different religions and still continues with hatred today and I'm afraid will go on for a long time yet."

Sofija got out of her chair, asking grandma if she had enough talk for one day. Baba said she was all right with it because it brought back a lot of memories, some she likes to remember, and some she would like to forget, but talking about it refreshed her memory, especially personal ones of her family.

"Did my great-grandfather, your husband, Petar, have a similar upbringing to yours," Sofija asked.

"Yes, he did, but he was 11 years older than me and in 11 years, things changed a lot even in a small village like ours. Your great-grandpa wasn't much of a talker and when I used to bring the subject up, he would say, 'That's the way it was at that time and now we can only reflect on those memories, but let's leave it in the past.' That used to be his answer."

"Do you truly have happy memories of your childhood, Baba?"

"Yes, of course I do. We were happy most of the time. Nobody is happy all the time. There was not much comfort, nor luxury, but as I told you many times before, we didn't know better, we were happy. Everybody around us was the same."

"What about school?"

"After the Second World War school was mandatory. You had to go to school. Parents could not see any benefit in school, especially for girls. They thought it was Communist propaganda—nothing more. Parents would bribe officials in some cases to declare their child incapable of learning. They needed their daughters to mind the livestock. My parents didn't do that. We were grateful to them for that. I had to walk four kilometres every day to school over rugged terrain. I remember classes always started the same way. When the teacher walked in, all pupils rose, and all together said our allegiance to Tito and the Communist party. We had to sing the Communist hymn every morning and every time at the end of the class.

"We were always asked what we did during our absence from the school. We were always worried about what to say, because if you lied they would give you a failing mark. Our parents often reminded us not to say anything negative about the Communist party, especially Tito. They didn't like Tito's regime but they knew they could not do anything about it. One could have some freedom in abusing people, stealing or similarly bad things, because you could bribe officials and get off easy. But one could never, ever try to offend Tito or his party.

"The punishment was too severe and even bribes didn't work in that case. Nobody could save you from being punished. A number of years after the war, punishments eased off a bit, but it always remained a very threatening situation.

"I remember one old man in my village who was hard of hearing; he said something to his neighbour about the Communist party, which was not that drastic, but he ended up in jail for six months. People were rewarded for reporting to the authorities that others had said something bad about Tito and the party. A spy was in every village. The same man was a good friend with my parents prior to that incident. After that, he didn't want to talk to anybody. When my father was alone with him, he asked him why he didn't want to talk to him. He wasn't the one who reported him to the Communist authority, he only told him he could not trust anybody, 'even the ground underneath our feet talks.'

"That is how much people were frightened, because a lot of people ended up in jail, just like my parents' friend. The Communists always put an emphasis on the young people and brainwashed us to think the way they wanted us to think. We used to parade through the village carrying Communist banners and singing Communist propaganda songs. For us kids, it was very exciting. We didn't know any better. Our parents or other grown ups who understood the Communist propaganda were afraid to say anything disparaging to us because there were cases where even children turned in their parents. We kids followed Communist propaganda wholeheartedly, because we were convinced of it being a complete, glorious truth.

"Yes, there was a lot of brainwashing when I think of it now. We thought that our country was the richest, the most powerful, the cleanest, the freest in the world. Children believed that the Communist system was the best, but some older people did too, at first. Later on, they saw more clearly that Communism was a utopian way and camouflaged the real truth. They were very disappointed but couldn't do anything about it. Some took their own lives."

"Wait, Baba, what did adults do when they learned they were misled?"

"What do you think they did? Bite their tongues—nothing. What could they do? They could not jeopardize their life, especially the lives of their family."

"Wow, Baba! Was it that bad?"

"Oh yes, my dear, it was very, very bad at first when the Communists took over. Oh no, it was not an easy life. There were a lot of bribes. Everything you wanted you had to bribe somebody to get it. Sometimes Communists prosecuted people who took a lot of bribes in order to slow it down. But such restrictions held for a while and started again soon after.

"I remember your grandpa and I went to visit Yugoslavia in the late '60s. We wanted to travel by train overnight to visit our relatives. We asked to get a sleeping coach, but we were told 'all sold out.' When we came outside and told that to my brother-in-law he asked, 'Did you offer the teller some money?' Your grandpa replied, 'No, why should I offer her any money? I'm paying for my ticket, is that not enough?' My brother-in-law replied, 'What do you think? This is not Canada. You don't get anything here without a bribe, *kapish*."

"Your grandpa swore at the system. My brother-in-law looked around to check whether anybody heard what your grandpa said. 'Please do not say anything like that while you are here—that is dangerous.' He asked great-grandpa Petar for 10 dollars and went inside to the teller and quickly came out with the sleeping cabin reservation. Grandpa and I were left dumbstruck. My brother-in-law said, 'This is the way our system works. Take it or leave it, as they say.'

"We discussed that when we came back to my brother-in-law's house. My husband said to his brother, 'Don't you people know that you are destroying your country with the way you are doing things?'

"'What is the matter with you, my brother?' answered my brother-in-law. 'Who cares about the country? You have to fend for yourself and your family, not think of the country. What can the country give you when all that is good and valuable is seized by those who are on top? You have to be careful not to talk negatively about the regime; otherwise you can get in trouble. There were lots of decent people who refused to be in that category at first but little by little they saw the light, and many changed.'

"Your grandpa and I were looking at each other, thinking we better listen and do what my brother-in-law suggested. There was truly a lot of good changes since I left in the midfifties. People lived better. We were surprised to find a lot of well-educated people. Your great-grandpa did not like anything because he left after the war ended and the Communist rule came in. He fought against the Communist party."

"Baba, are you sorry you came to Canada?"

"I was only 20 years old when I arrived in Canada. I did not know anyone, and I was very scared of everybody and everything. Your grandfather, my husband, was a very nice and affectionate man—his friends too—but they were strangers to me. I was very well looked after by your great-grandpa. He did not buy for himself, but he bought things for me: nice clothes, chocolates, and for a special occasion, flowers. I remember when our doctor told us we were going to have a baby; he said to your great-grandpa, "Mr. Milutinovic, you will soon be a father, congratulations. After that I became more relaxed and started to think more about my family's future and less about the things I had left behind.

"We were so excited; your great-grandpa more than me. I was still scared about how I was going to look after the baby. You cannot describe such feelings unless you go through it yourself. Yes, right after I came, I was sorry that I came to Canada and left my parents, friends, and lots of other things, but your great-grandfather and our coming baby made up for it. I was very lucky to have your grandpa's understanding. Slowly, I started to learn English and made some friends.

"The baby came. I was very busy looking after my baby, my house, and my husband. Loneliness and fear dissipated, and every day, week, month, and year brought big changes. I became very happy. When I left my country, everybody cried as if they were burying me. People in our village couldn't imagine they'd ever see me again or that the day would come when we could travel back and forth between Canada and Europe. Six years after, I went with my husband and our two children to visit for the first time. Everybody was envious of me and how perfect my family and I looked.

"After I had two babies, and after my first visit to my village, I became very happy with my family, and my new country,

Canada, and I was very glad that I was here. My life has been full, and I have no regrets whatsoever."

"Baba, how do you really feel at the present time? Are you disappointed in us, your family, because we did not keep you at home instead of putting you into an institution?"

"You didn't put me into the institution. This was my choice and mine only, not yours. No, child, I'm not disappointed in my family. I have a wonderful family and I'm sure if I insisted on being at home you would keep me home, no matter how hard it would have been for you. But let's be realistic. It would not go smoothly. I know you would not say anything to hurt me in any way. But we are not talking about one week, one month, or even one year, but who knows how many years I could live. Only God knows; I'm very happy, more than happy that I'm capable of making my own decisions."

Chapter 8

Sofija did not want to ask Baba again whether she truly was all right being where she was. Sofija knew she would get the same answer. Instead Sofija asked her if she would like to come home next weekend and enjoy spending time with them around the pool.

"I will teach you how to swim, Baba."

Mitra never learned how to swim because one time, when she was still a kid, her friend pushed her into the deep end. She told Sofija how she started to choke, probably because she was in a panic more than anything else. When Sofija asked who saved her she said, "Me, I saved myself."

"But how did you do that since you did not know how to swim?"

"My friends were yelling out to me, 'Come on Mitra swim, swim. You know how frogs move their legs, you can do the same.' I was grabbing water around me like crazy, trying to stay above the water and trying to push water down under me as if the water was a tree and I was trying to climb up. Boy, that was such a scary moment for me."

"Once you got out of the water, what did you do to your friend?"

"I tried to fight her but since she was older and stronger than me, I could not do anything. She just held my arms, so I could not move them. She kept saying to me, 'I did you a favour, teaching you to swim.' I was calling her all sorts of names out of anger, but she just kept on telling me, 'I pushed you because you were always afraid of water and the deep end; now you know you can do it and keep doing it.'"

Mitra never wanted to venture into the deep end after that experience. She would always stay in the shallow part of the swimming pool.

She smiled at Sofija, "You little brat, you know the story of my swimming lesson but if you were to push me now into the deep end, I'm sure I would not come out because my hands and legs could not extend and help me to stay afloat. But you know, Sofija, that would be a good and quick way to end the life of an old woman."

Sofija's eyes went wide, "Baba, what are you talking about? How can you say such a dreadful thing to me?"

"Sorry, my dear, for saying something stupid like that. I know you love me. I promise I will not say it again. Let's talk about something that is more pleasant."

"I agree with that, Baba."

Just as they were going to change the topic, a nurse came by with a beautiful bouquet of flowers.

"These are for you, Mrs. Milutinovic."

Mitra's eyes went wide seeing such a beautiful bouquet.

"Oh, my Lord, who sent me such beautiful flowers?"

While Mitra was opening the card to learn who sent them, Sofija was teasing.

"Aha, Baba, I did not know you have a secret admirer. I would have sworn you didn't have one, but now I'm not so sure. C'mon, c'mon hurry up—open it."

Sofija was trying to peek inside the envelope but Mitra covered it up in order to tease her. She pulled out the card from the envelope and when she saw the name of the sender, she had tears in her eyes.

"Mrs. MacDonald's daughter, she was my best friend and neighbour when I came to Canada.

"She was such a wonderful person and good friend. She taught me English. She is in a nursing home too. She is my own age. I am sure her daughter Sarah has sent these flowers in her mother's name. How wonderful to have a good friend. True friendship is worth a lot."

"Baba, it is very easy to be a friend with you. I wish I could find some people who are smart, good natured, and able to reciprocate good friendship in many important ways. But it is not so easy to do that," Sofija said.

"There are still a lot of good people in this world who have such qualities; you just have to look for them. Friendship goes through the test of time. The longer friendship lasts, the better it becomes. Once you go through such trials and errors together, you become friends for life. Many people call others their friends, just by knowing them. Usually that does not last very long because they are still in the acquaintance stage and really should be referred to as 'the acquaintances,'" said Mitra.

"Baba, did you have many friends in your life?"

"Yes, I had and still have two of my good friends. The third died two years ago."

"So altogether you had about three friends in your life."

"Yes, only three," Mitra confirmed. "One of my three friends was extra special, one to whom I could express my true feelings about everything that happened in my life. I knew full well my close confidence with her would not be revealed to anybody and that is my friend Mrs. MacDonald."

"But, Baba, how come you were not as close with the other two?"

"I could not be because even though they were very good people and my good friends, they were not the types to hold something within them—they just were not capable of doing that even though they would give you the shirt off their backs. For that reason, I could not trust them."

"Baba, you are saying you had one exceptional friend, two good friends and the rest you considered as acquaintances?"

"Yes, my bright great-granddaughter, you summed it up nicely. Now, I know about my friends, and I hope you will think about how to make friends and be a good friend yourself."

"I will remember your words about how to make good friends, Baba."

Sofija and Baba got off the subject about her past life in Yugoslavia. Sofija said, "We covered some interesting things." No sooner had they finished their talk, when Mitra's friend called to ask her if she wanted to go to see a good movie. Sofija asked Baba if she wanted to go—perhaps, it would be nice to see a good film. She could not stay longer because she had to study.

"You mean you have to meet a nice guy," Mitra smiled.

"No, Baba, no boys yet. I'll let you know when I meet someone."

Sofija teased, "I don't know why I bother coming when you are always on the go with your friends: you're worse than a teenager—always busy."

"What's wrong with that? It shows I'm still alive because I have good friends and a lot of hobbies. Sofija, develop good hobbies to pass time pleasantly when one day you cannot do physical work. I know you are young now and you do not think of getting old and feeble, and that is good that you do not occupy your mind with that. When I was young like you, I never thought I would get old one day. But the truth is if we live long enough—and we all strive to live— we become old pretty quickly. It creeps into every muscle, blood cell, and even wreaks havoc with our neurons. I'm thankful to God that so far he did not mess up my brain terribly, so as long as I have that I'm all right and I can enjoy my time."

"Baba, which hobby do you enjoy most?"

"When I was younger, I enjoyed gardening, knitting, sewing, playing cards, and chess."

"Yes, Baba, I remember how you made me a wonderful dress when I was about 10 years old."

"Really, I don't remember, but I'm glad you do."

"Yes, you did, Baba, and that day I wore that dress to my friend's public school graduation party."

As the two of them were talking, Baba's friend, Evica, called to ask if Mitra was ready to go.

"Yes, yes, I am. My great-granddaughter and I had a lot to talk about."

She turned to Sofija.

"All right sweetie when are you coming back again? If you have a lot to study, take your time. I'm going to be fine. My new friends and hobbies will keep me busy. Bye, Sofija dear— Baba loves you."

When Sofija left, she was thinking of what Baba said to her about how important it was to create some hobbies. Sofija was struck by that and she felt as if old age was not that far off.

"Oh, what am I talking about? I am only 18. Of course, old age is too far for me. But how long would it take for me to develop some good hobbies. I can practice and use them to occupy my free time even now. Baba is so right. Oh, what kind of hobbies do I like? Let's see; I like sporty kinds of hobbies: baseball, soccer, skiing, and skating. But they won't be good for my old age, because I won't be able to do them.

"I have to create hobbies that don't involve strenuous effort. Baba warned me not to depend too much on weak eyes in old age. So that means sewing, embroidery, and knitting are out.

Oh, I have to develop playing different games of cards, domino, chess—that is what I like to play but not too many people like to play chess. Chess is a European game. Baba told me she loved to play chess with her brother when she was small, even though girls were not allowed to play chess because it was considered a man's game."

Sofija remembered that she played chess with her great-grandma when she was younger, but she did not recall why they stopped playing it.

"Baba had some good ideas and when I come next time, I will ask her to suggest what kind of hobbies I should practice."

Sofija had thought enough about hobbies so she put the radio on to hear what was going on in the world. The first news was about an accident in Toronto, which took two young lives, a 16-year-old girl and the 19-year-old male driver of the vehicle. They slammed into a guard rail and died instantly. When Sofija heard this, she felt sorry for the two young lives lost. Likely, just before they died, they were contemplating the good things in life to come. How can we make plans for the future when we're not sure about it? Sofija wondered. When we make plans for the future, we seldom anticipate the likelihood we won't be here anymore.

Sofija's enthusiasm about finding the right hobby for her old age was tarnished. After hearing about these two people's lives cut short, she wondered if she would live as long as Baba. On the other hand, it would be terrible and frightening for one to think that one could die soon. It was better to think positively and be confident about the future.

"It is best, my baba says to leave that for God to decide," Sofija thought.

After Sofija repeated her baba's statement, she thought she was becoming a believer in Baba's spiritual reasoning. It took the load off her shoulders to trust God's decision-making.

When she arrived home, she found grandpa Marko. She was very happy to see him because she had not seen him for a while. He was very pleased to see Sofija and, at the same time, asked her about his mother. If his mother would confide to anybody about her real feelings, it would be to Sofija. Somehow, they had a special bond with each other. That made Marko very happy for both of them.

"How is your baba doing, Sofija?"

"She is doing pretty well so far, grandpa."

"I'm sure she confides her inner feelings to you," Marko said.

"I don't know, grandpa. Your mother has very strict rules about what she allows people to know and what she keeps for herself."

"Are you sure?" Marko asked. "If that is true, then you know your baba better than her own son, me."

"That is my opinion, grandpa. I could be wrong, but I don't think so."

Marko got off his chair and came over to give her a hug and kiss. When he sat down, he asked Sofija how their project was going.

"What project?"

"You know what project, Baba's project."

"Oh, that project. It is going very, very well. I'm glad I started it because I want to know everything about Baba's life. She is so, so interesting I could not believe some of the things she was telling me about, when she was growing up. I'm sure the worse ones she is not telling me about. You will see, grandpa. Once I write it all down into a book form, you will be surprised."

"Thank you, Sofija. We're all proud of your project. You are a very smart girl. I mean it when I say that."

"Thank you, grandpa; you must know, grandpa, how much I love and admire my great-grandmother."

"Yes, I know, Sofija."

Sofija excused herself and went to her room. She told grandpa that she had some studying to do.

"Okay, dear."

When Sofija heard how grandpa Marko was excited about Sofija's and Baba's project, she became even more enthusiastic about it. She couldn't wait to go back and be with Baba, listen to her stories and write them down. Two days later, she visited again. After giving her baba big hugs, a few kisses, and her small coffee with double milk, Sofija started with questions.

"Baba, what was the event of your biggest celebration?"

"The biggest celebrations were Christmas, Slava, weddings, christening of a child. That's about it."

"Wait, wait, you forgot birthday celebrations."

"No, I did not forget; we never celebrated birthdays."

"What do you mean you never celebrated birthdays?"

"I meant, we did not celebrate birthdays. You think people kept track of when they were born. If they wanted to know when they were born, they would go into the city hall and find out from the registrar. Even then, you were not sure what the exact date of your birth was. Sometimes, in remote villages, if it was bad weather in winter or at harvest time, you had to take care of things more important than registering the baby."

"Baba, what are you talking about? Was it that bad?"

"Why do you think that everything was bad, Sofija? No, it was not such a terrible thing if a baby was not registered exactly when they were born. Legally, parents were responsible to report a child's birth right away, but sometimes they needed a few days to do that."

"The baby could be older by days, even months."

"That was almost normal, but so what's the big deal? A few days, one month or even two, it didn't make such a big difference, not when I was growing up."

"So, nobody knew their exact birthday."

"No, not really, it was not so important for us to know. You usually visited the registrar's office for marriage, army duty, or in the case of death. For these three or four times in life, you need to know your birthday; otherwise birthdays were usually quiet days. Do you think we celebrated birthdays like you do now? No way."

"Don't you agree that a birthday is an important day in person's life? Everybody celebrates birthdays big time nowadays with family and friends."

"Oh, I know that, child."

"By the way, Baba, what do you think about that?"

"About what?" Mitra asked.

"About birthday parties."

"It is nice to remember it with your immediate family, but I don't know about a big bash. I was never for that. But if somebody wants to celebrate, let them, it doesn't bother me."

"Baba, did you ever wish you were born in Canada instead of Yugoslavia?"

"I don't know, I never thought about that. I had a good childhood and wonderful memories of my parents, siblings, grandparents, cousins, friends, and all the people there. I don't know what it would be like if I were born here. My dear child, not everybody is happy here either. Happiness always depends on the immediate surroundings of the people around you, the conditions at the time one is growing up. I don't know if I would change anything. I was happy with my life."

"Baba, what about the other holidays? For example, Christmas, how did you celebrate it?"

"Oh my God, that was a fun time. I already told you about that and how we celebrated it."

"Yes, yes, I forgot about that. You did love those holidays."

"Yes, I did. They were a lot of fun, and more than a day of celebration."

"Could you tell me something about marriages?"

"As I said before, marriages got a lot of attention because the marriage of two young people connected two families."

Sofija liked this topic. She begged her baba to tell her every last detail. Mitra started to laugh, "Oh, my child, you probably want to compare it with marriages here. Yes, we had a wonderful traditional celebration during the process of marriages.

"We must first start with the engagement, that's how the process takes place."

Sofija's heart started to pound. She twisted a bit on her seat in anticipation of hearing something exciting. Mitra noticed Sofija's excitement and said to her, "Don't be so anxious. I will tell you everything. Be patient. When a boy turned 17 or 18, which is the age before army service, the boy's parents started looking for the right girl for their son. The most important thing was her family status, how well the family was respected in the community, and their financial and moral status. The old saying was, 'When a tree is being cut down, its slivers do not fall very far away from the tree.' The same was believed about the girl or a boy; they are what their parents are. It was important that a girl was healthy physically and mentally.

"Skinny girls were not preferred: more popular were the fuller and red-cheeked ones who could bear strong healthy children and were able to work hard in the field. When the boy came back from the army, he would usually be 21 to 23 -years-old. This would depend on the rank he served, because some ranks were two years and some three years."

"What about the girls' ages, Baba?"

"Girls' ages at their prime were 16 to 18 years. Girls over the age of 20 had a hard time marrying because they were considered old maids."

"Did young people date before they got married?" Sofija asked.

Mitra's eyes opened wide in surprise at Sofija's question.

"What are you talking about? Often times they didn't know one another before they got engaged. The boy's father and closest male relatives played big part in the engagement process. The girl's parents also played big roles in trying to find out through relatives and friends who would ask for their daughter's hand. They were quite prepared with the answer they would give to a young man's father, or the one who was asking the question. The girl's parents would consider similar qualities about the boy's background. Only, the girl's parents would pay more attention about the young man's financial situation.

"Marriages and engagements always took place outside of harvest time; usually, early spring or late fall. It was also usually in the evening time, called *prelo*, when the girl's hand was asked for. The male from the young man's side popped the question to the parents of the girl, mostly her father. The decision had to be made right then and there. It was shameful to ask for a girl's hand more than once. The girl's parents would somehow know what their daughter was thinking about the young man. The parents would consider her feelings but sometimes in a situation when they knew their daughter would not be happy marrying the young man, they would say no, even if she said yes. Girls would elope sometimes.

"The parents of the girl pretended to be ignorant or unaware of the young man wanting to marry their daughter. If they were against it, they would say so before they asked their daughter for her opinion especially if she was in love with him. If they wanted their daughter to be married into his family and to that young man, they would pretend not to know their daughter's answer but, in fact, they would always know their daughter's feelings for the young man, and they would ask her if she would like to marry him. When both parents and the girl agreed, then congratulations started by first giving the girl a red apple as a symbol of engagement.

"An apple symbolizes never-ending happiness, sweet as her future life in the new family. Red as the blood that symbolizes procreation."

"Oh my God, doesn't the girl get an engagement ring?"

"What ring? It was hard to get a nice red apple, never mind a ring. First of all, it wasn't customary and second, nobody had money for such a thing. An apple was enough."

"This is so interesting to hear. If you were married there, would you have been married the same way you just told me about?"

"Of course I would have," Mitra exclaimed. "Why do you think mine would be any different?"

"Please, Baba, just continue; I love your stories very much. So, what happens after the girl receives the apple?"

"It's easy to know what happens. Lots of hugging, kissing, drinking, eating, and singing. Most men would get drunk."

"What would happen between the boy and the girl? Would they kiss?"

"Of course they would. They would even make love. There was no such thing as a man and woman kissing in public unless they were closely related. The young man would be allowed to exchange a few words with the girl. She would be busy serving her guests and future in-laws."

Sofija kept insisting that Baba continue the story. Mitra said, "Yes, yes, I will but first I need some water. My mouth is so dry from talking so much and also our bean soup today was too salty."

"I will get you some water."

"Yes, please," said Mitra. After she downed an almost full glass of water, she said to Sofija, "Please let me stretch my legs a bit. I feel so stiff from sitting too long. It is not good for my old bones to sit too long or walk too much."

"That's fine, you rest while I go through my notes from today."

Sofija went through her notes. She was very happy with them. She was learning so much about her baba's young life and the unusual customs she grew up with. Sofija was pondering how to ask proper questions so she wouldn't miss anything, because it was all very interesting. Although she lived with her baba all her life, she never knew many of the things she'd learned in the last few sessions—not in such detail anyway.

"So, Baba, I have to go back where we left off. Now that you told me about the engagement, or so-called engagement, how did the ceremony proceed from there?"

"Well, it depended on the family's financial situation and the success of their last year's crop, because preparing for even the simplest wedding was a tremendous and expensive effort. It was never a big wedding; only family members on each side, very few close friends and a few godparents, best man, the second-best man—who was in charge of the groom's wedding party—were invited to carry on the customs of the day. Neighbours were always offered drinks or even some food. Neighbours were very important, because we depended on each other."

Sofija was intensely interested in each part of the wedding ceremony.

"The date for the wedding was always set for the weekend but the celebration was carried on for at least three days. Once the date was set, both sides got ready for the big event. The custom was that the groom's side would go and fetch the bride.

Once they were at the bride's house, they had to ask to see the bride. Usually, the groom's brother or one of his closest relatives asked for the bride to come out of her house to meet the wedding party. The bride's side usually brought out someone else instead of the bride.

"The groom's side would keep yelling, 'No, no, that's not the right one, we know who the right bride is.' Once the right bride was presented, there was a negotiation to compensate the bride's brother or whoever brought her outside of the house. It was usually a symbolic amount of money, but it produced a lot of fun and laughter. Usually, that money was given to the bride and groom.

"Once the bride was taken into the groom's family she was placed among the ushers and the groom's best man—not with the groom.

"The ceremony started with eating and drinking the whole night long. No one went to bed. Lots of food and drinks were consumed. Most of the men would get drunk while the women refrained themselves from drinking. It was shameful for women to be drunk in public. In the morning, guests washed their hands and faces in a basin, and left a modest amount of money for the bride and groom beside it. Breakfast was served. There were a lot of leftovers from the night before, but especially smoked ham and cured and aged cheese, that was so, so delicious.

"The wedding party then prepared to leave for the groom's house. As they continued on their journey, there was continuous singing and dancing and especially drinking. Usually the bride's and groom's families lived close by, two to three villages apart, and as they went through each village, people greeted the wedding party, had a drink, and extended their good wishes. But if a groom was from somewhere farther, horses and buggies were used for transportation.

"The bride usually had a dowry, which consisted of bedding, linen, her wardrobe and perhaps a few garments for the groom. This was put into a wooden box that was made especially for the bride. All this was loaded onto donkeys, or into a cart pulled by a horse."

"Baba, you never mentioned if there was music or some kind of dancing?" Sofija asked.

Mitra was surprised that Sofija didn't ask this question much earlier, but she was getting smarter and realized that there was no music. But there were some wedding party members singing appropriate folk wedding songs. It was simple, but at the same time very nice. The bride was greeted by the groom's parents with an assembly of relatives and neighbours. The bride was given a red apple in front of the house. She was required to throw the apple clearly over the roof onto the other side. The stronger and clearer the throw meant a successful marriage and a house filled with a lot of good and healthy children. Many brides were lucky in their successful throw because houses were small and low. Young girls were more praised if they looked strong and not skinny, particularly if they had rosy cheeks."

"It was opposite to what girls are praised for today, slim and tiny," Sofija asked.

"Exactly," Mitra confirmed. "It's different now. At that time, girls and young women were expected to work hard and bear a lot of children. Today, everything is about pushing buttons. Modern women bear their children at 30 to 45 years of age while back then, women of those ages would have grandchildren."

"Oh my God, if I lived at that time, I would already be married and have a couple of kids."

"Yes, my dear girl, but today is better than then. Women went through a lot of hardship, especially if their husbands were bad men. Today, women have far better protection and because of that, a better life."

"I agree. Let's go back to the wedding ceremony."

"What I'm telling you about, all these cultural ceremonies, would have happened during the time of my marriage. Lots of things have changed and I must say for the better. When the bride arrived at the groom's house, she first kissed her in-laws and gave them some presents, usually socks, kerchiefs, or something little because nobody had much to give. Then the bride would kneel down at the entrance of the house and kiss the entrance. After that, the ceremony continued well into the night. When it was time for the bride and groom to go to sleep, the bridesmaids prepared the bride for the bed and the ushers prepared the groom. When the bride was ready, the groom was brought to her and the bedroom door gets shut."

"So, that was the wedding."

"Yes, of course, but only people from far away were accommodated with some kind of sleeping place. The rest of the guests went home. In the morning, the bride would be first to get up and wait on her in-laws. Some guests would come back for breakfast and give some money to the newlyweds, the same as they had the previous morning. It was always a small amount, but even a small amount meant a lot."

Sofija's eyes had widened more and more as she was listening to her baba's explanation of the unusual customs.

"So, it's over," Sofija exclaimed.

"Yes, it is, my child. The reward after nine months, a newborn in a lucky house."

Sofija hardly moved on her seat. Mitra asked her, "Are you all right? You look as if you're stunned."

"Yes, I'm all right. I am amazed by your stories. Please continue. I am making short notes because it is so fascinating. As soon as I get home, I will go through my notes and add in all the details. Next time when I come, I will read them to you and you will tell me if I have missed anything."

"That's good. I don't think you missed anything, I have told you enough for today," Mitra said.

"I agree," replied Sofija. "I won't be able to come tomorrow because I have to study for my test the next day. I have to brush up on my subject in order to get good marks."

"That's smart," Mitra agreed, "I will be fine for a day or two."

"What are you going to do for the rest of night, Baba?"

"Oh, I will go over to Evica's room, or I'll call her to come over and we can play cards, or just talk."

Sofija turned around, kissed and hugged Mitra, and said goodbye. As she was leaving, she told Baba to call if she needed anything.

"Don't worry about me; I will call if I need anything."

Chapter 9

When Sofija left, Mitra called Evica, but she didn't answer. She decided to call her again and if she didn't answer she would go over to see if she was all right since she had the key to Evica's room. As Mitra thought this, there was a knock at her door. It was Evica asking, "Is your Sofija gone?"

"Yes, she is," Mitra answered.

Evica came in, saying, "What a lovely great-granddaughter you have."

"Yes, she is," Mitra answered.

"I see her with a notebook in her hands whenever she visits you," Evica said.

"When we talk, she likes to take notes. She likes to know about my life."

"What did you talk about that was so interesting to her?"

"She wants to know what it was like when I was growing up."

"So, what did you talk about today?"

"We talked about the wedding ceremony."

"How did she react to your story?"

"Oh my God, she was stunned. She did not move while I was talking. Today's children cannot imagine hardships and poverty. Can you imagine how these kids would survive if they were suddenly faced with the situations we were in?"

"Not so easily," Evica replied, "but they would find a way to adjust."

"It would be very hard for them—really hard. Do you want to play cards, or do something else?" Mitra asked.

"You know what, let's go to the big sitting room and watch the movie on the big screen."

"What's playing tonight?" Mitra asked.

"They said it's going to be *Gone with the Wind*, but because it's too long, the other half will be shown tomorrow night. Oh, that's a classic with Clark Gable. I would like to see it again."

"Let's go watch it," Mitra said.

The room was almost full, including the new Italian lady, who'd moved in a couple days earlier. The two of them sat next to each other. The Italian woman was a couple of seats away from them. She kept talking to the woman next to her, but this woman never replied. Eventually, the woman, upset by the constant chatter, got up and left. The Italian lady kept talking to the next person closest to her. This woman also got mad at her and told her to shut her trap or she would shut it for her. The Italian lady asked Mitra what the woman was saying to her. Obviously, she did not understand the meaning of trap.

Mitra said, "She's asking you to be quiet because she wants to watch the movie."

"No, no, she no say that. She says bad thing, bad. I no care she say. I pay big money no care here," the Italian woman complained.

The woman sitting beside them got mad at her and said, "We all pay big money for living here, not just you. It would be nicer here without you."

The Italian woman got up quickly. Mitra thought she would leave the room; instead she pushed the other lady against the wall, saying to her, "You pig. You no good. I tell my son beat you. Tomorrow he comes, tomorrow you see."

The other woman struggled to get up, but couldn't. Suddenly, the nurse appeared because she'd heard the commotion and asked what was going on. She helped the lady up, but the Italian woman still tried to push her again.

"Oh, no, no, Mrs. Velenosi, you don't do that to people in here."

The Italian woman just kept talking, calling them all 'stupid bad people.' An orderly appeared and tried to persuade Mrs. Velenosi to come with him downstairs. She kicked him in the shin and kept saying things in two languages, English, but mostly in Italian. It sounded like swear words. As they tried to calm her down, they led her away from the others. The only words Mitra heard clearly were, "I no like here. I want go my house where is my son. Oh, God help me, help me."

Even after they left the room, Mitra and Evica could still hear the woman yelling and screaming. They went to Mitra's room. Both were shaken. They sat quietly for a while. Evica spoke first, "Poor Mrs. Velenosi is so upset and unhappy being here. I am not very happy being away from my home or my family but what can I do? It does not help me to make a scene as Mrs. Velenosi has. I try to put up with it. That is the only thing I can do."

Mitra kept quiet. A couple of times, she moved her head to show her own frustration. They were not in the mood for playing games. Mitra's phone rang. The caller's voice was so loud that even Evica clearly heard it.

"Hi, Mitra, are you in a bad mood already?"

Once Mitra started talking, Evica motioned to her that she would leave, and come back later.

It was Mitra's brother, who was younger than her and in very good health. She considered him a very lucky man because he had a very good wife, a few years younger than him. Mitra felt sorry for herself: if her husband was still alive, things would be different. She would not be living in this institution. He would see to that. At the end of her long talk with her brother, he promised that he and his wife would come to see her tomorrow, asking her if she needed anything.

"Mila will bring you some homemade strudel; she knows that you like cheese strudel. She will make it tomorrow morning."

"Okay, see you tomorrow."

Evica came back, but neither of them felt like playing cards. Evica asked what her brother said. Mitra told her and asked her to leave some room for cheese strudel.

Since both of them were not in the best of moods, Evica got up to make a phone call to her daughter. When Evica left, Mitra started to cry, feeling sorry for herself, questioning the meaning of her life and why she was living when life had no meaning at all. She remembered her own grandmother when she died on a warm June day. At least it wasn't cold. She died with dignity. All her family was around her. She was never alone. Mitra was wondering why she was thinking about her grandma's death all the time.

In the summertime, older people stayed together while adults and children played near them. There was life, love, and happiness around them. Kids were trained to be polite and respect old people. Sure, they did not have the comforts of today, but she would give up all this comfort in exchange for the way her grandmother lived her final years. What did she have here among these thrown away lives? Wherever she looked, all she could see was lost souls waiting to stop breathing to free themselves and the rest of their families.

Evica called to see if she would come over but Mitra lied that she felt tired and would rather rest. She just did not feel like having any company. Mitra thought about Mrs. Velenosi and the meaning of her life. She felt as if she were a thrown-away object. She must have worked very hard raising her family. Her vitality was used to make a better life for her family.

Mitra questioned how it had come to such a system. Long ago, Mitra heard a story from someone about how a man who was building a thin, long stretcher. His little son asked him, "Dad, what are you making?"

"I am making a stretcher for grandpa," said the father.

"Where are you going to put that stretcher?" the youngster asked.

"This is for grandpa when he gets really old and cannot help himself. It will help me carry him over the mountain to the other side where there's a place for the old and sick."

The next day, his father was looking for his little son and found him in the garage. The man asked, "What are you doing, son?"

The boy answered, "I'm building a stretcher for you, so I can take you over the mountain like grandpa."

That was the best reminder for that man about what awaited him, and very similar to what awaits all of us.

Mitra turned on the television to see what was going on in the world. After changing channels, she did not find anything interesting. To Mitra everything was irrelevant or made up. She decided to read the book *The-Hundred-Year-Old Man* that she'd started reading a few days ago. She found it to be very interesting. It was very well written and extremely imaginative. Mitra read a couple of pages but her eyes started to blur. That was not unusual because it happened all the time.

She closed the book, turned off the television, and started to prepare herself for sleep. She was lucky she still had most of her teeth, so she brushed and flossed them. She washed her wrinkled, sagging, spotty face, wondering, "Where are all these coming from? So much skin hanging around creating a lot of intersectional highways, without any precision or order. The age spots are so anxious to come to the surface in order to show how much in command they are, to smear my once beautiful rosy cheeks."

Mitra got mad at herself asking, "What is wrong with me tonight? Why worry when nothing can be done about it. It's simply old age."

So, Mitra got into her night clothes, lay in her bed and began her regular night prayer, which was usually the same. Tonight, she had to pray more.

"Lord, my God, my Father, protector of me and my family, please forgive me for being so negative tonight. Please put me straight by reminding me to be thankful, accepting life's changes because it is normal to go through these stages. Please God, let me have wisdom and peace in my soul and let me ignore my physical imperfection. I had that when I needed it but now it's not important any more.

"Please, Lord, help me have a good day tomorrow; protect me and my family and all the people from bad things. Amen." After the prayer she became much calmer. Turning off the light, her last thoughts were of her granddaughter Sofija. Mitra thanked God for her wonderful great-granddaughter, Sofija, "She gives me more joy than anybody else."

When Mitra woke up in the morning, she felt refreshed. As usual, Evica came to fetch her for breakfast.

When they got to their table, the Italian lady was not there. Evica asked at the office later on about Mrs. Velenosi. She was told that her son came and took her home. Whether that was true or not, they didn't know; she was no longer among them. They were not surprised that she was removed because she made a lot of people stressed, which was not allowed in such a place. Nevertheless, Mitra felt sorry for her. Evica asked Mitra how she slept. Mitra's reply was short: "good." She did not need to remind herself of the previous night's negativity.

They went for the regular programmed exercises. This was the first time Mitra participated, and she liked it very much. She promised herself to do it every morning: "It's good for the body and mind instead of sitting and being nagged by negativity."

After the exercises, Mitra went to her room to stretch out and have some rest before lunch and the visit from her brother and sister-in-law. After a few hours of rest, Mitra felt like a different person. At that time, she promised herself that she would not let herself be so negative. She picked up her book to read a few pages before lunch. She found her eyes more cooperative. She read about 10 pages with great enjoyment, even had a few smiles about the fascinating events that took place on the man's journey.

As Mitra was getting ready, Evica appeared at the door: "Are we ready to go for lunch?"

"Yes," Mitra answered.

The lunch was pretty good: roast beef, mashed potatoes, and green peas. Dessert was mixed, diced fruit. But the two of them did not eat their full meal because they were waiting for the cheese strudel. Evica went to her room to have a nap as she usually did every day. Mitra remained sitting in the lobby waiting for her visitors. While she was sitting there, a nice lady sat beside her and introduced herself as Sandy Jonson.

"I understand you are a new resident here," the lady said.

"Yes, that is true," Mitra answered.

"I have been here for two years," Sandy said.

"Oh, that's nice. You must have gotten used to this place."

"Yes, but I didn't like it when I first came, I hated it."

"I hope it will be the same for me," Mitra said.

The lady nodded as she was saying, "Yes, it will. We do not have many choices at our age. It's best to get involved in some activities offered here. You have to occupy your time in order not to think too much about yourself. Those who occupy their time with something, they feel pretty good, but those who do not, they are very unhappy."

Mitra asked what kinds of activities were offered.

"There is exercise in the morning twice a week, water aerobics, and swimming every day. The big community room has bingo, card playing, chess, a big television screen. There's even bowling once a week, but for that they take us out."

"That's nice," Mitra confirmed and at the same time she remembered the discussion with the Italian woman last night.

"We really enjoy all those activities. I went to watch community TV last night, but it did not end very well," said Mitra.

"Yes, I heard there was some commotion," Sandy acknowledged. "Of course, that happens sometimes with newcomers, especially if they do not speak English. Don't forget, it's a big shock at first because you leave your family and your personal comfort behind, and you're being thrown into a strange place where you see only old people around you. It's not fun."

"I know I talk too much," Sandy added, "but you seem like a nice person and I wanted to remind you of what this establishment offers."

Mitra asked, "Can I call you, Sandy?"

"Yes, please do."

"Thank you very much for giving me all this information."

As Sandy was leaving, Mitra's brother and sister-in-law walked in. Mitra said, "This is my new friend, Sandy Jonson."

They extended their hands and gave Sandy warm greetings. Mitra asked Sandy what floor she lived on.

"Same as yours, fourth floor, room 14."

"Thank you," Mitra said.

Mitra and her visitors went to her room. Both of them were very curious how she liked it there.

"I am well. I still have to get used to it. I was just reminded by the lady you just met to get engaged in various activities. I think I will take her up on that. She has good ideas. Somehow I think she is worthy of friendship."

"That's very good," confirmed her brother, Dusan. "Next time we come to see you, we may not even find you in your room."

"Probably," confirmed Mitra.

"How's Evica doing?"

"She is good. We spend a lot of time together."

Mitra told them about last night's commotion and about other things going on.

"How is the food?" her sister-in-law, Mila, asked.

"Pretty good, but it's not like home-cooked meals."

"Of course not," Mila said.

"Don't worry, I will get used to it. I should not eat too much anyway," said Mitra.

Mila looked around the room and said to Mitra, "I'm surprised that your room is so splashy and bright. I really like it a lot; I like the way your furniture is arranged too. Who did the arrangement for you?"

"My sons carried the stuff, but my daughter-in-law, Doris, and Sofija arranged where things were put."

"Of course, your daughter-in-law, Doris, would do anything for you unlike other daughters-in-law who wouldn't even bother," Mila said.

"Yes, I'm a very lucky mother-in-law," Mitra said.

"Where did you get this size-and-a-half bed? They went out of stock a long time ago," Mila said.

"This was our first full-sized bed for our Marko. We bought it for him when he was five years old. I like the bed very much because it reminds me of him when he was a baby. I asked Marko to buy me a new mattress and he did, but he had to order it in memory foam. I like it very much because it forms around my body and makes me feel very comfortable. I couldn't bring my double bed because it's too big for here and this one is just the right size," Mitra said.

"That is true," her brother, Dusan, confirmed.

"The dresser is from my old bedroom set. They stripped it and painted it together with the headboard, so it looks like the same set," Mitra said.

"They did a very nice job," Dusan agreed.

"You were always a practical person," Mila added to his remark.

Mila pointed at the TV and said, "Look at the size of the TV. It's bigger than ours."

"Okay, okay," Dusan said, "I can see that everything is nice; you don't have to compare."

"You even have a microwave. That's good; we can warm up the strudel if it gets cold."

"Of course we can," Mitra said.

"Do you still correspond a lot? I see a lot of writing equipment: nice table, chair, computer, and telephone," Dusan asked.

"Yes, I still correspond with people but not as often as I used to. I like it best when I talk to people directly, hear their voices, and instantly ask them questions about what interests me."

"That is the best way; I like that kind of correspondence too," Dusan said.

Mila was quiet for a while and she said, "I'm surprised you don't have as many family portraits as you had in your house."

"Sofija doesn't have that much time to put them up, but as soon as she has free time, she will do all that for her baba," Mitra said.

"I'm sure she will," Dusan said.

After they talked for a bit, Mila pulled the strudel out of her bag. Its aroma spread throughout the entire room, reminding Mitra of her own cooking, the divine aroma of wonderful food. As Mitra took a piece, she first looked at it, smelled it, and then nodded as she bit into it.

"Thank you, Mila, for bringing it. I appreciate it very much."

"You are very welcome," Mila said.

As Mitra took another piece, Mila joked, "Are you going to save anything for Evica?"

"There is plenty left for her and me. She is having a nap right now. We did not eat very much lunch; we saved ourselves for strudel. I like strudel while it's still warm and crunchy."

It was almost close to dinner time when Dusan and his wife left. Mitra took a little rest. Shortly after, Evica was knocking at the door.

"Are you ready to go for dinner?"

"Yes, I am," Mitra answered.

They went down to their usual table, but this time there was only three of them. The Italian lady wasn't there. Mitra wasn't hungry and only took some pea soup and a cup of coffee. The waitress asked her if she was feeling all right because she refused to have a complete meal.

"I'm fine," Mitra confirmed. "I cannot eat because I had treats given to me from home."

Mitra gave a piece of strudel to the Dutch lady and two pieces to Evica. She would have invited Evica to her room, but she felt tired from her visit with her brother and sister-in-law. She'd enjoyed their company and homemade strudel very much.

Sandy passed by their table to say hello to Mitra. When she left, Evica asked Mitra how she knew that woman.

"She introduced herself to me in the afternoon while I was waiting for my brother and sister-in-law. Her name is Sandy

Jonson. She told me about many activities they have in here."

Evica's tone was unfriendly.

"You don't need a stranger to tell you about these activities. Why didn't you ask me? I could have told you."

Mitra was surprised with Evica's reaction and said, "I didn't ask her, she willingly told me. What is wrong with that?"

Evica calmed down a bit.

"Nothing, nothing, I'm just surprised."

As they parted, Mitra realized that there would be problems in the future because of Evica's jealousy. Mitra hated to be controlled by a jealous person. She hadn't yet realized Evica was like that. While Mitra was thinking about this unexpected conflict, there was a knock at the door.

Mitra said, "Come in."

Sofija appeared at the door with coffee for the two of them. Mitra asked her if she'd had her dinner.

"I just had a bagel, so I could come here quicker."

"You didn't have to rush, I wasn't going anywhere," Mitra said.

"Oh, I don't know about that. You are still an interesting and charming lady. Some man might ask you on a date."

They both laughed.

"Yup, anything is possible. If I am not here, I have gone to heaven."

"Baba," Sofija raised her voice, "don't talk nonsense. You are going to be around for a long time. What would I do without you?"

"Come on, child, your life and happiness don't depend on me. Let's stop this talk. Here is some strudel your uncle Dusan and his wife brought this afternoon. Would you like some with your coffee?"

"Yes, of course. You know how much I like strudel. But I'll leave some for you."

"Don't worry. I had enough this afternoon. I could not even eat my full dinner."

"All right, I will have some."

Sofija finished two pieces of strudel while Mitra was telling her what happened since she'd last visited two days ago.

"I'm sorry you had to go through such unpleasant incidents, Baba."

"I'm all right. I feel sorry for people being in trouble due to somebody else, or through their own making."

"I know you can't stand unpleasantness, but what can you do?"

"Nothing," Mitra said. "Don't worry, everything will be all right."

Sofija got up and kissed her Baba, asking her if she would like to come home for the coming weekend.

"What is going on at home this weekend?"

"Just a normal weekend. Nothing special."

"I think I will stay here for this weekend. I need to get a little more settled in my new place. It's not that bad here."

In order to convince Sofija, she told her she had met an interesting acquaintance. She would like to spend some time with her.

Mitra wasn't happy spending the weekend in the establishment, but she didn't want to admit that to Sofija. Mitra knew her family had been hesitant to go anywhere after she fell three months ago. She wanted them to have some free weekends without worrying about her.

"Are you sure you want to stay here? I will come to keep you company on Sunday, but tomorrow I won't be able to come. I promised to help my friend study for her French exam."

"No child, please have your Sunday to do some fun things with your friends or your parents. I'll be fine. Do not worry for me all the time. You are young, and you should enjoy yourself."

"Thank you, Baba. Grandpa and grandma will be here tomorrow to see you."

"Good, that will be nice. Next week I will come because it is the long weekend, Labour Day. They say a lot of people go home on the long weekend. Maybe that weekend won't be so pleasant in here."

"Ok, Baba, now that we finished with the wedding and the baby on the way, what then?"

"Well, happy times again," said Mitra. "Once the baby arrives the mother of the bride's side comes over with a lot of homemade food: smoked ham, aged cheese, breads, pastries like beaver tails. Then there has to be wine and whisky. There is also clothing for the small one."

"All these are minimal, right Baba?"

"Yes, child. It was all that people could afford at that time. By today's standards it was nothing, especially from the point of view of people in your position."

"Did the baby have a lot of clothes?" asked Sofija.

"Not really, only three to four washable diapers dried outside in the summer, and by the hearth's fire in the winter. One more thing that was practised and considered important, for the first couple of weeks, was swaddling the baby. After two to three months, the baby's hands would be free, but the rest of the body would still be rolled in a long piece of cloth."

"That's awful, Baba. How did the poor baby survive such treatment?"

"I agree with you now, but at that time I was thinking like the rest of my people. Customs and tradition are powerful, and people conform to the social norm, often without questioning it."

Sofija took a deep sigh, "So was that the way you were treated as a baby?"

"Of course I was. Why would I be any different from the rest of the children born in that tradition?"

"But, Baba, what was the reason for that?"

"The reason was for the baby's hands and especially legs to remain straight. They did not know what was proper, but they believed such treatment guaranteed a straight, solid structure for the baby's skeleton."

"Oh boy, I was lucky I wasn't born there," exclaimed Sofija. "Probably I would have died like many other babies died at that time."

"But you have to look at the other side of the story; perhaps you would have lived and had a straight solid body," Mitra said as a joke.

"Baba, you are being funny. Don't scare me please," Sofija said. She looked at her grandma as she was weird for saying that.

Mitra seeing that Sofija was so serious said, "Come on, child, I meant that as a joke. We should stop talking about different customs, especially the ones from my background, which you can never understand."

Sofija asked if they were going to continue on the next point. "Maybe we can talk about the baby's christening since you said it was a very important part of the custom."

"That is true. We will talk next about that, but right now I will have to go for a short walk to stretch my legs. Is that okay with you?" Mitra asked.

"Yes, it is of course. You go ahead while I look at my notes to see what I have written down so far."

"All right," Mitra said and left. She walked in the long hallway and at the end of it, Sandy came out from her room. They exchanged greetings.

"So, you are going outside?" Sandy asked.

"Not now," Mitra answered, "It's too hot and my great-granddaughter is in my room. I am just taking a short walk to stretch my legs."

"You're doing the right thing," said Sandy. "See you around. I am going out for dinner with my friend. She's picking me up."

"That's good," Mitra said.

"Do you go out for lunch?" asked Sandy.

"Sometimes," answered Mitra, "see you later."

Sandy disappeared in the elevator and Mitra returned back to her room.

"Must have been a long walk. Did you meet 'him' behind the door?" Sofija said.

"No. But I met my new acquaintance, Sandy."

"Oh, looks like you like her a lot."

"I don't know about that; I certainly find her interesting."

"What would you do if she suggested you go for lunch together?"

"I think I would like that," confirmed Mitra." I would like to know her better. That reminds me to get some money from my bank. I know they are warning us not to have any cash with us, but I would not tell them about it. And if it gets stolen so what, it's not a big amount."

"Would you like me to get you 50 dollars from your bank?"

"Yes, you can do that, but do it when you're ready to go home, not now."

Mitra got on her bed and motioned for Sofija to come and sit next to her. She stroked Mitra's fine grey hair and kissed her baba on the cheek, saying, "I love you, Baba, most of all for your fairness, justice, and wisdom, which you've taught us our entire lives."

"It is nice to hear that from a girl who is sensible and loving."

They looked at each other and kissed again.

"How do you feel? Do you want to continue with our project?"

"I don't know, maybe we better leave it for the next time you come. In the meantime, I will think about what would be important to remember. I've forgotten a lot of things. It has been 70 years since I came to Canada. I did not go back that often because our children were small. We had no money. The more I delay telling you about my life, the more often you will come to visit me," Mitra said, laughing.

"But Baba, I would come to visit you without any other reason but just to see you and be with you."

"I know you would, my child, but these visits have more meaning for you—that's what I am saying."

"You're right, Baba."

"Don't worry you will be here many, many times before I go to the other world."

"Oh, Baba, don't talk nonsense. You will live forever, not exactly forever, but I believe a long, long time yet."

Sofija left Mitra stretched out on the bed to rest a bit before Evica knocked on the door either to play cards, go for a walk or go to the community room to watch TV. They usually put on some good films from the classical selection. If the film was interesting Mitra found that time flew. It made her feel good being engaged in something pleasant. She would fall asleep more easily when her mind was relaxed and happy.

Chapter 10

Mitra's thoughts and tiredness made her sleepy. When she woke up it was almost 8:00 pm. She was surprised that she'd slept so long. It was all right, now she felt well rested. Mitra was very surprised that Evica had not already called on her. If she had, Mitra didn't hear her.

Mitra got up and went to knock on Evica's door. There was no answer. She tried to open the door, but it was locked. She got worried and tried not to panic.

"Maybe she knocked on my door and since she did not get an answer, she locked up her own door and went somewhere."

Mitra kept saying, "She is all right; she has not gone too far. I am going to find her soon."

When Mitra saw Evica in the community room watching a film all alone, she was shocked.

"I have been looking everywhere for you; why didn't you call me?"

Evica turned her head saying, "I thought you left with your new friend—what's her name, something warm, Sunny?"

"Evica, what are you talking about? I hardly know the woman much less consider her my friend."

"Go and look for her; I will be fine."

Mitra sat down, looking at Evica and wondering what was happening to make her behave like that. She was well aware that Evica was very angry, but she could not understand that her meeting and talking with another woman could make Evica so jealous and angry. Mitra realized she'd never experienced something like this before in her life.

Mitra got up and went to her room. She thought at first that she had found a peaceful corner in this establishment for the short remainder of her life. But now Evica's behaviour threw her security out the window. Mitra felt that the centre was no longer a comfortable and peaceful place for her. She felt all alone. Even her family was suddenly far, far away. She wished for her death, thinking it would be best for her and everybody else.

She sat on the bed. Tears were running down her cheeks. Suddenly she heard the knock at the door. Mitra quickly wiped the tears with the corner of her sheet and said, "Come in." The nurse walked in. She noticed Mitra's unhappy smile and asked if she was feeling all right.

"Yes, yes, I'm fine," Mitra answered.

"I noticed that you were watching TV in the community room with your friend. When I saw that you left, I thought I should check on you," the nurse said.

"I'm feeling a little tired but otherwise, I'm all right. Thank you, nurse."

"Please, Mrs. Milutinovic, call me if you need anything."

"Thank you, nurse, I will."

Mitra tried to convince herself that she should not take this incident so hard. It's a well-known fact you cannot be in charge of other people's feelings and their reactions. But just the same, she could not understand how somebody could be that way. Such people are not happy unless they get what they want; in this case, to stifle someone else's freedom and choice. They always want to be the centre of attention.

"Now I have learned, more like discovered, what kind of person Evica is. Oh well, let it be, I don't have to have a relationship with her. There are other people besides Evica. I'm reacting too strongly again; by tomorrow, everything will go back to how things were. I should go to bed a little earlier because there is nothing else to do."

When Mitra got into such moods she usually took a pill to relax herself and sleep it off. Tonight, she really needed one of the pills she'd been taking since her fall. She would ask the nurse for a pill. She got the pill and she was ready for bed. She said her usual prayer, mentioning also that she forgave Evica for her behaviour.

Mitra had a good sleep. She did her normal morning procedure and got ready to go downstairs for breakfast. She hoped that Evica would knock on the door any moment and ask her to go for breakfast. There was no knock on the door. Mitra went down by herself. When she came into the dining room, Evica was sitting at a different table. Mitra sat at her regular table with the Belgian lady, who for the first time smiled when Mitra sat down. Surprisingly, she was very pleasant and attentive to Mitra, as she kept moving things on their table so that Mitra could reach them easier.

Mitra was very surprised how different reactions came from Evica and the Belgian lady. When breakfast was done, Evica quickly got up and disappeared without even throwing a glance at Mitra.

Soon after Evica left the room, Sandy came over to Mitra saying, "What is wrong with your friend? She's behaving differently than usual."

"Oh, I don't know. She had some unpleasant news from home and she had to leave quickly. She will be all right."

Mitra did not want to talk about Evica in any unpleasant way. She still hoped everything would be all right between them, once Evica calmed down and realized that she did not have any reason to get mad.

Sandy asked Mitra if she would like to take a short walk outside in the fresh air: "It's a beautiful morning and that will be good for both of us."

"Yes, please, I agree with you." Mitra hoped that Sandy wouldn't talk about Evica. Mitra did not think much of people who talked down about others. That would change her intention to befriend Sandy.

Sandy never said anything about Evica; instead she asked Mitra if she was going home for the weekend: "I wasn't planning to go home this weekend, because I wanted my family to have some free time to relax or go somewhere since they haven't gone anywhere for two months."

"They were busy?" Sandy questioned.

"Not only that, but because of me. I fell about two months ago and they didn't want to leave me alone, or only with my great-granddaughter who found me on the floor."

"Is that the young lady who often comes to visit you?"

"Yes, that is my dear great-granddaughter, Sofija," Mitra replied.

After saying all this to a perfect stranger, Mitra was surprised with her openness towards Sandy. But somehow, she had a good feeling about her. When Sandy heard this, she patted her on the shoulder: "You'll be all right here. You seem to be a very pleasant person. The nurses took a liking to you I heard."

"Thank you," Mitra said.

"I'll tell you what. I will give you my phone number and you can call me if you'd like some company. I won't be going home for the weekend either. My reason is the same as yours. My daughter and her family went to Toronto to visit their friends. They will stay there for two nights."

Mitra was surprised and appreciative for such kindness, and thanked Sandy again. She promised Sandy she would call her if she got bored; "I have a large extended family. They usually call me or visit me on the weekend. Please do not think that I didn't want to call you; if anything, I would like to know you better because I find you to be a very interesting person."

"Thank you," Sandy said.

Mitra asked Sandy how long she'd been at the establishment.

"Tomorrow, it will be two years since I arrived."

"So, you have been here longer than Evica?" As soon as Mitra mentioned Evica's name, she felt sorry for bringing it up in conversation.

"Yes, of course. Evica came here about a year ago," Sandy said.

They both fell silent for a while, then Sandy said, "I would like to tell you something about Evica. You will hear the same thing from others so please do not think I'm talking Evica down. I'm telling you the truth. When Evica came in here she quickly warmed up to me, and we became very good friends until a new lady came named Dorothy. She was a very pleasant person but not pushy for friendship. One day Dorothy got sick and the nurse told me that Dorothy was not feeling well. I asked the nurse if Dorothy would like some company because before she got sick, she told me that her only daughter went on a holiday with her husband.

"The nurse said, 'I think it will be very nice of you to visit her. She doesn't have very many visitors.'

"When I started spending time visiting and being with Dorothy, Evica became furious with me, protesting my visiting Dorothy everyday. I explained the situation, but she would not listen to any reason I gave her. She stopped talking to me. Even if she did not break up our friendship, I would have because she was very unreasonable. Poor Dorothy died a week after and that's how it all ended up. I am sorry for telling you all this."

Mitra ended up saying, "Thank you for telling me."

"I hope she doesn't behave towards you as she did with me; I heard you speaking the same language and being together a lot," Sandy said.

Mitra nodded, "Whatever will be, will be."

When they entered the building, the same nurse who was very pleasant to Mitra asked her whether she was going home for the weekend. Mitra confirmed what she had already told Sandy. The nurse said, "That is all right; we don't mind having you around."

"Thank you," Mitra said. "I think with such good people around me I should be fine. Now I think I will go to my room and have some rest."

"That's a good idea, I will do the same," Sandy said.

Mitra thanked Sandy for her company. Sandy replied, "You are welcome. See you at lunch."

When Mitra left Sandy, she thought she was going to be fine, but she kept thinking about what Sandy said about Evica: how much should she believe? Sandy seemed like a nice lady, but one could never be sure, especially when one was in a vulnerable situation as Mitra was now. Well, somehow things would be all right. She thought Evica would come down and everything would be as before. Mitra would like that to happen. She enjoyed Evica's company and she could not believe that Evica would want to lose her friendship. But just in case, if Evica didn't want her friendship, nothing could be done. It wouldn't be the end of the world.

"I lived without Evica for 90 years and I certainly can live the rest of my life without Evica; if Evica wants it that way then she will be granted it. Friendship cannot be forced, bribed, or begged for, but has to come from one's own will and heart," Mitra said angrily.

This day, Mitra preferred stretching out on her bed instead of sitting on the chair. She felt a little tired from walking and she dozed off. Her husband, Petar, came into her dream. She dreamt that he was floating above her head and wanted to touch her. He had that mellow passion, the one he always had for her. In her dream, she tried to stretch her hands and touch his face because it was so close to hers. Somehow, she could not reach him. He remained in the same position but with a smile, as if he was trying to reassure her that everything would be all right, even if she couldn't touch him.

Mitra was so excited that he was there. She tried to move to one side and make room for him to lie beside her. She became upset when she could not move. Suddenly, she couldn't see his face anymore. Mitra started to scream, asking Petar not to leave. At the same time, she heard somebody knocking at the door. She hoped it was Petar coming back.

She woke up with a smile on her face. When she looked up, she saw the same nurse who greeted her at the front door a while ago.

"Are you all right, Mrs. Milutinovic?"

"Yes, I am."

The nurse asked what had happened. "I don't know exactly. I was tired when I came back from the walk with Sandy. I lay down and fell asleep. In my sleep I dreamt my husband came. At that moment I screamed. That was how it happened. I am very sorry, for startling you."

"It's fine, Mrs. Milutinovic. I may have startled you too because I rushed so quickly into your room. I thought something had happened to you. I am glad you are all right."

"Yes, I'm fine, thank you for your concern."

"Thank you, Mrs. Milutinovic. It is my job to take care of our residents."

"You are doing a wonderful job for us," Mitra said sincerely.

After the nurse left, Mitra uttered a big sigh and tears started running down her cheeks. She became sad again, "No, I'm not fine and I don't understand this life—this new and modern way of life; self centred and greedy living has become the norm. It is far removed from the way people thought and felt when I was young."

Mitra wondered if she was right in thinking like that. She concluded she was because all the comfort and wealth were meaningless if one is not happy.

"And I'm not," Mitra confessed. "No, no, this is not the happy ending of one's life, but the ending that comes to all of us."

Mitra heard the knock on the door. She quickly wiped away her tears, and said, "Come in."

Sandy entered.

"I came because the nurse told me you had a bad dream."

"Oh yes, yes, I did." She told Sandy what had happened.

Sandy knew Mitra was sad as they all were when they first arrive.

"I am all right," Mitra said. "It is a little hard to get used to a new place, away from the family."

"Of course it is. We all know what it's like at first. But don't worry, you will get used to it slowly and after a year, it becomes like your own home and your new family. That is why we are in here."

These remarks changed Mitra's thinking, "Sandy is saying the right thing because there is no other way. There is no way out."

She repeated Sandy's thoughts, "This is now my home and my family—how sad, but true."

"I tell you what; we will go out for lunch. There is a nice family restaurant close by. We will see some young faces there. It will take our minds off this place a bit. It will be refreshing to spend some time among people. If you do not have money with you, I'll pay for everything and you can pay me back when your family comes."

"I have my own money. My great-granddaughter brought me some money yesterday, but thank you for offering, Sandy."

"We'll both pay for the taxi to take us there and bring us back. I'm sure you cannot walk that long. We don't need to hurry back."

Mitra agreed to Sandy's idea. She was already feeling better.

"Thank God for Sandy," Mitra thought. "Sandy is my family now. I hope it won't end up like it did with Evica. That would be devastating."

Mitra felt that Sandy was a totally different person. Mitra had a wonderful time. She felt so good hearing families' conversation, laughter, and children crying. Sandy was an especially good companion. She even had a good sense of humour, as she cracked a few jokes.

The outing took about three hours. Mitra felt tired, but still in a pretty good mood. Sandy asked her just before they parted if she would be coming down for dinner.

"Yes, I will. I don't think I can eat much after such a good lunch, but I will have a little bit and a drink. I need to be with my family," Mitra said.

"That's right, you have to think that way," Sandy agreed.

Mitra thought, "The morning started badly but the afternoon was quite nice—as a matter of fact, really nice. So, I should not panic at every negative thing that happens. Thank God for Sandy, she is a very encouraging person and makes me feel good."

Mitra lay on her bed to get some rest. The phone rang, and it was her brother. He wanted to know how she was doing and, at the same time, to tell her he wouldn't be able to visit her because a friend from out of town had stopped by.

"That is all right; come when you have time."

After the call, Mitra wondered whether that was another excuse for not visiting.

It was time for dinner. She dressed up and went down. Lots of people had gone home, judging by the almost empty dining room. Sandy was waiting for Mitra and they sat together. They had an interesting conversation.

Mitra learned that Sandy was a linguistics professor but was acting like a lay person. She was not infatuated with her profession. Mitra was so pleasantly surprised and honoured to be sitting next to a person of such calibre who at the same time, had a down-to-earth attitude.

Sandy said to Mitra, "Please, Mrs. Milutinovic, think of me as a person who enjoys your company, not as a professor."

"Can you please call me Mitra, not Mrs. Milutinovic? I like to be called by my first name."

"That's fine. From now on you will be Mitra, and I'm going to be Sandy," Sandy said.

"I like that," Mitra said.

"What are we going to do for the rest of the night?" Sandy inquired.

"I'm open for suggestions," Mitra said.

"Would you like to watch a movie? Tonight, there's a very nice film, *Rain Man*, starring Dustin Hoffman," Sandy said.

"Oh, that is a very nice film. I saw it once a long time ago but I wouldn't mind seeing it again," Mitra said.

"Okay, in that case I have a big screen in my room, and we can watch it together," Sandy said.

Mitra was quite surprised with Sandy's friendly approach, and she asked, "Is that all right with you Sandy?"

"What's not to like about company?"

Mitra felt a little uneasy with such quick bonding and wondered whether Sandy could be a lesbian, "But what would she do with an old woman like me?"

Sandy looked a few years younger than Mitra. Then again Mitra's mind changed thinking, "What is wrong with me that I have to question everything. I have to stop that because such thinking makes my life miserable and very insecure."

Sandy offered Mitra a drink, but she declined. The film was wonderful; it was on the public channel that had no commercials. When the movie was done it was close to 10:30 pm. Mitra thanked Sandy for a lovely day and evening and left. For the first time, she was a little more comfortable in her new place. She prepared for bed, said her prayer, and thanked God and her new friend for a pleasant day.

She had a good night's sleep. When she woke up and looked through the window it was a beautiful, warm, and bright day. Around the retirement centre was nicely cut green grass with lots of flowers at the edges.

"Yes, mid-June is a beautiful time of the year. This will help me to settle down."

Mitra said a little prayer of thanks and also asked God to let her have as beautiful a day today and the next as she'd had yesterday. This morning she felt much better. She got herself ready to go down for breakfast. She heard the knock on her door. It was Sandy, saying, "Good morning, Mitra, are you ready for breakfast?"

"Yes, I'm ready."

Mitra felt good for having good company again. The dining room was still almost empty. People had not returned from the weekend. Mitra and Sandy had a table to themselves. As they ate, they were chatting about yesterday, especially how good the film was. Sandy complimented Dustin on how well he played his role.

"What are we going to do today?" Sandy asked.

"You are very good with planning things. I will leave it up to you and I will follow," Mitra answered.

"I suggest we get a taxi and go bowling."

"Bowling! You think I can bowl if I am not even very steady on my feet?"

"Don't worry, they have everything prepared for people like us. We can even have lunch there," Sandy said.

"That seems very nice, but I doubt if I can bowl."

"Have you ever bowled?" Sandy asked.

"Very little, when my grandchildren were old enough, I did some bowling with them. But at that time, I was much younger."

"I'd like you to keep me company. It's better for you to get out even if you do not bowl at all. You can watch me. We will have a good time," Sandy promised.

"I guarantee you that," Mitra said.

Mitra agreed to go if only for company because just being with Sandy was fun enough.

"I don't know if I have enough money for all of that," Mitra said.

"Don't worry. I have enough money for both of us. You will pay me back when you can."

When they got there, Mitra was surprised how many older people were there. She felt good as soon as she saw that. They paid for three sets of rounds. It took them quite a long time to finish each set. They both had coffee and a couple of small chocolates.

Sandy said, "There is a lot of energy in chocolates."

After they finished all three sets, Mitra was surprised that she was not feeling very tired. This was a good deterrent against stressful, negative thoughts. When the time came, they decided to have a hamburger and also to split medium French fries, and a large ginger ale.

Mitra felt like a teenager. She felt really, really good.

"Whenever you are ready to go, we will go," Sandy said.

"I still feel pretty good. Unless you would like us to go, let's stay a little longer."

"So, you like it, huh?"

"Yes, I do very much. Thank you for suggesting this great fun," Mitra said.

When they came back to their establishment, Mitra felt quite tired, but happy. Soon she sprawled on her bed and fell asleep. She slept until supper time. She did not feel hungry, but she decided to go down and have something to eat, and a drink. Most of all, she liked to be with Sandy. Dinner was delicious. It was a nice piece of roast, mashed potatoes, salad, and nice crème brulée for dessert. They both agreed to have a slow walk outside, because the weather was so great. They talked about their day and how wonderful it was.

As they were parting, they both agreed that they had had a wonderful weekend together. That was Mitra's first happy weekend after one month in the establishment and surprisingly a very nice weekend with a newfound friend: "I think God heard my prayer. Thank you, Lord, for your kindness."

Mitra was going to her room when she met Evica. She came over to Mitra and put her hand on Mitra's shoulder saying, "I'm sorry I rushed out on Saturday! It was an emergency; you know how we react in emergencies."

"Really, I don't know how you react to anything, but I'm finding out how you do your stunts."

"No, that was not a stunt but a real thing," Evica said.

"That's fine, we are going to leave it like that—it's your business."

Mitra went to her room without even saying 'good night' to Evica. She closed the door and soon after there was a knock at the door. Mitra opened the door; there was Evica acting slimy and saying, "Are you mad at me?"

"No, why should I be mad? You have a right to behave and act the way you want, but you cannot tell someone how to respond," Mitra said.

"Now I see, you are mad at me."

Mitra just shut the door saying, "good night." She did not hear Evica's reply to her, neither did she care. Mitra felt tired, got ready, and just about when she was going to bed, Sofija called with her cheerful, lovely voice, "Hi, Baba."

"Hi, honey."

"How are you?"

"Good, very good, I have had a very nice weekend with my new friend Sandy." She told Sofija everything they did.

"I'm so happy for you, Baba."

"And what did you all do?"

"We went to Kingston to see mom's parents. We had a great time. Grandma and Grandpa and the rest of their family asked how you've been. They all send you their regards."

"How are Gordon and Helen?"

"They are good. Only grandma Helen complains about her hip."

"Who doesn't have sore hips at our age?"

"Baba, is it all right if I come tomorrow around one in the afternoon?"

"Of course it is all right. What kind of question is that? You know how happy I am to see you."

"I like to hear that, Baba. I just thought you may be busy with something."

"No, no, not for you, you know you are always first in my book."

"Thanks, see you tomorrow. Good night."

"Good night, honey."

Mitra slept well. She was fully refreshed and happy. Downstairs in the dining room sat Sandy, at her usual place.

Mitra knew that Sandy was sitting with two ladies who went home for the weekend and had come back. There was room for one more person at Sandy's table. Sandy came over to ask Mitra if she wanted to join them. She brought Mitra over to the table and introduced her to two ladies saying, "This is Mitra Milutinovic."

They all said, "Pleased to meet you."

"Mitra, this is Mary and this one is Joan."

"Pleased to meet you, ladies."

They were very polite, speaking in light low voices about how bad the weather had been—so much rain making Lake Ontario overflow in areas low and closest to the lake, and flooding beautiful Toronto Island. "What can you do? We have ruined our environment and now we will have to pay for it. But the last few days, the weather has been very nice."

"Yes, that is true," Mary added.

Joan turned to Mitra asking her how she liked it here since she was the newcomer: "It's always difficult at first to adapt to a new environment."

"The first couple of days, I did not like it very much, but thank God for Sandy. I had a wonderful weekend with her."

"That's good. I'm very glad for you," Joan said.

"Thank you, Joan," Mitra replied.

After breakfast Mitra went back to her room. She needed to call her son Marko because when she checked the messages this morning, she found his message asking her to call him at home. He had been on holiday with his wife, Doris, in Italy. She had a good and long conversation about his trip. He told her how he loved everything he had seen: "It was a wonderful holiday. We could not have asked for a nicer gift."

"I'm glad you had such a good time."

"Mom, we are a bit tired today, we will come to see you tomorrow. Is that okay with you?"

"Of course it is. Have a rest, will see you tomorrow."

Mitra sat down, took a piece of paper to mark down some of her memories from back home because Sofija was coming after lunch and she would ask her a lot of questions: "I better not think about it now. I don't know what she is going to ask me anyway."

She went downstairs to the front entrance. Evica was sitting there all alone. Mitra did not bother to say anything to her. She just passed by. She looked on the wall where the bulletin board was. There was a note: "New exercise program, three times a week for free. It is really easy for everyone to do it. Start time: 10:30 am."

"It starts in a few minutes in the gym," Mitra said. "I better go and see for myself what is going on."

Mitra found others there: Sandy, Mary, and Joan. When they saw Mitra, they welcomed her, "Glad you came. You will love it."

"I hope so. If not the exercise, I love the company."

"I did not want to ask you to come with us because I thought you wanted to make up with Evica," Sandy said.

"Not yet," Mitra said.

The lady who was in charge of the exercise said, pointing at Mitra, "I see we have a new face."

Sandy introduced her, "This is my friend Mitra."

The lady came over and shook Mitra's hand saying, "Welcome. Do not worry; you just do the simple things you are comfortable with. I guarantee you; you will do much more, even more by next week, if you keep coming."

"Thank you," Mitra said. "I'll do my best, I have plenty of free time."

"The only thing you need is the will to do it," said the lady.

Mitra did exactly as the lady told her. Sandy and her companions were doing much better. They were younger than

Mitra, and also had been involved in the programs in the centre for some time already. At 11:00 am the exercise session was over and Mitra felt a little tired, but optimistic and hopeful for improvement. She was happy that she was getting involved in the community program, as Sandy said, "in the family."

When she came out, Evica was still sitting there in the same place, talking with another resident.

Mitra went to her room to get some rest and prepare for lunch. Lunch was really good: spaghetti with meatballs and cabbage and kale salad with nice mild dressing. Dessert was fruit cocktail. Sandy asked Mitra what she would be doing in the afternoon. She told her that her great-granddaughter Sofija was coming.

"I don't know when she will go home, usually she stays for a few hours."

"Good for you," Sandy said.

"Thank you," Mitra answered. "What about you, Sandy, what are you going to do?"

"My friends and I are going to play cards. Would you like to play?"

"I don't know how to play your cards. I only play 52 and sevens."

"It's not hard to learn. After dinner, you come to my room and I'll teach you."

"You will?"

"Of course. Why not?"

"Thank you, Sandy. You are a lifesaver and my true family in here." They both laughed.

Chapter 11

Sofija came with coffee and a few Timbits. This was her usual way. They first talked about simple things while drinking coffee. After they finished Sofija said, "Let's go, Baba."

"Go where?" Mitra asked.

"Baba, how come you always forget our project? Your life in the old country."

"I thought we were all done with it. I don't know what else to say. I told you plenty of everything I remembered."

"No way. I'm sure there is more. Please tell me about your coming to Canada."

"And what do you think I can tell you?" Mitra asked.

"I'm sure there is a lot you could tell me. I'd like to know how you were asked and who asked you if you wanted to go to Canada to marry my great-grandfather?"

"My family and Petar's family were not from the same village but knew each other through Petar's relatives, our neighbours. Petar's mother saw me at a church gathering. There was always a big celebration at the church's Patron Saint feast. At that time, I was only 18. Petar's mother told me later on, after I said yes to marrying Petar, that she was sure I was the right girl for her son."

"Baba, what happened after Petar's mother saw you at the church?"

"After a couple of days, she and her husband came to our house to ask my parents whether I would agree to go to

Canada to marry their son. I was not home at that time. When I came home, my parents told me about the proposal. Remember, parents were the ones who first proposed to a girl's parents, not to the girl. My parents asked me what I thought about that. I didn't know what to say, but I wasn't enthusiastic about it, mostly because it was too far, and I would be away from my family forever.

"At that time, in the midfifties people never thought it would be possible to visit back and forth. For our villagers, Canada was a different planet from which you never came back. I had a boyfriend in the village with whom I was in love and he was in love with me, but his parents wanted him to marry another girl, and eventually he did. Parents had a lot of influence on their children. The same day Petar's mother saw me in the church, I saw a very nice young man. He asked me for my name, and I told him. He told me he would come one evening with his friend for *prelo*. *Prelo* meant gathering in someone's house in the evening. He said he wanted to know me better. I liked him, and impatiently waited for him to come to *prelo* in my house. Mr. and Mrs. Milutinovic came a couple more times, trying to convince me to agree.

"They told me that any girl would grab such an opportunity to go to Canada. Indeed, people in our village were saying positive things about Canada, just as if they were there. Two weeks later, I got a letter and picture from Petar. He looked very handsome, formally dressed in a black suit, white shirt, red and black-striped tie. The letter was very, very skilfully composed. I always wondered whether a professional wrote that letter. He later reassured me he wrote it. The words of the letter were very convincing.

"In his letter, he told me how Canada was a wonderful place to live: 'A lot of our people live here. I promise you, you will never feel lonely. Imagine the prosperity of your children here in comparison to the village life there? My mother highly praises your good nature and your beauty. I am already in love with you, my sweet neighbour. I wish to get your letter and a picture, so I can fall even more deeply in love with you.' The letter was quite long."

"Baba, he was very clever and obviously in love. So, what happened after that?" Sofija asked.

"Petar's parents kept pressuring for an answer because a month had passed since they first asked. The second letter came from Petar within 10 days after the first one. He sent another picture with him and his friends sitting on the grass having a picnic. In the background were many people, sitting, walking, standing: 'You can see there are many of our people in Canada, especially in Hamilton,' he wrote in his letter, 'You will not feel lonely.'

"The young man whom I met at the church never showed up. He may have heard about the offer I got, so he stayed away. One and a half months after Petar's parents' proposal, my parents agreed I would go to Canada to marry Petar. In order to start processing papers, Petar and I had to be married in city hall, or civil court. Petar sent his consent for marriage. Soon after, we were married and had a small wedding organized by our parents; there was no groom at the wedding. It took me about two years to get the papers. My parents and I were not so sure whether I would get the papers or not. Spending my prime time without my husband was threatening my ability to have a family."

"Poor Baba," Sofija said. Mitra did not say anything but just shrugged.

"How did you travel to Canada? By ship or by plane?" Sofija asked.

"I came by plane."

"How was the flight?"

"I can't tell you much about it. I only understood that I was high up in the sky. There was a lot of noise and shaking. I did not like that. I was sitting by the window. I was afraid to look down. I didn't like it when the plane was ascending or descending; I was glad when it landed."

"Where did you get the second connection when you were flying from your homeland? At that time, planes didn't make direct flights from Yugoslavia to Canada," Sofija asked.

"That is true. We stopped in Paris; it was a French airline."

"How were you feeling? Were you scared?"

"I think I was beyond being scared. I felt as if I was put in a balloon and was being tossed around, without any idea where I was going or what would happen when I finally arrived there."

"Was it that bad, Baba?"

"I don't think you can imagine my position. I lived in a village among 50 neighbourhood homes and the people I knew all my life. As I told you before, I never ventured even to the smallest city that was closest to us except two or three times."

"How long did it take to arrive in Canada?"

"It took me two days, but I don't know how many hours I was in the air or waiting in the transfer area. At that time, planes were not as safe or fast."

"How was it when you came to Canada?"

"The airport wasn't as busy as today; the service person at the airport kind of guided me until I met Petar. I recognized him right away from the picture he sent me."

"How did you feel when you saw your future husband for the first time?"

"After I landed and finally met him, I felt safe and relaxed. Petar came with his best friend who had a car and did us a favour because Petar didn't have a car or a license at that time.

Generally speaking, not many people had their driver's license or owned cars."

"What time of the day did you arrive?"

"I think some time in the afternoon."

"So, what happened when you came to where Petar lived?"

"Nothing special, because Petar wasn't a very extravagant person. He was good natured and in control of his emotions. There were a few people who met me at Petar's house, mostly men, and two younger women. Everybody was very pleasant, attentive, and full of questions about life and the situation in the old country under Communist rule. I told them what I could and what I knew. I noticed right away their hatred towards the Communist party, but I could not understand why because I thought it was the best social system.

"I was lucky; Petar sensed I might say something they would not like and cause bad feelings between me and his friends. Petar asked me how my flight was, even though I'd already told him in detail. This was meant to change the subject. After his friends left, Petar warned me about saying good things about the Communist regime. I wasn't pleased that he was putting down my Communists, until I realized later how badly brainwashed I was. People in democratic countries are surprised that others can like regimes such as Communism. The leaders of all regimes cleverly capture the hearts and minds of the younger people, while they keep older people under strict control, so they cannot make any moves. In that way, the regime keeps itself safe."

"Were you tired when you arrived?"

"Yes, I was very tired and doubtful about my life in Canada."

Sofija was excited about what Baba was going to say next.

"What happened after everybody was gone?" asked Sofija.

"Nothing really, Petar was looking at me. I blushed every

time he looked at me. He took my hand gently in his, telling me how very glad he was to see me in his house and with him."

"Please do not worry, everything will be fine. We will take things slowly—as slowly as you want. Just remember, I love what I see in front of me. I am ready for close relationship whenever you are—you know what I mean," he said.

I looked at him shyly.

"But it is not only up to me but equally up to you. I will wait for that moment," he said.

He showed me where the washroom and bathtub were and how to flush the toilet and to turn the faucets on and off. He encouraged me to have a bath. I did. It felt so wonderful to have hot water. I'd never experienced that before.

He took me to my bedroom. The furniture looked nice and the bedding was very white and beautiful. He told me, "This is your bedroom from now on, until you are ready and willing that I join you."

He asked me, "Is that all right with you?"

I said politely, "Yes, yes, it is."

He took both of my hands into his and looked again into my eyes.

"Is it all right if I kiss you?" he asked.

I nodded my approval. It was just a simple, gentle kiss. He stroked my hair saying, "Sleep well my angel and do not worry about getting up early. Sleep as long as you need and want. I will be downstairs waiting for you, and then you are going to tell me what you want for breakfast. I will prepare it for you."

He kissed me gently one more time without waiting for permission, turned around and closed the door behind him.

After he was gone, I looked around the room and straight above the headboard hung a big picture of me, the very first picture I sent him. Under the picture was written: "My girl, my future wife." When I saw that, I had goose bumps.

"Me too, Baba, everything you are telling me looks so simple and romantic. My great-grandpa truly was a wise and kind man," Sofija said.

"Yes, indeed, he was," Mitra replied.

I was tired and slept long. When I woke up, I looked at the clock; it was 9:30 am. I jumped out of bed, got washed and dressed. When I got downstairs, Petar was sitting in the kitchen reading newspapers. When he saw me, he got up and came over to me, "Good morning dear, did you have a good sleep?"

"Yes, I did. I slept really well, who wouldn't in such a comfortable bed."

"I'm happy your bed was comfortable," said Petar. "What would you like to eat? You are young; you must be hungry."

"I'm not too hungry, but I can eat. Can I help you with something?"

"Do you know how to cook?" Petar asked.

"Yes, I do, but only our village-style cooking. I don't think cooking in Canada is the same as in our village."

"Don't say that," Petar said, "I remember my mother and my grandmother made tasty food. I like sauerkraut and smoked meat or a good homemade soup. I didn't like cornmeal very much, but every house cooked that. Are those meals still staple foods?"

"Yes, of course they are. These foods are still prepared in every home. Those who have enough food are lucky. There are some families who don't."

"How do these families survive?" Petar asked.

"Some survive and some don't; usually the well-off families help out. Winters are the worst because if you don't have anything stored for the winter due to a previously poor harvest due to drought or some kind of natural crop destruction, you are doomed."

"So, nothing has changed," Petar said.

"No, not much, but slowly it's getting better."

"In what way?" Petar asked.

"More young people are moving into the cities to find work. There is only so much arable land to grow crops. Families are expanding in large numbers and require more food."

"Do families still have 7, 10, or 15 children?" Petar asked.

"Yes, of course they do," I answered.

"Here in Canada, families don't have that many children, usually two to four," Petar said.

"Oh, that's one third of our village families," I answered. I was tempted to ask how many Petar and I would have, but I thought I'd better stay silent.

Getting back to cooking, Petar asked if they still cook on a hearth fire or on the stove.

"We cook on a wood stove. We have made some advancements in our domestic life, but there are still a lot of families using a hearth," I said.

"That's good; it's about time that you did. Is that Tito's progress or have people become wiser on their own?"

I only nodded without saying anything. My father warned me not to say much about Tito or the Communist party to Petar or his friends before I got to know them better.

"Sorry, sweetheart, for saying that," Petar said.

To shift back to cooking, I said, "You know we don't have electricity in our village. It will be very hard for me to handle electric utilities."

"It will be much easier for you to cook on electric or gas ranges."

"I hope so," I answered.

Petar admitted that he didn't have any breakfast yet because he was waiting for me to come down. "I wanted us to eat breakfast together. I will have two eggs, bacon, toast, and coffee. What about you?" He was talking to me in Serbo-Croatian, but it sounded awkward.

"I will have the same," I said.

"I watched what Petar did and tried to help a little. Every moment together, made me more relaxed and happier. He was in his prime at 31. He was also a very handsome, very pleasant man who smiled all the time. His eyes were so amazingly happy, bright, and blue, reflecting his healthy body and mind.

Petar asked me what I would like to do that day. I shrugged, "You ask me what I want to do. I don't know. I'll do whatever you tell me to do."

He smiled, "You're acting like an obedient young wife. You don't have to be that. You can speak your mind; you're no longer in your village."

I smiled back, "I will remember that in the future."

"Stupid of me, I'm going against myself. Can I change my statement?" Petar joked.

"Not a chance! It stays now and forever," I said.

"Can I suggest we go downtown?"

"Where is that?"

"That is about two to three kilometres away. It's the centre of the city."

We leisurely enjoyed our breakfast as we talked, teasing each other and laughing a lot.

"We need to buy some things for the house and some clothes for you. Let's go downtown and spend the day there," Petar said.

We hopped on the bus and went on our way, as a couple.

When we boarded the bus, I looked around to see what was going on. I saw a lady walking a dog on a leash. I'd not seen someone walking a dog before. The dog itself looked unusually clean and happy, marching forward like a soldier.

Even its head was held high. Everything was contrary to the way dogs were treated in my village. Our dogs were usually dirty, skinny, and afraid of people because people always chased them because they would be so hungry and sometimes kill a small domestic animal for food. I was wondering how I would get used to Canadian culture. I was sure it would take some time.

When the bus stopped to pick up and discharge passengers, an older lady entered the bus. Petar got up and politely offered her his seat. The lady sat beside me and said something. I did not have a clue what she said but Petar told me the lady said, "Your young friend is a very nice and caring young man." Petar made a joke of it telling me, "See, even old ladies like me; I hope young ones will too." We both smiled at Petar's comment. More people got in and Petar was pushed away from me. He told me not to worry, just keep sitting until he came to get me. I needed reassurance in order to feel safe.

Without Petar nearby, I paid full attention to the scenery outside. I was surprised that people kept their grass like a carpet, all evenly cut. There were also a lot of flowers around houses. There were some very nice bushes, some of them neatly shaped into various shapes. "Quite amazing," I thought. Back home all the bushes would be broken by the animals or children. There were not many decorative bushes around the houses in my village. There was no way that villagers could keep their landscape around the house because there was no opportunity for that. I saw a man watering the grass around his house, and wondered if Petar had been doing the same around our house—our house was a very pleasant thought for me, and I smiled happily. In my village, we scarcely had water to drink and wash with in the summer much less to water the grass with.

The bus stopped again. I saw a beautiful house, quite large in size, and wonderfully kept. A man sat on the grass next to a little girl. The girl was truly a beautiful child. She had a beautiful dress, red with blue polka dots, white trim around the arms and the neck, and two to three inches of white layer trim at the hem. The dress was puffed up and well above her knees. She had long, brown, soft curls hanging down almost to her waist. But what attracted my attention was the child's beautiful and happy face. The beautiful rosy, clean cheeks were pink and lively. She was running around the man saying something to him that I could have understood if I knew English.

I wished I could have understood what the little girl was saying to the man—probably her father. I wished to have such a beautiful little girl, but I was pretty sure Petar would prefer a son in order to preserve his family name. That was so important in our tradition. I was sure Petar would want to start a family right away. Since I came from a culture in which a girl's purpose was to marry and have children soon after, I was thinking along the lines of starting a family right away. But I wanted to have a girl first. I remembered my brother's ballads when he sang about how a princess wanted to have girls before boys. Among other reasons, the princess thought that her girls would marry off before her sons would marry, so there wouldn't be any quarrels in the family. I confirmed my wish again, but whether I had a girl or a boy, it would be all right. This was not my village where girls were less valued than boys, I hoped.

We came to a large-sized building. Small children were coming out of it. They were noisy: screaming, talking, laughing, and running in every direction. A couple of older people came out and they were talking loudly to the children. I assumed it was a public school because the children were small and the grown-ups—teachers, I assumed—came out to keep the children in line. The children soon forgot what they were told and continued playing and making noise.

At the last stop, before we got off the bus, a large black man boarded the bus. I'd never seen a black person before. Since the bus was full, he was holding on to the pole near me. I could not see anything but his pants and his shoes. I wished I could have had a picture of him to send back home to my family to see what a wonderful country I'd come to live in.

If I could have spoken English, everything would have been much easier. The bus stopped; people began getting out. I heard Petar say in Serbo-Croatian, "Remain seated until I come to you." A moment later, he was beside me, putting his hand on my shoulder. "We're here," he said, asking me to get up. I walked off the bus hand in hand with Petar.

There were a lot of young men and women holding hands. I was surprised to see that, because I never saw this public affection in my village. Such a thing would be indecent. People were not supposed to display their affection in public. That was considered immoral. As we were walking slowly down the street, I heard two people conversing in Serbo-Croatian. I was surprised to hear my language spoken in this big city. Petar heard them too. He said, "Don't be surprised to hear our language in this city. Many of our people came here after the First World War. We call them old settlers. Many more people came after the Second World War, like me. We will go to church on Sunday. You are going to see our community.

"Hamilton is a very important place with two large steel plants. Since many of us who came here do not have much education and didn't know the language, this was the easiest place to find a job. Our people are hard working. They welcome the opportunity to have a job."

Now, I understood a little better about the mixture of different people, "What about the black people? Where did they come from?" I asked.

"They are either new Canadians like you or descendants of Americans who escaped slavery. They like it here very much, I think. It is better in Canada but not perfect: many white people are unkind or ignore them."

There were lots of people going every which way. Many different stores displayed their products. I never saw so many different things. I felt overwhelmed and a little ashamed for the lack of knowledge because I felt lost to the point that it was disturbing me. What will Petar's friends think of me? I thought again that I had to try to learn as fast as I could in order to feel more comfortable here.

Petar sensed that I was deep in thought and he asked me if everything was all right.

"Yes, yes, I am all right. Why do you ask?"

"I ask because you are so quiet."

"I was quiet because I was thinking how wonderful everything is and how am I going to get used to all these things?"

"Don't worry, you will get used to it. You are young and young people adapt to things quite fast."

"Yes, that is true, but you understand where I came from. It overwhelms me to be exposed to all these changes so quickly."

"Yes, I understand. You've got lot of time to adjust to these changes. I hope you will accept our living together and be happy with it. That is what is important to me."

I smiled because I was happy that Petar was wondering whether I was falling in love with him. I surely was overtaken by his charm, looks, and the care he was showing me. I still did not feel comfortable to tell him I had fallen in love with him.

My upbringing didn't allow me to admit this so quickly. Hopefully, he would soon see how much I desired to be intimate with him.

We were entering a very big store. Petar told me, "This is Simpsons-Sears, a very popular store. We will look for some clothing and shoes for you and whatever else you would like to have."

"Are you saying you are going to buy the whole store for me?" I asked.

"Not exactly," Petar answered. "As much as I would like to, I'm limited with my money."

I admitted I was joking with him. We walked through the store. Petar urged me to pick up some clothing I liked. "I'm not sure what to chose; you better pick up something that you think would be nice and not too expensive. Everything looks so beautiful," I said.

We walked through the store for some time. Petar asked me again to pick up something I liked. I wasn't sure what to choose because I was afraid to look foolish. Many sales people talked to Petar suggesting what would look nice on me. They were pleasant, assuming I knew what I liked. They did not know that I had no experience in shopping. When I was home my mother would buy some material and make a kind of dress worn by girls in our village. It would be an old-fashioned dress that would be fitted for the size of the girl's body from the waist up. Buttons were sewn from the waist up to adjust for comfort. It would have long sleeves. Girls did not wear short sleeves at that time. The dress would be pleated from the waist down for fullness on the hips and would reach to the ankles.

The only modern dress I'd worn was when I was preparing to go to Canada. My parents bought me two dresses and shoes for the trip. That is how much I knew about shopping.

Petar picked some clothes that he thought would be nice for me. He asked me to try them on to see if they fit. Petar didn't mind if I displayed cleavage. I had a beautiful body. As I was trying garments on, the sales lady said, "Your wife has a beautiful figure. Everything looks so perfect on her." Petar smiled as he agreed that he was a lucky man to have such a beautiful woman on his arm.

"Yes, you are," the sales lady said.

The sales lady tried to push some more clothes for us to buy, but Petar said, "Thank you; this is good enough for now."

After we bought everything Petar suggested we stop at a restaurant and have lunch. "Lunch at this time of the day, isn't it too early? We just had a breakfast not long ago. If we ate this much in my village, we would have consumed all our food before the winter was half over."

"Well, we are lucky we are not in our villages."

As we were talking about this, a young girl about my age, walked by us; her face was very pretty, but her body was twice the size of mine. Petar said, "If she lived in your village, she would be slim like you. Not exactly but definitely she would be smaller. She could eat a little less even in Canada."

We walked into a huge store. It was called Kresge's. It had all kinds of clothing and household utensils. In one corner they had a few smaller tables and one very large counter. We sat down at the counter. Petar looked at the menu and asked me what I would like to have. I felt excited as I was looking at the girls preparing different orders of food on a very long hot grill. They were handling food so quickly; I was amazed at their skill. I told Petar to order whatever he liked. Petar said he would order a hamburger and French fries with a Coke for himself.

The waitress wrote down exactly what Petar ordered. Petar pointed out to me, "This is the same as what I ordered for you."

"Oh, no, no, that will be too much for me," I said.

"Don't worry about that, I will finish what you cannot manage," Petar said.

When the waitress brought us the order, I looked at the hamburger, lifted the upper part of the bun and saw underneath something yellow like baby's poop, with something green and white. All this debris covered the meat and the bun. I put back the top part of the bun. Petar looked at me knowing that I didn't like it. He asked me, "Do you still eat bread separate from everything else and you don't put anything on it that is gooey and wet?"

"Yes, that is the way we eat in our village. Bread is the main staple; we eat a little piece of meat or cheese with a big chunk of bread."

Petar asked me to try it, "Take only one bite."

To please him I took a bite, but I could not swallow it. I started to gag; I was ready to bring up. Petar saw what was going on; he took my hand and rushed me back to the toilet. He was anxiously waiting for me to come out. I came out all red with puffy eyes. "Thank God you are all right; I was worried about you." The waitress asked if everything was all right. Petar said, "Yes everything was good." Turning to me, "I am going to order you another hamburger because you loved it so much."

We both laughed.

After that experience, I didn't eat hamburgers for years. Petar finished both hamburgers. I looked at him as he ate them, amazed that he could like them so much. I finished my French fries. I truly enjoyed those. Petar even give me some of his. After lunch we wandered around looking and enjoying each other's company. As we roamed around, Petar pointed at different buildings and told me what each building was used for. "This is Hamilton City Hall where Hamiltonians' property taxes, roads, and police are administered."

Petar wasn't sure if I understood what he was talking about, so he said, "Don't worry about it now. I am sure you will learn all that in the future."

He pointed out a big building.

"This is the post office. My letters to you were sent from this building. Your letters were also received in this building and distributed to my mailbox."

Petar asked me if I liked his letters. I gently smiled and said, "Yes, I did like them very much, and I read each one more than once."

"Thank you," he said.

I asked him whether he liked my letters, "Probably they were not as interesting as yours were."

"Oh, yes," Petar said, "I loved every sentence, every word, you wrote because they were coming from you, my sweet lady. I truly found your letters very interesting and your thoughts sensible."

I was pleased with his compliment, but just smiled gently. I wasn't used to saying many thank yous. It was not in my upbringing. Petar told me, "When someone says nice things to you or if they give you something, or you do any other favour, say 'thank you.' It is customary here to make an acknowledgment with 'thank you.' I know back in Yugoslavia, this is not customary, instead they would say, 'Thanks to the Lord.' Here also people expect you to say that you're sorry for doing anything unpleasant. I hope you understand me correctly. I'm not trying to be smart or to offend you in any way. That is not my reason for saying it. I know where you've come from and our customs from there, which I don't think have changed very much since I left the country. In Canada, customs are different.

"I mentioned to you before, don't get mad or disappointed. I'm sure you will get accustomed to Canadian ways."

I felt a bit guilty, but I was not mad at Petar for telling me that. I finally said to him, "Thank you for everything."

"You're welcome," Petar answered.

"And what is the welcome for?"

Petar started to laugh, "It's another gesture that means, I appreciate your thank you."

I said, "You spend a lot of time with these different gestures."

"Yes, we do."

"I think one day I will become a true Canadian. You wait and see."

We both laughed.

We sat in Gore Park on the bench holding hands. We were encircled by tall buildings: The Royal Connaught Hotel, The Canadian Imperial Bank of Commerce, Eaton's, Kresge's. Inside the park were statues of Queen Victoria, Sir John MacDonald, the first prime minister of Canada, and some other statues.

It was almost 4:30 pm. Petar suggested we go home. The bus was tightly packed because it was rush hour. People were going home from work. Petar and I were pushed all the way to the back of the bus. People kept pouring in. Petar and I were holding onto the bar facing one another. Every time the driver stepped on the brakes, they hurled us into each other. We didn't mind that at all. My face was getting red. It felt so wonderful. At the next stop we were supposed to get off. Petar pulled the cord to let the driver know and also to let me know what to do when I went to the city by myself.

Chapter 12

We came home at five. We sat in the sitting room. He sat on the chesterfield, I sat on a chair. We relived our pleasant day in the city. We began to feel relaxed with each other. Petar tried to take off his tie, pretending he couldn't do it. I got up and came over to help him. When the tie came off, Petar playfully pulled me down onto his lap. I totally melted in his embrace but was not sure how to react. I expected him to initiate the action of love. He stroked my hair and kissed me gently a few times.

I said, "Everything we saw today was very interesting."

"I'm glad you liked it," Petar said. "We will go again soon since you like it so much."

"Is the bus fare very expensive?" I asked.

Petar smiled, "Look at my little lady; she is already concerned about spending our money."

I blushed believing that I must have expressed myself the wrong way. Petar noticed that I felt uncomfortable because of my red face.

"Mitra, please, I didn't mean anything bad; I only wanted us to have some fun and to be more open with each other."

I smiled at him very pleasantly to show him that I was very happy to be with him.

"That's my girl; I like to see you smiling, that makes me very happy. No, Mitra, the bus fare downtown is very cheap. You should not concern yourself about that."

Petar got off the chesterfield and took my hand. He told me that he would like to show me certain things I should know when he is away.

He first showed me a little window on the side of the house.

"This is the mailbox. The newspapers come in the early morning hours. I always pick them up because I like to read them before I go to work. The milk and bread are delivered between seven and eight. You will need to pick them up as soon as you hear the delivery man, especially the milk. Leave the milk in the fridge and the bread in the bread box. The mail, such as letters and bills, comes around 10:00 am. Take them inside the house. I will explain to you about the bills, so you will know where our money is going. Will you be all right with that?" Petar asked.

"Yes, of course, I will do anything you want me to do. Sometimes I might forget something. I'll ask you more than once to show me and tell me again. That is if I have already forgotten how to do certain things."

"We agree that we will cooperate," Petar said.

"Yes, we do," I agreed.

"I must remind you that sometimes for different reasons deliveries do not arrive on time or even not at all. Don't worry about that. We have a corner store nearby; we can buy what we need there. We won't starve, I promise you. Please don't worry, we will do things together. One more important thing," Petar said, "you have to learn how to use the gas stove. It can be dangerous and it can even harm you."

He didn't want to scare me by telling me, "It can kill you and blow the house up. I will show you how to use it safely until you are comfortable using it."

"Thank you," I said.

"There you are! You are already my little Canadian!"

We went back into the sitting room and sat the way we were sitting before. Petar made light conversation with some questions about back home; mostly how young men and women teased each other. Petar was in love and he wanted to raise my desire for lovemaking. He knew his gestures were effective because I kept blushing and kept shifting in the chair. Finally, he said, "It's dinner time and we have nothing to eat. What would you like, another hamburger?"

"No, no, more muddy hamburgers," I answered.

"Then, I'm going to buy roast chicken and potatoes, you seem to like them."

"Yes, I do."

"Do you like chicken?" Petar asked.

"Yes, I do," I replied.

Petar went to get the food. I was alone in the house. I was surprised how everything was delivered to us at the house. I started looking around the house. My new way of life felt overwhelming and strange to me. I sensed that Petar wanted us to become intimate. I wanted the very same thing with all my heart, but I was afraid I wouldn't please him the way he expected. I was taught that sex was dirty and was not to be enjoyed, but only to be done for procreation purposes. Sex was a taboo word for girls. Nobody had told me anything nice about sex, yet I was burning with desire to have my first lovemaking experience with my husband.

On the way to the store, Petar thought about how to make love with his bride. "I desire her very much, I am sure that she feels the same for me. I know our old-fashioned upbringing stands in her way." Petar planned how to do it: "I am going to take her to the movie now showing at Ottawa Street's Tivoli Theatre. It's a perfect movie to arouse a young woman's sexual desire, *Cat on a Hot Tin Roof.* After we return home, I will think of something to get from her room."

Petar felt that his plan was pretty clever, and it would work. When Petar came back with chicken and roast potatoes the table was already set. Petar thanked me for that. He cut up the chicken asking me what part of the chicken I preferred. I pointed to the leg. We were very hungry and enjoyed our meal with a glass of red wine.

I took some more potatoes and salad. I asked Petar if I had taken too much chicken.

"No, you take as much as you can eat," Petar said.

"We don't eat this much meat back home."

"I know you don't; this is not back home, this is Canada."

"The chicken was very tasty," I exclaimed.

"I know, it was baked for you. Was it better than hamburger?" Petar said.

"Please don't mention hamburger, especially when I am enjoying such delicious food."

"I won't. I am sorry about that."

Petar brought two Cokes because that was considered a young person's drink. He pulled a chocolate bar from his pocket and offered me the first piece. I took the first piece saying, "You are going to make me fat if you continue feeding me like this."

"That is my intention, God willing."

I got the idea that he was not talking about fat, but something more important.

After we finished dinner, which I enjoyed very much, Petar suggested that we go see a good movie called *Cat on a Hot Tin Roof*, starring Paul Newman and Elizabeth Taylor. I didn't know what all those words meant. I had never seen a movie before. I didn't know the people Petar mentioned. I thought the easiest thing for me was to agree with my husband's idea.

The film was too much for me. It was sexually explicit and disgusting, especially Elizabeth Taylor's acting, which would put any decent woman to shame. I didn't understand English and didn't know what the movie was all about, neither did I care to know. Petar tried to explain certain points, but I only responded with, "a-ha, a-ha," without letting Petar know how I felt about it. People were getting annoyed with Petar. At one point, a man behind us got really angry, "Why did you come to watch the movie if you don't understand the language. Go back where you came from and watch the film in your language; stop disturbing people here."

I was afraid that Petar would start a fight. I couldn't wait for the movie to end. When the movie finished, Petar asked me how I liked the movie. I didn't want to hurt his feelings so I told him I liked it but liked the popcorn and pop more.

People were pouring out of the movie, mostly young couples holding hands. Petar grabbed my hand. For a moment, I felt uncomfortable being held by a man even though he was my husband. I relaxed after a few minutes after seeing that everybody was doing the same thing.

Petar suggested we walk home because it wasn't very far. When we came home, Petar poured a glass of wine for himself. He asked me to join him. "Wine is good for relaxation, and that is what both of us need." I guessed what his motives with the movie and wine were.

We sat down on the chesterfield, this time close to each other. Petar asked me if I wouldn't mind sitting close to him. The wine glasses sat on the coffee table nearby. He cut up some cheese and bread into little squares. Petar wasn't used to fancy food; sometimes, he went with his friends to a Serbian restaurant for some special occasions. He liked the food there better than other countries' cuisine, because he hadn't developed a taste for foreign foods yet.

Petar was very busy as he kept entertaining me. He kept alternating between kissing and stroking my hair and lifting the plate and offering cheese, bread, and wine, saying, "Cheers, my darling." I felt that the time for intimacy was getting closer. I was confused between my desire to make love with my husband and the little voice whispering from back home, "Watch it, sex is a dirty thing; be careful."

I downed a full glass of wine and since I'd seldom had more than half a glass before, I felt giggly and light headed. I slowly became less on the defensive. Petar thought that was a good time to go off to bed. He suggested, "It's time to go to bed. It's already past eleven." I was disappointed, even hurt, when we had to stop and go to bed, but didn't say anything. I just followed Petar upstairs to my bedroom, where I'd slept the previous night alone.

He walked into my bedroom, kissed me a few times and stroked my hair, before saying, "Good night, my sweetheart, sleep well."

At this point, I was wondering why we stopped. Was it because Petar said that we should move slowly towards intimacy. I was ready and wanted that moment to happen right then. All the warnings from back home didn't stop my desire to make love with my husband that night.

Prior to going to bed, Petar pretended he was going upstairs to the bathroom. He left his watch on the night table half hidden from the full view beside my bed. After Petar left me in my bedroom, he knew this was the right moment to make love. He waited for a few minutes for me to undress, wash up, and prepare for bed. He did the same thing but tonight he would share the bed with his bride.

When Petar thought it was the right time, he knocked on my bedroom door. I was already in bed crying. I quickly wiped away my tears and said, "Come in." Petar told me he'd forgotten his watch on the dresser and he needed it. Once he got into the bedroom, he sat on the side of my bed. He kissed me a few more times. He told me he was cold; he went under the covers with me. When our bodies touched, we melted into each other. That night we made love more than once.

After our first night of intimacy, I wasn't shy anymore. I felt relaxed and enjoyed our intimate moments. We acted like two teenagers playing and teasing each other. My feelings changed from uneasiness to full enjoyment in the new environment with my husband.

I often teased Petar about how clever he was in preparing me for lovemaking. I would say to him how about a glass of wine but we didn't need anything to help us have our intimate moments. I was happy. I learned to handle all the chores around the house, even how to operate the gas stove. Mrs. MacDonald and Petar were helping me to learn. It was going slowly, not as fast as I expected. After a few days, Petar told me it was the time to get together with our friends to celebrate our wonderful union. That would be our wedding ceremony.

"What does wedding mean?" I asked.

"It's a special celebration for the two people who are marrying."

"Oh, are we marrying again?" I asked.

"Yes, my darling, we are."

"But we already got married in Yugoslavia."

"Yes, we did, but we are going to get married now in our church, Saint Nicholas. Are you all right with that?" Petar asked.

"Yes, yes," I answered quickly.

"Don't people get married in the church in Yugoslavia?" Petar asked.

"Only a very few couples marry in the church; most others marry at City Hall," I said.

"This is not a Communist country but a democratic one where everybody can do what they want without being persecuted, unless they do something illegal," said Petar.

Mitra felt a little bit confused about how people could think like that, but never said anything for fear of saying something wrong. "We young people were convinced how lucky we were to live in a system of brotherly love, respect for all, and wealth equally divided among all. Now when I think of how sure I was about that system, I can truly admit all young people were totally blinded by clever Communist propaganda."

"Baba, when you came to Canada and your husband and his friends tried to convince you otherwise—were you unhappy about it?"

"Yes, that is true, Sofija. In one way, I did not have a choice and in the other way, I trusted your great-grandpa that he would be a better judge than me about which system is better: democracy or Communism."

"Baba, let's go back to the wedding ceremony. I'd like to hear about your wedding."

"Great-grandpa arranged everything with the lady at the church; food drinks, the ceremony. She even helped me with my wedding gown and some fancy lingerie. Everything was arranged within one month. Petar invited everyone he knew, and his best man was his own godfather from back home, a very nice guy, Pavle Jovanovich. His children were much older than our children and they were the godparents to our children"

"Our godfather for many years," Sofija said.

"In our custom and religion, godparents are considered to be family members and the church requires godparents to take care of their godchildren if for some reason, the parents cannot."

"We have been told by all of you how important godparents were and that they should be respected by their god-children. So, Baba, let's go back to your wedding day. I want to know the details; how it was and how did you feel. Were you happy, or scared?"

I think I was both of these things. I was happy because I was so much in love with Petar and I knew I didn't need to worry about anything, because Petar reassured me everything would be fine. The truth is I was not worried about the ceremony and what was going on. I was very concerned about how to approach people, and how to behave properly. Petar used to say all the time, "Just be yourself, I am sure you will be fine."

My neighbour, Gloria, helped me get dressed properly. She put some make up on me including really red lipstick. I was not used to lipstick and my tongue kept wetting my lips, so the lipstick disappeared quickly. Later on, when we got to know each other better, Gloria reminded me, "Don't eat your lipstick like you did on your wedding day."

We went to the church; the ceremony started at 2:00 pm. The priest went on and on. It was quite long. Our best man and maid of honour held large candles burning behind our backs. The priest tied our hands together asking us if we're committed to one another and nobody else. Petar was asked first; he said to the priest he was truly committed only to me until his death. When Petar was saying these words, my heart pounded so hard from happiness. Then I was asked the same question; I answered like Petar.

Our best man handed over the rings. He put the ring onto Petar's finger, but Petar put my ring on my finger. It was a beautiful shiny ring. I loved it. They told me that my ring had diamonds but that did not matter to me because I knew nothing about diamonds and their value. I liked it a lot because my husband bought it for me.

After the ceremony, we signed the church records, and all was done. People congratulated us cordially. Then we went to the studio to take a few pictures: the two of us, with our best man and maid of honour, our bridesmaids, ushers, and all the wedding party together. Altogether about 10 to 15 different poses. The wedding party went to the hall for dinner without the photographer.

Everything was beautiful. The band played and sang songs in our language, to me. Tables were covered with white paper instead of tablecloths. All the food was our national cuisine. Soup was served first, then cabbage rolls, baked potatoes followed by roasted pork and lamb with salad. We had a white wedding cake nicely decorated.

After dinner it was customary to collect gifts for the newlyweds. There was a big man with a very strong voice announcing donors' names and the amount of their gift. I didn't know if I liked that part. Guests who had families brought their children with them. At that time, a lot of men were still single awaiting their brides from Yugoslavia.

"Did people give generously, Baba?" Sofija asked.

"Yes, they did, usually 10, 15, or 20 dollars. Twenty dollars was considered a very generous gift in the '50s. That was the time when your great-grandpa laboured for less than $3,000 a year in the steel industry, which was considered good employment. It was the time when you could buy a very decent house for $10,000 to $12,000. The gifts we received covered all our wedding expenses and our honeymoon to Ottawa."

"But did people buy wedding cards and put the money in an envelope, instead of doing the collection in such a primitive manner?"

"Nope, that was the way it was done for everybody."

"You were following your village custom?"

"You could say that," Mitra agreed.

"It was a fun day for you?"

"Yes, it really was. I felt like a true princess."

After the wedding, a few close friends came to our house to keep the celebration going on. We stayed up the whole night.

Some slept on the floors, chesterfield, chairs. The lady who cooked for our wedding packed up the leftover food and the drinks and gave them to Petar. He prepared coffee and put all the food on the table. He told his friends, "Enough drinking for now." We had breakfast together and soon after they left.

After the wedding, Petar suggested we go for a honeymoon in Ottawa. I didn't know what a honeymoon meant. I asked Petar to explain, "It means that we are going to celebrate our wonderful and sweet life, so that we never forget how it began."

I smiled and said, "It is wonderful and sweet, my darling."

Petar was surprised that his shy wife said these words to him. He smiled saying, "Thank you, darling. You have come a long way from your village upbringing—welcome to Canada."

"It is beautiful and wise to celebrate our life together since we are so happy. Where is the place that we are going to? We really don't need to go anywhere from our home—your home," I added.

"Oh no, no, my darling, you said it right the first time—our home. That is the way it will be from now on, our home, not mine or yours separately. You are starting to tease me."

He chased me throughout the house, and we ended falling into each other's arms.

We took the train to Ottawa. Petar explained that Ottawa was the capital city of Canada, the seat of the Canadian government, the parliament, military, and justice branches.

"Everybody says that Ottawa is a beautiful city to see," Petar said. "And lots of newlyweds go there for their honeymoon."

"Nice, had you been there before?" I asked.

"No, I was not married before. I waited for you to come so we could go together."

"Thank you," I said.

"You're welcome, my darling."

"As long as we are together it will always be beautiful."

"Yes, I think so," Petar added.

We went to Ottawa in the afternoon. We found a hotel, left our suitcases in the room and went out to find a restaurant to eat. We were very hungry. Petar ordered pork schnitzel, roasted potatoes with salad, and two pieces of bread. Both of us ate a lot of bread.

I cannot remember all the details since it was a long time ago, but I clearly remember walking around the parliament buildings admiring the well-kept landscape and statues and busts of famous Canadians. Petar showed me many interesting sites, including some foreign countries' embassies.

It was too much for me to grasp. I just kept saying; "a-ha, a-ha, a-ha." Everything was overwhelming; I thought I was imagining things. I could not comprehend such a huge difference between my small village and this grandiose city. I also could not understand how lucky I was to fall into this way of life. I will never forget sitting on the bench looking down at the Ottawa River.

Petar didn't have a car, so we had to cover a lot of ground walking. That didn't bother us. We were young, in love, and very happy to be together. We used the bus to go to a market called ByWard Market. We took a cruise on the Ottawa River, saw Ottawa's famous canal. Petar bought two trips: one was to see the city's foreign embassies. We saw the Yugoslav embassy. It was just a little larger than a house, not much to see compared to the embassies of richer countries. Petar also bought a trip to see the city's outskirts and Lookout Hill.

It was interesting and beautiful to look down upon the Ottawa valley and across to the Quebec side. Petar took me through the Parliament buildings and to the mint where coins were made. He bought me a gold ring with my birth stone in it.

"That ring is still on my finger. I will give it to you, Sofija."

When Sofija heard this, her eyes filled with tears.

"Thank you, Baba."

Sofija was intensely listening to the story about Baba's beginnings in Canada. She sensed how much her great-grandmother enjoyed talking about these memories and how important they were to her.

Finally, Sofija said, "I can't imagine being matched with anyone because it is so different from how we get acquainted today. When we meet someone who we think is the right match for us, we explore how well we get along in all aspects of life. Traditional marriage is no longer the first priority. Both men and women have careers and if they want a family, both of them contribute equally, otherwise it doesn't work in my world today."

"I know there is no gender divide with family responsibilities in the way it was in my time," Mitra said.

"That is why, Baba, your system of family is outdated in today's world."

"That is fine. You keep your system if you like it that much, but don't forget I loved mine the way I lived it with your great-grandfather."

"In your opinion, what would be the most important characteristic to look for in order to select a good life partner?"

Mitra cut in, "A good husband?"

"Yes, a good husband. When I find someone who I believe is good, can I bring him over for you to meet, so you can tell me what you think of him?"

"Oh, I don't know if you should do that. You're a smart girl and you can decide for yourself. But, believe me, too much love can blind you and there is a big possibility you won't see the person for who he or she is truly all about."

"So from what I can tell so far, your life began well in Canada."

"Yes, my dear girl, I was very happy while sharing my life with your great-grandfather."

"Baba, you were quite young when grandpa died. Did you ever think of marrying again?"

"Never," Mitra said. "When great-grandpa died, I had my three beautiful children who needed me, especially Sava and Stefan, who had not yet graduated from school. I had my daytime job working in the shoe factory, and occasionally when I needed extra income, catching worms at night and on weekends."

"Baba, you worked hard and sacrificed a lot for your kids."

"Yes, my child, I did but I didn't mind because I was working for my children and me."

Sofija had the urge to ask her baba something personal. She thought this was the right moment.

"Baba, will you tell me the truth about anything I ask you?"

"Yes, I will. You know I always tell you the truth."

"Did you ever regret being matched with grandpa by your parents?"

"Never, never," was Mitra's quick answer. "I do not think I could have picked a better man with my own choice than your great-grandpa."

Sofija noticed that Baba was getting tired.

"I think we've had enough serious business for today," Mitra said after a while.

"Yes, Baba, I think so, I have to go," Sofija said. "Need to meet my friends."

She hugged and kissed Mitra and was gone.

Chapter 13

After Sofija was gone, Mitra thought of her loving husband and how wonderful he was in all aspects of life.

"I was very fortunate, unlike some of my acquaintances who were beaten by their husbands."

Mitra crossed herself and thanked the Lord for her good fortune while Petar was alive before an unfortunate accident took him away from her and her children, very early in his life.

When the accident happened, a man came from the company Petar was working for. When she saw a strange man at the door, she was surprised and didn't know what he wanted because at that time there was no soliciting.

"Are you Mrs. Milutinovic?"

"Yes, I am," she answered.

"Mrs. Milutinovic, my name is Stan," he said, while extending his hand. "I come from the company your husband works for."

These words scared her right away.

"Is everything okay with my husband?"

The man said, "I wish I could tell you that everything was okay, but it is not. There was an accident. Your husband was involved. The company sent me to let you know and take you to the hospital. Can you go Mrs. Milutinovic?"

Before she quickly changed her dress and left with him, Mitra asked the man to tell her the truth about her husband.

"I don't know, Mrs. Milutinovic. They only told me he was alive and asking to see his wife."

Driving towards the hospital was the longest trip Mitra endured in her life. All kinds of thoughts went through her head: "Is he badly hurt? Is he still alive?" There were no answers to these questions.

When they reached the hospital, the man introduced Mitra right away, telling the nurse she was the wife of the injured man. The nurse answered, "Mr. Milutinovic is in intensive care," indicating to Mitra to follow her. When Mitra entered the room and saw Petar as white as a ghost, she imagined the worst thing: "is this end of the happy life I lived with him?"

The nurse said, "Mr. Milutinovic, can you open your eyes? Your wife is here to see you."

He opened his eyes, but they were not the eyes Mitra was used to: big and beautiful like the brightest blue sky. She tried not to cry and upset him.

He moved his hand and gave the sign to Mitra to sit on his bed. Mitra sat looking at him. The nurse guessed that Mitra did not kiss Petar because she was there. At that time people did not kiss openly when someone else was around. The nurse got out. Petar made a gesture that he would like to kiss her.

When she kissed him, she knew these were not the same lips she'd been kissing all the time and for many years. The coldness and trembling of Petar's lips stayed with Mitra long after Petar died. He tried to say something to Mitra, but the sound wasn't coming out of his trembling lips. Even though Mitra never heard any sounds from him, she was sure she knew what he wanted to tell her: that he was sorry it was the end for them and thanking Mitra for their wonderful life together, to watch out for their family and herself.

While Mitra was imagining all this, the nurse came back asking Mitra if she could step out for a few minutes. The doctor had to treat Petar. Mitra did as she was told hoping they could save him.

In a few minutes, the doctor came out.

"Mrs. Milutinovic, your husband just passed away. We could not save him even though we tried our best," he said. "He was very, very badly injured in the accident. I am sorry to tell you that."

Mitra burst into tears and the doctor gave her a gentle hug as he kept repeating, "I am very sorry Mrs. Milutinovic for your loss. Can we call anybody in your family so that you're not alone?"

The children were either working or in school. At that moment Mitra could not remember the school Marko worked for or the school Sava and Stefan attended. Everything was blurred. She was so badly traumatized with sorrow, she couldn't remember anybody's name or phone number. After she recuperated, they took her home. Even later she would not recall the funeral or the people who attended it. She fainted several times and had to be sedated.

Mitra shook her head, trying to shake away her memories. She left her room for the dining room. The meal was nice: chicken breast, brussel sprouts, carrots, and tossed salad. The company was great and Mitra felt that she was getting used to the place, and her new family.

She told Sandy she would not come over tonight for cards because she felt tired, but she hoped that she could have a rain check. "Besides that, my brother and his wife are coming to visit me."

"That's fine, Mitra. It's not something that has to be done tonight."

Her brother, Dusan, and his wife came with a nice package of fruit and some cheese strudel. They talked a lot about their children and grandchildren. Mitra was glad when they got up to go. She did not ask them to stay longer. After they left, she prepared herself for a good night's rest. There was some news that she wanted to hear more about. There was an ISIS attack in Manchester, England, where many people died and over 300 were injured.

Mitra could not understand what was happening; people willing to blow themselves up in order to hurt others. She wondered what went on in such a person's mind. They must be emotionally disturbed for some reason to end their lives. Mitra thought how unsafe the world was today. The news was the same all day long. She shut the TV off before the news ended. Oh, let the world and the people in it continue, she certainly could not do anything about that.

Once in bed, Mitra usually said her prayers but tonight she did not finish before she fell asleep.

Not long after falling asleep she dreamt that she heard steps and the closer the sound of the steps came, the more certain she was they were Petar's. In her dream, she was rushing around putting food on the table because he liked to eat soon after he came home from work. She always tried to please her husband. Suddenly, she smelled burning coming from the kitchen. She was in panic; she forgot to take the chicken out of the oven. She quickly grabbed the roasting pan from the oven. Since she did not have oven mittens, she burned her bare hands. The flesh sizzled; she let the pan go. Both the pan and chicken ended up on the floor. She started to cry.

She woke up and crossed herself, "Oh, my dear husband, forgive me for disturbing you today. I talked about you and our life together and how wonderful it was. Rest, my darling, I will join you soon."

Mitra thanked her lucky stars that she didn't scream and wake up everybody the way she had before. She got up, went to the washroom to splash her face with cold water to shake off the dream. She calmed down after that, sat in the chair rather than on the side of the bed and rested a bit. Her thoughts went again to the happiest time of her life. She would be asked about that part of life by her dear Sofija. Best to go to sleep and try to get a good rest.

She had a good sleep and felt rested and in pretty good spirits. She was hoping that Sandy would suggest going out for lunch today. She got ready to go down to the dining room. In the elevator she met Evica. Before recognizing it was her, Mitra looked at her thinking it wasn't Evica, until she turned her face towards her. She was surprised how much Evica's face had changed. Mitra felt sorry for her but neither of them moved towards each other.

Mitra went to the table where Sandy was sitting because she had been sitting with Sandy's group for a while. She found them all in good spirits. She felt sorry for Evica. Breakfast was fairly good; there was even bacon. Mitra loved bacon and she took three strips. They usually gave two, but if you asked for more they let you have it. Mitra's taste for bacon went back to when she was a little girl. Her father would cut her some lean smoked bacon. It tasted so, so good. She still felt her father's bacon in her mouth.

Sandy asked Mitra what she was planning to do today.

"I haven't thought about it."

"Would you like to play cards with us?" Sandy asked.

"Oh, I don't know if I can play cards right away. I've got to learn how you play and if I get it, then I would be glad to play with you."

"Come and watch us play and we will explain it to you."

"That is a good idea if that would not interfere with your playing," Mitra said.

"Nonsense, you won't bother us," said Mary.

So Mitra sat and watched as they were playing. She grasped the idea of how to play. From then on, Mitra was a regular player and she enjoyed it very much. When she was going back to her room, she heard voices a few doors from hers. The voices were not in English, but one voice in English was the nurse who greeted Mitra when she first came.

The nurse was very patient and seemed to come up with soothing words to make one relax and hopeful. Mitra guessed right away that a new person was brought in a couple of days ago. Mitra heard that the former tenant in that room became very sick. She was told the woman was transferred to the hospital, but she heard from the housekeeper that the lady had died, despite being transferred.

When Mitra walked into her room and closed the door, she found her son Marko and his wife, Doris, there. They jumped up from their seats, came over to hug and kiss Mitra. They told Mitra about the many things they had seen in Italy, especially in Rome.

"I am glad you had such a nice holiday," Mitra said.

"Yes, we did have a wonderful holiday."

They asked Mitra if she was getting used to the new place.

"Not too bad," Mitra answered, "I am slowly getting used to it. I met a few nice ladies. That helps me because they include me in everything they do."

Mitra told them all the things she had been doing with her new friends.

"Do you spend a lot of time with Evica?"

"Yes, I do," Mitra answered but she didn't want to tell them what had happened. They stayed for one hour and told her they had to leave because they had to be somewhere soon. They did not say where they had to go, but Mitra did not want to ask if they were not willing to tell her. Mitra wondered if this was the usual excuse of needing to leave quickly.

Sandy was right, they were her family now. How true when one thinks of it in a sensible and true way. After Marko and his wife left, Mitra felt tired. She lay on the bed to get some rest before dinner. She skipped the full lunch and only picked up a banana and apple to tide her over to dinner.

Also, Sofija with her questions had stirred up so many of her happy memories and that kindled her heart into a happy and uplifting spirit.

Mitra's daydreaming made her forget about dinner. She quickly got ready and went downstairs for dinner.

The dinner and company were good. The ladies asked Mitra what she was planning to do after dinner.

"Not much," Mitra answered, "Today I had lot of visitors and they tired me out. Old bones can only take so much."

"Ha-ha," said Sandy.

"It's true," Mitra answered.

They all laughed, and they continued to joke on further about different things.

"How is your beautiful, young great-granddaughter? We saw her earlier on when she came into the building. We said 'Hi' to her and she answered with a very nice smile. She is gorgeous," said Mary.

"Sure, she is," Joan added, "just like her grandmother in her prime."

"Thank you, ladies, for the compliments you gave to my great-granddaughter, but I only deserve half of your compliments."

Jokingly, her friends warned Mitra to beware, "You are still a good-looking lady and there are a lot of available bachelors in here."

"Really?" Mitra exclaimed, "If four of us stand side-by-side, I would be the last one picked, if at all, that's how much value I have left."

"Now, now, Mitra, what you are saying is not right at all. You have the most important things that everybody values: a good and positive attitude, and nice manners. What else do you want?"

"Thank you, ladies, for giving me many compliments. You're all nice yourselves, and I'm glad I have you as my friends."

"That is right. We are not going anywhere without you."

"Thank you," Mitra answered with a giggle, as she joined her companions.

On the way to her room there was yelling coming from somewhere. As Mitra got closer to Evica's room, the voices got louder. Mitra recognized Evica's voice mumbling some words that were not clear. Mitra also recognized one of the pleasant nurses. Her voice was saying to Evica, "Please calm down Evica, Mitra is not to blame. You made her angry."

"She made me mad for dropping me for that whore, Sandy."

"Be quiet, Evica, please, you cannot say something like that about other people. The rules in here say nobody can call someone else names."

"She is a whore. I know she is; she's had so many men. She told me about them."

"But what do you care, if she did or did not. That is not your business."

Mitra heard the thump. Somebody must have fallen, but she did not think it was the nurse. Only when she heard Evica's voice again saying, "You are a whore too for trying to convince me Sandy is not a whore. Now you lay down there, you whore."

It was clear to Mitra, Evica must have pushed the nurse or she'd tripped on something. Mitra called the office, but nobody answered. She called again and an orderly answered, "Yes, Mrs. Milutinovic, what can I do for you?"

"I'm not calling for myself, but to tell you there's a big commotion in room 14, just next to my room."

"What kind of commotion?" orderly asked.

"You better come and see."

"All right, Mrs. Milutinovic, I will."

"Please come right away, Tony."

"It's that urgent? Has somebody killed someone else?"

"I don't know."

Sure enough, Tony came up right away. He opened the door and found the nurse on the floor bleeding from her nose. He knew right away, it was serious because she was groaning. Tony called the ambulance. The ambulance came within five minutes. All the residents gathered in the front lobby and outside to see what was going on. The nurse was taken to the hospital.

Everybody was in shock over what had happened. Somebody yelled out, "Where is Evica?" She was missing. After the altercation with the nurse, Evica took a taxi and disappeared. Somebody from the crowd confirmed that they saw her leaving. In no time, police came to question what had happened. Tony pointed out Mitra, saying to the policeman, "This lady, Mrs. Milutinovic, called me to go to room 14."

The policeman came right over to Mitra and asked very politely, "Are you Mrs. Milutinovic?"

"Yes, I am," Mitra answered.

"Can you please tell us what you heard and how did the voices sound to you?"

"I heard two persons talking loudly but I did not hear exactly what they were saying to each other. I'm a little bit hard of hearing."

The policeman asked, "How far were you from the room where they were arguing?"

"I was coming from the elevator when I heard them, but soon after I heard a thump, and I became concerned and called the orderly to come to room 14."

Mitra did not want to say what she'd heard because she wanted to spare Evica's reputation despite her rotten attitude. Mitra did not feel good about lying either. She was only hoping that the nurse wasn't badly hurt.

Mitra went into her room and closed the door. The policemen were still in Evica's room. Soon after Mitra heard the voice of Evica's son and some more voices. She heard Evica crying but Mitra did not want to interfere—what could she do? Evica should not have behaved like she did. She was her own worst enemy.

Mitra heard them talking about charges, because the nurse was hurt badly, and her family were demanding charges against Evica. Evica was yelling and crying, "This place has some bad people in it, lots of whores who make other people's lives miserable. That whore, Mitra, forgot all I did for her, and this is how she pays me back. I treated her like my own sister; she threw me away for another resident."

Mitra heard her son saying, "That is not true mom; Mitra is a very good person. It is not Mitra but your own jealousy as always. When are you going to stop that nonsense and be a normal person?"

"Now you're blaming me for always being wrong and while other people are right. My own son, my own flesh and blood turned against me."

"Nobody is turning against you and if we are, it's only with good reason. You know what you did in the other residence. You did exactly the same. Where are you going to go now? You've closed all the doors, and nobody will take you."

They were both so loud that Mitra could hear everything they were saying.

"Mrs. Petrovic, you have to get ready and come down to the station with us," the policeman said.

"What for?" Evica protested.

"The nurse was hurt in this room and we want to know what happened."

"What do you mean what happened? The nurse turned around and wanted to leave hastily. She tripped, and she fell. I did not do anything to her."

She said in her own language, "Sama pala, sama se ubila."

The policeman asked Evica's son what she said. He explained to the officer she meant, "She alone fell and alone got hurt."

"I'm afraid, it's not so simple. When we came in, she did not tell us that the nurse tripped. Come on, come on, hurry up, Mrs. Petrovic."

Mitra heard Evica crying again. Now her son said, "Come on, mom, everything will be all right. I'm going with you; I will look after you."

She asked if she could sleep in his house that night. She did not want to come back ever, especially tonight.

"It's all right, mom, we will figure out something. Come down, everything will be fine," he repeated.

Mitra heard more voices and soon after that the door shut. She was contemplating whether to come out and tell Evica she was sorry for the incident and that everything would be all right, but she never opened the door. Evica's incident brought back Mitra's memory about her own aunt.

Mitra remembered how back home her father's sister was exactly the same as Evica. She would do anything for you such as helping you or doing work for you or giving you little gifts always, and was always pleased to be in your company and always, always was so pleasant. But if she thought you crossed her in any way, even though you knew you hadn't, her friendship would turn into passionate hate. She wasn't speaking to half the village. This reminded Mitra to make her children aware of such relationships.

Sandy called her to ask what was happening up there so Mitra told her what had happened but did not tell Sandy everything she'd heard. Sandy asked Mitra, "Are you all right?"

"Oh yes, yes, I am. I feel badly for Evica, but I could not do anything for her."

"What can you do for someone who wants to behave like that?" Sandy said.

"I guess nothing, nothing at all; I won't be coming down tonight. I have to make a few phone calls and when I finish. I think I want to go to bed a little earlier," Mitra said.

"Good night; see you in the morning. Have a good night's sleep."

"Thank you, Sandy," Mitra replied.

Sandy knew that Mitra was shaken up a bit, but she did not want to push. She left it to Mitra to ask for company if she wanted it.

This was Mitra's final break from the person who was instrumental for her moving into this place. Mitra didn't even feel like calling anybody as she thought she might. She was truly shaken up by the incident; more than she wanted to admit. Now she felt sorry that she said to Sandy she wouldn't be down tonight but she could not go back on her word. She felt that she really needed company in order to remove the incident from her mind or at least to distract her thinking about it.

As she was thinking about this, her darling Sofija phoned. Her happy voice was so welcome and soothing to Mitra's feelings. She said, "Hi, Baba."

"Hi, honey, you're home?"

"Yes, Baba, I'm home, I just had my midterm test. I took one course to make it easier for me when I go back in September."

"What kind of course did you take?"

"I took a science course. You know I always follow your wishes. You call me, 'your future doctor' who will make 'Baba feel better.'"

"Are you serious about studying to become a doctor?"

"Yes, Baba, I'm very serious about it. But do not let me down, you have to witness my graduation."

"I wish you all the luck in the world, but I don't think I will be here for your graduation as much as I would like to. It's not likely to happen. But don't worry I will watch you from above. You have your dreams and will do well in your life. I will be very happy and proud of you as I am always."

"Thanks, Baba," Sofija said.

"That is very nice, dear. I'm looking forward to seeing you soon."

"I'm going to Ottawa tomorrow to visit aunt Sava. She asked me to come for a few days. She paid for my ticket. I will come to see you tomorrow before I go. Please, Baba, be prepared for my questions. I'll have lots of questions for you when I come back because I find your life story very, very interesting."

"All right, dear, I will try to dig deep into my memory and see what I can come up with. Don't forget it has been a long time since I was young and some of it is more sand than pebbles now. Good night, dear, go and finish your studying."

"Good night, Baba," Sofija said.

Just as Sofija hung up the phone, Sava called and asked how her mother was doing. Mitra reassured her that she was doing well and not to worry about her.

After Mitra talked to Sofija and Sava, she felt much better. "It was very nice that they both called," Mitra thought. "I really needed these calls in order to divert my attention from what happened to Evica."

Mitra felt much better. She started thinking about her daughter, Sava. She remembered how Sava was devastated after her father, Petar, died. She was her father's little angel. She used to hang around him constantly. A couple of years after Petar's death, Sava fell in love with an older man, Robert Peterson.

He had similar features to her father and it's likely that is why she blindly fell for him. He was also charming and a very good actor. Mitra wasn't sure he had a good character, because occasionally she would notice his selfish nature. She tried to discourage Sava from marrying him, or at least to wait a little longer.

But Sava sensed her mother's reservations and she refused to hear or discuss them with her. She told her mother that she would marry Robert and that was the end of the discussion. She swore that she would never marry if she did not marry Robert.

They were married when Sava was 22 and Robert was 33. She was a happy and beautiful bride, but Mitra never stopped worrying. She noticed that Sava wasn't as happy as she claimed to be, but that was for a good reason. She tried to get pregnant and after trying so hard, she became pregnant but lost the baby after two months. She got pregnant two more times but they ended in miscarriage.

Sava was devastated; she feared she was going to be childless. That didn't bother Robert that much. For that reason and others, Sava's feelings towards Robert started to change. For four years they lived together, but actually, they were very much apart.

Mitra wasn't surprised when Sava told her she was going to divorce Robert. She told her she was sorry to hear that. Sava admitted to her mother that she had not been right about Robert. She didn't have her mother's eyes; her own were not able to see the warning signs.

"It is what it is. It's best to end it. Thank you for your understanding, mother."

"I wish I could ease your pain and make it easy for you, but correcting a mistake is neither pleasant nor simple," Mitra said.

"Yes, mother, I sure know that now, but just as you said, it is not easy."

"Don't worry that much. Once you divorce Robert, you will soon feel relieved. It has been said that, 'When one door closes, another one opens.' There is always hope when one is healthy. You really should not worry. You have a lot of time to find yourself a good man," Mitra comforted her.

"Thank you, mom, I will never rush into a new relationship as I did before," Sava said.

"Good thinking, dear," Mitra agreed.

After Sava got divorced, she landed a good position working for the government of Canada as a constitutional lawyer. She was now very happy, but it was very hard to get in touch with her because of her position with the government. Sava was now involved with a man of the same age with a similar profession named Don. His wife had died, and he had three children. Sava was very pleased with his children's acceptance of her. She had grown close to them.

Mitra did not ask anymore if she was going to marry. Sava was happy now with her life and Mitra was exceptionally happy that she did not have to worry about her. She thought Don was the right guy for her daughter because she'd met him once and instantly believed he was a good person.

It was time for bed. Mitra was pleased that her friends didn't say anything bad about Evica. They knew that Mitra would not have liked to hear anything negative, and out of respect for Mitra, they kept quiet.

Surprisingly, Mitra had a good sleep and she felt relaxed in the morning despite the bad ordeal the night before with Evica. After Evica left, everything seemed to change. Mitra felt no more stress because of Evica's unstable behaviour. Sandy and her friends became Mitra's friends too. They were always together and always doing something so there was no time left to think of anything bad.

Mitra could not believe how her situation had changed in a very positive way. She thanked God for her new family and the fact that things were not so bad for her any more. She no longer thought that the place was horrible. She could not believe that things had changed within a month and a half. She was told by other occupants how Evica was a horrible person who spread lies and quarrelled with everybody.

Chapter 14

The day was going as usual, and after lunch Mitra's darling Sofija came. Mitra was sitting in her room expecting her. Sofija snuck into Mitra's room like a fox who spies her prey.

Sofija said jokingly, "Is this the residence of Mrs. Milutinovic?"

Mitra said, "Yes, it is, Mrs. Milutinovic just stepped out. I'm her assistant."

"Oh, I didn't know Mrs. Milutinovic had an assistant."

"Oh yes, yes, she does. Would you like me to call her?"

"Tell her that her great-granddaughter is here."

"Are you sure you are Mrs. Milutinovic's great-granddaughter?"

"Yes, I'm sure," Sofija said.

Just when Mitra pretended to reach for the phone, Sofija started to laugh.

"Baba, you are really good actress."

"Oh, it's you, sneaky intruder."

They both laughed about their pretentious acting. As usual, Sofija brought two Tim Horton coffees. She hugged and kissed her baba, making up with kisses for each day she didn't visit her. They sat for a while looking at each other and catching up with news from home. Nothing new was happening. Sofija asked Mitra how everything was in her residence.

"Everything is fine with one exception."

She told Sofija about Evica's ordeal, but not the whole truth.

"Are you sorry she is gone, Baba?"

"To tell you the truth, I'm sorry for her. Evica had become a very nervous, jealous, and quarrelsome person. One could not be friends with her without worrying when she was going to flare up."

"Then maybe it's better for you that she is gone knowing how sensitive you are and how much you dislike ugly scenes," Sofija said.

"Oh, what can you do? Some people cannot help themselves. I'm thankful to her for helping me come to this establishment. We got along at the beginning, but something went wrong, and she changed tremendously. God help her."

"I'm sure you are not to blame for her trouble."

"Well, I didn't try very hard to help her either. The problem is when people are in trouble, we can't grasp the depth of their trouble. We tend to blame the person in trouble for not doing the right thing or correcting the problem. Despite what she thinks of me, I am very sorry for Evica."

"Baba, you're sorry for everybody. Stop worrying; it's no good for you. Evica will be all right."

"I hope so," Mitra said.

"Baba, I can't stay too long because I have to catch a plane at 9:00 pm. Let's start on our project. You've told me a lot of things already, but I would like to hear about some things we bypassed."

"Do you really want me to dig up the smallest things about my life? What would you like to know?" Mitra asked.

"When you came to Canada, what was hardest for you at first?"

"The hardest thing for me was the language. I felt badly that I was not able to engage in any conversation. It made me frustrated, lonely, and feel awkward."

"How did you survive without being able to speak English?"

"When Petar was at home, I was all right. I enrolled in English language evening classes."

"You mean the government sent you."

"Do you think the government sent me? There was no such thing. You did it on your own. The government did not give hand-outs like it does now. It was a very different time when I came to Canada in the early '50s. At that time Canada was a young country trying to get established. Everybody had to fend for themselves during the '50s and '60s, when most of us came to Canada. My Petar immigrated to Canada from England."

"Oh, he was in England before he came to Canada," Sofija asked.

"Yes, he was. He told me he was working in the mine. One day while he was down in the mine, he was badly frightened because there was an accident. He said his horse saved him."

"What do you mean his horse saved him? Why was the horse down there?" Sofija asked.

"Petar told me that horses pulled the wagons from the place material was chopped or dug out. They took it to the main lift that carried mining material up to the surface."

"Boy, that was a very primitive system," Sofija said.

"We are not talking about modern conditions and technology. Do not forget that happened when your grandfather was about 20 years old, which is close to a century ago. Things are different now," grandma confirmed.

"But how did the horse save him?" Sofija asked.

"I forgot the details he told me. I think when they were going down the main shaft, the horse did not want to move forward even though Petar tried to force him. Then all at once he heard thump and the earth closed up the tunnel."

"How did great-grandpa come up?"

"He came up all right because he was close to the elevator that was going up to the surface."

"And what about the other miners?" asked Sofija.

"He told me that within a couple of days, they dug out the earth to get the trapped men out."

"Did anybody get killed?" Sofija asked.

"I am not sure. I don't remember now exactly what he said about that. But after that incident, your grandfather didn't want to go into the mine anymore. He worked some hard jobs outside. They tried to force him back into the mine. He told them they could force him into the mine dead, not alive. After that they left him alone. He emigrated to Canada soon after."

"Baba, I'm glad you told me an interesting story about my grandpa's life. Thank you for that."

"You are welcome, my child."

"So far so good, Baba. Let's go back to the language. How did you learn the language and how quickly?"

"I think I mentioned before how Petar would write out English words and put the meaning in Serbo-Croatian. I learned a lot of words that first month in Canada, but I did not know how to connect them together into a sentence. When I started night school, it helped me a great deal that I already knew quite a few basic words. The teacher was very good and helped me because she saw my determination and eagerness to learn. She was an elderly person in her late fifties and after I started having children, she would still come to our house and help me with English. She was married but was divorced and never had had children. She loved our children very much. Sometimes if I had to go somewhere, she babysat for me. She would even help them with their English when they started school, especially when they were writing essays. Her name was Gloria. We kept in touch until she died. She died in her 80th year. She was more like a sister to me."

"That was very nice, Baba; you were lucky to have good people around you but then I'm not surprised; you're good with people," Sofija confirmed.

"Thank you, my dear. It always pays to be good with people, at least I think so," Mitra said.

"You are right, Baba, I'll try to remember that."

They both laughed.

"That was very interesting, Baba. What was the next hardest thing for you?"

"Customs."

"Interesting," said Sofija. "Customs, what was so hard about customs?"

"They were very interesting and very different from the customs I was born into. I found English customs to be more polished and less intimate when people talk. The custom from back home was always to acknowledge someone's presence in full measure."

"What do you mean, Baba, in full measure?"

"When people met in my village, they would usually say good... whatever part of the day was appropriate. After saying the greeting, they would pass without saying anything else. If they greeted you and also asked how you are, you would stop and exchange a few words about that person's health, family, etc. I found it very funny and rude when a Canadian would say to me in passing, 'how are you?' That's what happened to me the first day of school. Somebody said, 'How are you today, Miss?' I was surprised when that person just walked by, without stopping and saying anything else. I thought it was because I could not speak English. When I came home, I asked Petar to explain these strange Canadian customs. He said, 'When a person asks you in passing how you are, they're just acknowledging your presence, without meaning to know how you really are.'

"'If they didn't mean what they said, why didn't they say just good morning,' I asked. I told Petar it felt rude to me when one says something that really means nothing. Petar saw that I was upset, and he reassured me, 'I understand that the different customs here confuse and upset you. Please don't worry about that. You will get accustomed to Canadian customs, and the way of life very quickly.'"

"What else did you find was very different?"

"People constantly saying thank you for small or meaningless deeds or gestures."

"Why did you find that so strange, Baba?"

"I found it strange and monotonous because it was said too often."

"Did you not say something like that back in your village?"

"No, not really. We said it if it was very important. The receiver of thank you would not reply with the words of welcome but instead would say, 'thanks to God.'"

"That is strange, Baba."

"Well that was our custom. But now everything has changed, but not to the degree as it has here.

"The other habit, I found monotonous and overwhelming, was saying sorry, sorry, sorry for every little thing, like touching a person or just brushing against them in passing."

"What did you say in your country?"

"Unless it was something serious—nothing."

"Oh, Baba, that is really strange," Sofija said.

"Why would it be strange? That was our custom and we understood it," Mitra said.

"How did you get used to Canadian customs? How long did it take you to accept and adapt?"

"It took me some time. I forced myself to be phoney and to say things without meaning them in order to follow the customs. This prolonged my true acceptance of the customs.

Even today, I think we are saying too many thank yous and sorrys."

"That is very interesting, Baba, and strange that you still feel this way after being in Canada so long," Sofija said.

"Yes, I know it's impossible for you to grasp that, but I'm telling you the truth about how it was. Our custom back home was when you like someone, you tap them on the shoulder or arm, but I was warned here not to do that since such gestures are not customary here. That's how it is, my dear, when you come to another country and are faced with a lot of changes. You have to keep observing and following and eventually things fall in place. Funny how everything seems unusual and difficult when you are not familiar with the system. I guess that goes for everything in life," Mitra said.

"Did you like going back to your country of birth? How did you find things and people behaving? Were you pleased or disappointed?"

"After I came to Canada, I did not go back home for six years. The trip was expensive, and we had already started family. The Communist regime was still strong and ruthless and unpredictable and gave people very limited freedom. We did not want to expose our children to that. The Communist party still persecuted people like my Petar who fought against them during the Second World War, even though the Communist party had granted them amnesty. The Yugoslav Consulate in Toronto had a list with all the names of people who could not return to Yugoslavia. Petar wasn't on the list."

"But, Baba, how was it when you went there the first time after living in Canada?" Sofija asked.

"It was nice in a sense that my family and friends and the villagers were happy to see us. They were always very polite and loving. Things were much better than when I had left in the '50s, but it seemed far worse, compared to my Canadian comfort. Older people had changed so much. I was shocked how quickly they aged. My grandma was old when I left; it seemed as if she had doubled her years. My mom and dad had also changed so much. The little kids and all the younger people looked very healthy. They had rosy cheeks, nice brown skin, well toned muscles from working in the fields and playing sports outside. Nobody sat inside the house because it was summertime when we went. People were sitting under trees because houses had fairly large trees to give them shade. The custom of getting together had not changed. People were sitting in the shade and talking, laughing, gossiping.

"You know Sofija, sometimes you don't have to have much, but if you're in good company that entertains you and makes you happy and that really helps your spirits and makes it much easier to tolerate unpleasant things. That was the aspect of my village that I loved the best. I was never alone; I was with people that were known to me and cared for me."

"Did you ever get angry with each other, Baba?"

"Yes, sometimes we did, but it was mostly because animals got into the field and damaged crops."

"How did that happen?" Sofija asked.

"Very easily; kids would mind the stock and sometimes they played with other kids not watching the animals properly. The animals would sneak into a garden or cultivated field, and graze to satisfy their hunger. The owners of the damaged crops or gardens would be unhappy because of the damage done. That would cause quarrels between the owners of the stock that did the damage and the damaged party. The disputes were usually settled amicably."

"Didn't you have fences around your properties?" Sofija asked.

"Very few people had fenced in properties. It was expensive and impractical," Mitra replied.

"That was a tough life," Sofija said.

"People survived the best they could. Sometimes, they would clear up wooded areas to plant the crops in order to have enough food to feed the family. Sometimes men would go to the big cities and do some work, usually delivering things or moving household materials or working in the railroad stations, anything to make some money and feed the family. The main concern always was to secure enough food for family.

"My father used to tell us a story about how one man predicted that his family would have enough food for the winter. He predicted that his grandmother was old and would die, his daughter would marry, and his cat that wasn't feeling well would pass away. But it turned out differently. Grandma didn't die, the daughter didn't marry, the cat did perish, but instead the whole family starved. People were very much aware of such situations and tried everything possible to keep their families from starvation. It was not always easy to do that, especially if there were natural disasters such as drought, hail, and twisters that destroyed crops. Many families were poor, some were better-off and in the case of disasters, the better-off families would help the poor families."

"That is very interesting, Baba. You always looked out for each other."

"Yes, it is, but that is the way people lived their lives," said Mitra. "Nobody was homeless or hungry as they are in rich countries where food is so plentiful. People there depended on family and it was shameful for the family if one of their members had no place to stay. After a bad harvest, a member of a poor family would go on the road just before Christmas and beg for food. He would go to each family house and ask to be helped in order to save his family from starvation. It would always be a man asking for help. There were not many people who would do this. I remember there was only one poor family who begged. Usually people would be generous to the beggars, because the myth was if you do not help beggars, God will punish you for it."

"Looks like your God was prominent in everything around you," Sofija said.

"Yes, he was," grandma said.

"This was the situation while I lived there, but after eight years away, things had changed a lot. Young people were moving into cities, getting educated. I remember some young men I knew were highly educated. One became an engineer, another a doctor but most of them had trades. Very few stayed on the farm. Women were also getting educations, but not as often as men. I went back again for my father's funeral; that was 20 years after I left the village. I could not believe the tremendous changes for women of my age. We brought these ideas to our kids in Canada when we realized how important education was in the new world. The first generation born here were mostly highly educated because their parents made sure that their kids went to school and got a good education."

"So, you must be happy with what your children achieved: grandpa Marko became a high school teacher, aunt Sava became a prominent lawyer, and uncle Stefan, a history professor."

"Yes, I'm happy, very happy with my children's achievements. It was not always easy because there were many more expenses than money available to cover the costs. But it all ended well—thank God. I'm bragging too much, but I can't help it."

"Good for you, Baba, that is not bragging but telling the truth."

"Thank you, my dear," Mitra replied. "What do you think, Sofija? Have we had enough for today?"

"If you think so, Baba, we can easily stop."

"We will have a lot more time together."

"I hope so," Sofija said.

"God willing, we hope so," Mitra said.

"Baba, how do you feel now about this place after almost two months? I did not want to ask you before because I got vibes that you were not that happy about this place even though it's much nicer than some other places. I think you're much more comfortable in here now."

"You're right, my dear. That is true; I did not like it when I came. It's not so easy to make changes at my age and be comfortable."

Sofija's eyes got wet and she said, "I'm sorry, Baba, that we put you in that position."

"Please, please, my dear, it's not your fault. Do not feel guilty about that. I'm fine now. I have adjusted. I am telling you I'm all right here. I have a few good friends with whom I spend a lot of time. They are very interesting and knowledgeable people. We consider each other family."

"That is good, Baba, I'm very, very happy for you."

"Thank you, my dear, I'm happy for me too."

To change the difficult subject Sofija asked, "Would you like me to go and get us coffee?"

"It would be nice to celebrate each session with our favourite drink, coffee."

While Sofija went to get some coffee, Marko called to check out how his mother was doing.

"I'm good, son, very good. Sofija is here and she went to get us coffee."

"Oh, your great-granddaughter is better to you than your own children."

"You are all good to me, but I must say she is exceptional."

"I'm glad, mom, she is a good girl."

"Yes, she is," Mitra confirmed.

"How is everybody in your family, son?"

"They are all pretty good. Doris and I went to see our granddaughter Stefani, because we got the news that she and her husband, John, are going to have their first baby."

"That is good news. Please tell them that I'm very happy with their good news. How long have they been married already?" Mitra asked.

"I think about two years," Marko answered.

"Then it's time for them to have a child, but then they are not like I was during my young, productive days. I had you in the same year I came to Canada."

"Nowadays people are not in such a hurry to have families," Marko said.

"I know times have changed tremendously."

"Yes, mom, it has changed a lot. What did you do today, mom?"

"Not much. As I told you, Sofija was here and she wants to write down some things that I lived through in the old country and here."

"No kidding, that is wonderful that she does that. We will all be thankful to her. I'm glad she is doing it while you still have a good memory and a good mind, mom."

"Oh, I don't know about that, son. There are a lot of things I cannot remember," Mitra replied.

"No wonder, mom, it's hard to remember everything from 90 years. But I have to repeat I'm really, really glad Sofija is doing that for all of us. Do not tell her the bad things I did, please. Tell her all the good things about me."

Mitra heard Marko's laugh.

"Yes, I will tell her exactly what you deserve to be told about you. Joking aside, Sofija is really strict and demands the truth from me."

"You can lie a little; she won't know," Marko laughed again.

Marko heard Sofija's voice and asked Mitra to put Sofija on the phone.

"Hi, grandpa."

"Hi, my dear granddaughter. Your baba tells me that you're writing her memoir. How wonderful! Thank you very much. None of her children remembered to do that but her great-granddaughter has. Thank you again. I hope you will give me a copy too."

"Of course, grandpa, I will give whoever asks me from our family. Here is Baba."

Mitra took the phone just to say good night to Marko.

The two of them sat and had coffee together. Soon, Sofija was gone. Mitra always felt a pinch of pain when Sofija left.

Sofija told Baba that she was not sure when she was coming back. She promised to come as soon as she could.

"Don't worry about it, come when you can. You have to have time for yourself. You are too generous with giving your time to everybody," Mitra said.

"Only to those I love," Sofija answered.

Chapter 15

After Sofija left, Mitra couldn't decide what to do. She could watch her own TV, but she didn't enjoy watching it alone. She decided to go to the community room to see what was going on there. When she got there, nobody she knew was there. She figured Sandy and her friends were playing cards. She sat there for a bit watching television. It was the same thing all day long about American President Trump and the North Korean President threatening each other with war.

Just as Mitra was going to get up and go, the lady beside her said, "Are you leaving already? I don't blame you. TV has become a boring companion. It's not like when TV first came out, it was interesting to listen to and watch. We were all glued to our televisions," the lady said to Mitra.

It was clear that the lady was looking for a companion as Mitra once had.

"How true but I guess we all get enough of the same old thing," she said.

"My name is Sue."

"I'm Mitra."

"Nice name," the lady said and tried to say Mitra's name a couple of times but each time, it did not come out right, even after Mitra helped her.

Sue said, "I'm sorry, Mitra, I'm not able to pronounce your name right."

Mitra repeated how to say it and added, "You pronounced it very well."

"It's only when you try to get things right, you muddle it up. Thank you for talking to me."

"You're welcome," said Mitra. "You must be a new resident. I think I saw you in passing through the corridor yesterday."

"I came yesterday; it's difficult being away from home and not knowing anybody."

"I know what you are talking about," Mitra said, "but perhaps I was a little luckier than you because I had somebody here who was my friend."

"You talk about that person in the past tense so I'm sorry to hear that your friend has passed on."

"No, she didn't pass on," Mitra said.

Sue caught on.

"I'm sorry, how wrong of me to assume something that I don't know anything about it."

"Don't worry about it."

"So here I go again with my assumptions, but I hope you've gotten used to this establishment."

"It's pretty good," answered Mitra. "I've found a few good friends and I'm fine now. I'm sure you will be all right too. There are a lot of activities. There are nice people in here who welcome building friendships. We all need each other. I'm sure you will be fine."

She got off her chair, came over to Mitra and gave her a hug saying, "Thank you so much. God bless you; your reassurance already makes me feel much better."

"I'm glad to help. What room are you in?" Mitra said.

"Fourth floor, room 12," Sue replied.

"You are right next to my room, room 14."

Mitra thought, "This woman is looking for a friend. If I befriend her would Sandy behave the same as Evica? It looks like Sue would like someone to talk to. I shouldn't refuse her."

"Have you made a lot of friends? Is it easy to strike up a friendship in here?" Sue asked.

"Friendship is like everything else. It's like making a good meal. You have to have proper ingredients in the right amounts. Friendship is the same; you have to measure everything in order to keep a good balance. I hope this isn't worrying you."

"No, not at all. You're giving me good advice about how to make friends." They both laughed after Sue said that.

Mitra got up to go to her room and Sue got up too, asking Mitra if she minded that she walked with her since their rooms were so close to each other.

"No, no, I don't mind, why would I?" Mitra said.

"Thank you," Sue replied, "God bless you; you made my evening pretty good."

"I'm glad," Mitra answered.

They came to room 12 and Sue said, "This is my room."

"Good," Mitra said.

Mitra was glad Sue did not ask her to come into her room. She would not refuse, but she felt really tired and wanted to go to sleep. They bid each other good night. She had good vibes about Sue. She was not pushy, which would make it hard for her to make friends. She was going to be all right.

Mitra felt good that she could help Sue feel better. The thought of what Sandy said to her came to mind: "We're family." Mitra was reassured by her acceptance and adjustment to the residence. She felt the most relaxed she had in the two and a half months she'd lived there.

Mitra's cane fell on the floor. Soon after there was a knock on the door. The nurse asked, "Are you all right, Mrs. Milutinovic?"

"Yes, I am. My cane was standing by the head of the bed and it fell down, sorry about that."

"Don't worry—if you're all right, everything is good," the nurse said.

"Thank you, nurse, for your concern."

"You are welcome," the nurse answered. "We are concerned about our residents' well-being. Can I pick your cane off the floor?"

"Of course, you can, come in please."

The nurse put back Mitra's cane and at the same time asked her if she could do anything else for her.

"No, thank you, nothing else," Mitra answered.

"Mrs. Milutinovic, did you meet your new neighbour?" the nurse asked.

"Yes, I met the new resident from room 12. She introduced herself when we were watching television in the community room. She told me her first name is Sue, but she did not mention her family name," Mitra answered.

"She is a very nice person. I think she is going to be all right in here," the nurse said.

"I'm sure," Mitra answered, "Do you know anything about my former neighbour who was in the same room, Mrs. Petrovic?"

"I'm not supposed to say this because we're not allowed to talk about people after they have gone somewhere else. I heard that she was placed into a nice retirement facility but there was some problem between her and another patient, and because of that, Mrs. Petrovic was removed from the premises. I feel bad for her," the nurse said, "I think she has some mental problems that lead to anger and very bad behaviour, because I remember that she was a pretty good resident for a long time after she moved in here. You know, Mrs. Milutinovic, a mental illness is not like a physical one because nothing shows on the surface. And as people get older, a lot of changes happen not just in the body, but in the mind as well."

The nurse realized that she was talking too much about something that she should not; the management of the establishment would not like her behaviour.

"I think I have said too much tonight and believe me I would not talk to anyone in here this way. Somehow, I have full trust in you Mrs. Milutinovic and I feel I can say anything to you. My mother always told me not to talk too much; she too was born under the Communist regime in Czechoslovakia."

"Yes, that is true, Communism taught us to be very careful and to keep to yourself. Is your mother still alive?" Mitra asked.

"No, Mrs. Milutinovic, she died 10 years ago," the nurse answered.

"I'm sorry," Mitra said.

"Thank you."

"She was already quite old when she died. She had a good life and used to say to us kids how lucky we were and how happy we should be. We used to ask her what she meant by that because compared to other families, we did not have much choice in anything, be it food or clothing. She would always say to us, 'Are you hungry? Are you naked?' And then she would answer it herself, 'No you are not; you do not need expensive things to make you happy. Train your attitude to be happy without depending on luxuries. Now you have food, clothes, a fridge, an oven, a bed—what else do you want?'

"We were trained to be happy without striving for wealth. She was a very wise woman. I guess we are all in a pretty good position, my siblings and I."

"How many siblings do you have?"

"I have one sister and two brothers."

"That is very nice. Can I call you Dona?"

"Yes, of course you can."

"How old was your mother when she died?"

"She was 88. She was a very brave soul, Mrs. Milutinovic. In the last few years of her life, she used to say to us that she was ready to go whenever God called her home. We used to laugh when she would say that, 'But mom, this is your home here.'

"'Oh no, no, I'm only a passenger in transit, I have done my duties on earth. I put a link on the chain of life through my children. Now my duty is done and I'm ready to go home.'

"We would tell her, 'All right, mom, please do not hurry, we'd like to see you stick around to remind us how to be happy.' We all laughed a lot when we were together, and we were together a lot and we still are. We taught our children the way our mother taught us."

"That is wonderful, Dona. I am glad you told me about your mother and your family. It's very interesting indeed."

Dona got up saying, "I've got to go, Mrs. Milutinovic. They will be looking for me. Can I do anything for you?"

"Not really, I'm all right. I will go to sleep."

"Do you sleep well, Mrs. Milutinovic?"

"Sometimes I do and other times I don't, but since I have a lot of free time, I can sleep through the day—only naps one or two."

"That's nice, you were well-trained by your mother too."

"Yes, I was. I think my mother and yours had the same ideas about bringing up their families."

Dona said to Mitra, "Thank you, Mrs. Milutinovic. This was a really nice conversation, I enjoyed talking to you."

"I feel the same way."

Dona said good night and disappeared. Mitra got ready for bed by doing her regular things. When she lay in bed and said her prayers, Dona's conversation was still in her mind. "Hmm," Mitra thought, "So Dona's mother was an exceptionally stable individual. That is interesting. She must have brought her culture from the old country, or her own family."

That is exactly how Mitra remembered old people back home. Mitra thought that it was good to have such attitude in old age. "Yes, that is true, but fear of death is a powerful enemy that scares people to death. My God, what you learn as a child stays with you forever."

Mitra felt surprised and privileged that Dona opened up to her.

She got up and went to the washroom. She looked in the mirror and noticed that her cheeks were a little redder and warmer than usual, but she had been out in the sun today for a good hour and a half. She did not feel sick or anything unusual. "Everything is all right," she thought. Mitra did all the regular stuff that she normally did. She didn't even finish her prayers when she started to feel some heaviness in her chest. She first thought, "Everything is all right and it will pass." But it did not. Instead there was more pressure around her neck as if somebody was trying to squeeze her neck and choke her.

She understood something unusual was happening but still tried to convince herself that everything would be all right. Mitra called for Dona who came quickly. She knocked at the door and Mitra could barely say, "Come in."

Dona knew right away that something was wrong with Mitra. She entered quickly and found Mitra in distress.

"Are you all right, Mrs. Milutinovic?" the nurse asked.

"No, I'm not, something is choking me."

"What is choking you?""

"I don't know but something is."

Dona measured Mitra's blood pressure. It was 201 over 95.

"Did you take your blood pressure pills, Mrs. Milutinovic?"

"I did not."

"What do you mean you didn't? Didn't the other nurse give you your regular pills?"

"Yes, she did, but I thought I would be all right without them, and I did not take them."

The nurse turned around and went to get the pills for Mitra thinking, "If Mrs. Milutinovic doesn't improve quickly, I will have to call the ambulance to take her to the hospital."

The nurse came back to give Mitra her pills. She sat with her, stroking her arms and gently talking to her. Mitra asked Dona not to call the ambulance. She was already feeling better. The nurse waited for Mitra's blood pressure to come down. After half an hour, the nurse measured her blood pressure again and it was 185 over 85. It was still very high but much better than before.

The nurse said, "This is a lesson; don't fool around with your medication."

Somebody was beeping for the nurse and she told Mitra she had to go, since somebody needed her, "I will come back to see how you are doing and measure your blood pressure."

Mitra thanked the nurse for her help.

"There will be no more help for you if you do not behave, Mrs. Milutinovic," the nurse said smiling.

Mitra smiled, "I'm sure you'll come again."

When the nurse left, Mitra was much calmer thinking, "So much for my bravery, saying I'm not afraid to die. I guess it's different when you're faced with death."

Mitra remembered a story that she heard when she was a young girl when elderly women were talking about death. They usually told the story about a poor man gathering wood in the mountain. When he started to load the wood on his donkey, he couldn't do it because after he loaded on one side of the donkey and went to the other side to load, the load fell off. He tried for a very long time but could not do it. He sat down frustrated and started to cry, "Oh death, where are you? Come and take me. I've had enough of this wretched life and my poverty. It's better to die than to live and suffer as much as I do."

When death appeared, it was the scariest sight he'd seen or imagined in his life. Death asked the man what he wanted. The man quickly said, "Help me load my donkey so I can go home and warm my poor family with a fire."

This time the nurse didn't even knock at the door, she just walked in, asking as she was entering through the door, "Are you all right now, Mrs. Milutinovic?"

"Yes, yes, I feel much better thanks to you and your intervention. Can you please keep this incident between us? I promise I will always take my medication from now on."

"I don't know, Mrs. Milutinovic, if I do not record the incident and management finds out, I would be instantly fired."

"Nobody knows but the two of us," Mitra said.

Reluctantly, the nurse agreed. The nurse sat a little longer with Mitra and when she saw her blood pressure improved and Mitra looked tired and ready to sleep, the nurse got up to go, promising she would check on her during the night. "Don't worry, everything is all right now. You can go to sleep." The nurse left.

Mitra continued with her prayers where she left off. She shut off the lights, praying, "My Lord, I'm in your hands. Please protect me. Amen."

Mitra slept well and in the morning, everything was as usual. Nobody knew about her incident the previous night.

Morning proceeded as usual. Nothing new happened. The four friends did not have much to discuss, just small talk. Joan,

Mary, and Sandy went to exercise in the gym room. They asked Mitra if she would like to go. Mitra agreed, promising that if nothing else, she would watch them exercising. Each of them was a decade younger than Mitra.

Mitra introduced Sue to them and them to Sue. She told them that Sue just arrived yesterday—she was really trying to create a comfortable atmosphere for Sue. Sandy asked Sue if she knew anybody in the establishment. She quickly answered, "No, not really."

Sandy asked Sue to join them for the exercise session. Sue accepted the invitation instantly with a big smile saying, "Thank you." Everybody worked out in the gym according to their own ability. Mitra did some slower movements and enjoyed it. Everybody was happy. Mitra felt a little tired and went back to her room, so did Sue. The other three stayed behind to talk to some other people.

Mitra sprawled on her bed to rest a little and soon after she fell asleep. She had a dream of her and Petar walking along the shore of deep and very clear water. They walked knee deep, side by side, on a narrow ledge that divided the shallows from the very deep water.

Petar was walking ahead of Mitra. Suddenly Petar started falling into the deep water and Mitra watched him falling farther and farther down to the bottom. Mitra began to panic, seeing that Petar was about to drown. He was looking upward at her with his beautiful blue eyes, motioning her to come down to join him. Mitra didn't know what to do and just as she was going to jump after Petar, there was a knock on her door. Her son Marko walked in saying to Mitra that he came alone.

He brought Tim Horton's coffees and two Boston cream donuts, the ones he knew his mother enjoyed. Mitra asked, "How is everybody at home?"

"Nothing new is happening at home, just regular stuff. Sofija is gone for a few days to Ottawa to visit Sava," Marko said.

"I knew all about that," Mitra said.

"Of course you do. You know every little detail about your darling, Sofija."

"Now, now, you are not jealous of Sofija, are you?" Mitra asked.

"Of course I'm not jealous, I'm glad you are so close. It's good for both of you. I told you that already. How is Sofija's project going?" Marko asked.

"What project are you talking about?"

"Come on, mom, you know what kind of project: your diary."

"Oh, that," Mitra said, "I think that project is almost done; only a couple of points left, and it will be all done."

Mitra didn't want to mention last night's incident and dream. There was no use worrying her son. Everything was good.

Marko always asked his mother if she needed anything, but she said she did not. Even though she said that, he put an envelope in her hand, "You can have this and when you go anywhere out with your friends buy them coffee. Keep up good friendships, mom."

He stayed for a bit longer and left because he felt tired.

When he left, it was time for lunch. Her turn for lunch was at 12:45 pm this month. She did not mind that because she seldom felt hungry. There was always something to nibble on in the community kitchen. She seldom needed anything else, but many other residents did.

Mitra tidied herself when she was going out of her room. She always tried to be neat, not particularly worried about the latest fashion or even matching her clothes. She remembered how after Sava became a teenager, she would always remind Mitra to match her colours. She would even be angry if Mitra did not want to listen. That lasted for a few years, and then she finally learned that it was not important to her mother.

Sava also became modest like her mother. She mostly wore classical clothing, looking smartly dressed and beautiful. Mitra wished her Sava had a family of her own, instead of her stepchildren.

"I hope she is happy."

Mitra stepped out of her room when she saw Sue waiting for her. They went downstairs together. Sue asked who the man was who'd just visited her.

"It was my son Marko," Mitra answered.

"Nice man, I met him as he was coming into the building. I happened to be sitting in the lobby after I came back from my walk. Your son came over and asked me how I was today. I'm going upstairs to visit someone special, he told me, but he did not say that you were his mom."

"Yes, that's my Marko," confirmed Mitra. "He likes to goof around and keep people guessing. Yep, that's my boy."

"How many children do you have?" Sue asked.

"I have three children."

"Lucky you," Sue said, "I have only one son."

"Better one than none," Mitra said. "My daughter doesn't have children. I wish that she could have had at least one, but it wasn't meant to be."

Mitra was happy that Sue did not pursue the subject any further.

It was Saturday evening in mid-August, but the weather wasn't too hot. It was nice to be outside in the fresh air and do some walking. Sometimes Mitra went for walks but she really didn't trust her legs. She was very careful about every step she took, because even a small bump on the road upset her balance.

Chapter 16

That afternoon a lot of residents had left to visit with their families. Mitra was looking forward to tomorrow because her son Stefan was picking her up around noon. He said they were having a barbecue and his daughter, Marianna, was coming with her family. Mitra was looking forward to seeing them all. She liked Marianna's husband, Alfonso. He was such a nice guy. He was Brazilian. When Marianna first brought him home and introduced him to the family, Mitra wasn't very pleased because he wasn't white. As she got to know him better, the colour of his skin disappeared in Mitra's eyes.

They met at university studying medicine. They had two lovely girls. One was named Christina and the other one, Julia. Both girls were in school. Christina had just started grade nine. Julia was in grade seven.

Mitra found her regular companion at her table talking about a newcomer. She did not look around the room to see who the newcomer was. When she sat down, Sandy said, "Look at the corner on your right and you will see a newcomer."

Mitra turned around and saw a newcomer, a nice-looking man. She wondered what was so special about him. "We were told that he already had an argument with an orderly and told him off. We were told not to provoke him," Sandy said.

Mary said, "I don't know why they brought in such a man that will make us all feel unsafe."

Joan said, "I'm going to lock my door that's for sure."

Mitra said, "I will do the same thing."

Joan said, "I think they didn't know about his behaviour until he confronted the orderly."

"We are going to be all right. The staff will be extra vigilant about our safety, I'm sure," Sandy said.

"It seems most of us are going to our families tomorrow," Mary stated.

"We are going to play poker or watch the big-screen TV in the community room. Let's find out what movie they are showing tonight," said Sandy.

As we were coming back, the new man followed us. Once he was close, he said, "Good evening, ladies."

Then all four of us reluctantly replied, "Good evening, sir." When we saw he was going to the community room where the big-screen TV was, we changed our minds and went to Sandy's room to play poker. We played for a good two hours as we were continuously chatting about different things.

All of a sudden, we heard an ambulance and the police car sirens. We stopped playing right away. Sandy was the first to look through the window to see what was going on. Since she had a good view of the front of the building from her window, she saw a commotion between two policemen and what looked liked the new resident they'd seen in the dining room. Another person was being transferred into the ambulance. All four of them wondered what happened and who got hurt. As they were all wondering what had happened, the nurse Dona appeared at Sandy's door and told them not to fear anything.

"Romeo, the new resident, has been taken away by the police officers. Poor Roger got hurt. Romeo pushed him into the wall and gave him a few hard punches."

"Oh, no," Mitra exclaimed. "Roger is such a nice soul; he wouldn't hurt a fly."

"I don't think he provoked him," Joan said.

The sad part was that this new guy, Romeo, told police he didn't care who he hurt because he was hurt too. He was very angry at his family for putting him in the residence.

Mary asked where they took him. Dona said they took him to jail and will call his family. "So much for that," said Sandy. "We better behave. It's better in here than in jail."

They all had a little laugh. The nurse asked Mitra if she was going back to her room now, so she could give her the medication.

"I think I'll go now. We played enough for tonight—right, girls?"

Joan said, "I think so. Now that the bad man is gone, we are all safe."

They all said good night to each other and went to their rooms. The nurse Dona escorted Mitra to her room.

"I hope you will sleep well, Mrs. Milutinovic."

"Yes, of course, it won't be like last night. I already took my medication. I didn't want to say that in front of my friends because I don't want them to know what happened," Mitra said.

"Just keep doing the right thing and you will be fine. I am going to check on you later," the nurse said.

"I'll be all right. Don't worry about me," Mitra said.

It was nearly 9:00 pm and time for bed. When Mitra got into bed she started daydreaming. Sometimes, that gave her trouble because too many memories rushed into her head and kept her from falling asleep for two or more hours. The new resident came to her mind, "Poor man. He did all that out of frustration. He won't change anything with anger and frustration, taking it out on someone else. It will take him time to realize that he has to submit to the rules. We all do."

She adjusted her position and settled on her left side. When she settled down another thought came to her mind. She thought of her last dream walking on the shore and Petar sinking deep in the water. What did that dream mean? Mitra remembered that her mother believed in her dreams—not all of them, but only if the dreams were as clear as if it was really happening.

"Oh, why should I believe in dreams? A dream is a dream, not reality."

She thought again about her dream, "What if that dream is trying to give me a message? Petar went down under with a happy face motioning me to follow him. Does that mean that my time is coming soon to join him? Oh, you stupid old woman, don't waste your time dramatizing about this or that because there is no truth in it."

Mitra made another adjustment to her position. She knew that she had to stop daydreaming and sleep, otherwise, she would be tired tomorrow for the big day. She said her regular prayer asking God to sooth her mind.

In the morning, the nurse Dona came in to ask Mitra if she needed something. "Yes," Mitra said, "I would like your advice about what to wear because my son invited me to his house for a late lunch. He said his daughter and her family will be there. My son's daughter and son-in-law are both doctors. My granddaughter is a fashionable woman and her two daughters are as well."

"Oh, Mrs. Milutinovic, you're asking the wrong person about fashion. I'm only concerned that what I wear is clean and has no holes. Let's look at your wardrobe to pick out something comfortable and cool because today is going to be quite warm."

Dona looked through Mitra's clothes and suggested a nice light blue top and capri pants matching the blouse. She also suggested a light blue top with long sleeves because it was warmer, just in case it got cold around the pool or there was lots of splashing. She laid everything on Mitra's bed and left.

Mitra decided to go for breakfast and get dressed after that, just before her son came to pick her up. Mitra hadn't been visiting her children's homes often because she wanted them to have some time for themselves and their friends. Her children had so many good friends to visit and host. She felt like an intruder and she remembered again what Sandy said, "This is your family now."

"How true it is," Mitra thought. "Now, I'm feeling pretty good in here. When I came here, I was depressed, unhappy, and miserable and did not mind if I died. Now I don't feel that way, and certainly I don't wish to die yet."

Everything downstairs was as usual. People were lined up to get into the dining room. All of a sudden there was a big commotion. Somebody said that someone fell because of a stroke or heart attack. They told them to go back to their rooms. They would be informed when breakfast was served. They had to take care of the sick person lying on the floor. Mitra did not see who the person was, but Sandy was closer and believed it was the Dutch lady.

Outside, emergency sirens were blaring. The fire department and the ambulances were there. Mitra did as she was told and went straight to her room. She could not see anything from her room because her window wasn't facing the front of the building. Although she could not see what was going on, she certainly heard a lot of commotion. After an hour they called them to come down for breakfast.

Mitra felt uncomfortable eating breakfast after what they had just seen. She was curious who the person was and if the person was still alive. She looked at the table where the Dutch lady sat, but she was not there. Mitra thought she went home for the day. As she was thinking, the nurse Dona was passing by. Dona knew that Mitra wanted to know who the sick person was. Dona said, "It was the Dutch lady who used to be your partner at the table when you first came in here."

"Is she well?" Mitra asked.

"She was still alive when they took her to the hospital," Dona said. That was not true, but nurses were not allowed to disclose residents' private matters. Nobody was comfortable as usual. People moved out of the dining room quickly after getting coffee and toast.

The dreadful incident with the Dutch lady was on everybody's mind and everybody looked at the table where she used to sit. It was especially hard for Mitra because it reminded her of her first days in the residence; how the three of them sat together. Now, two of them were gone: Evica and Mrs. Decock. Mitra had only one toast instead of her usual two, and only a cup of coffee.

Her friends were ready to go out and they wished a good day to each other. Mitra went to her room. The phone rang and when she answered she heard Sofija's sweet voice on the other side.

"Hello, sweetie," Mitra said.

"Hello, my dear Baba. I called you twice yesterday but did not find you. Where were you galivanting, young lady? Is he good looking? Or more importantly, is he going to be good to you and to me?" Sofija joked.

"Yes, he will be all that or we will kick him out. No fooling around or no deal," Mitra answered.

"That's my smart Baba—something good or no deal."

After some humour, Mitra explained to Sofija what had happened this morning. Sofija was concerned after she heard what happened. "Are you all right? I will come home earlier if you would like me to."

"Oh, no, no, what are you talking about? I'm fine. I'm going to Stefan's house today for a barbeque. Your cousins Marianna and Alfonso are coming with their girls. I'm looking forward to seeing them all. You're staying with your aunt Sava. Is she treating you well?"

"Oh my God, she makes sure that I get whatever I want. I'm even afraid to mention that I like something. She has to get that instantly. She is too generous and too kind," Sofija said.

"That is nice. Is she there right now? I would like to say hi to her."

"No, Baba. She has gone to get something."

"Are you coming home on time or are you're going to stay longer?"

"No, I'm not staying longer. I have to finish our project before I go back to school. Try to remember as much as you can. I want to record everything. Aunt Sava is very excited about my project."

"Good, I hope you will have some memories when I'm gone to remind you of me."

"Baba, you are teasing me, right?" Sofija said.

"No, I'm not, just telling the truth."

"You have to get ready. You don't have much time. Uncle Stefan will be coming soon. Say hi to all of them for me." Sofija hung up.

Mitra was very happy that her darling Sofija had interrupted her bad thoughts; she was feeling a lot better now. She slowly got ready, being careful not to forget anything because lately she had been forgetting things. Mitra was thinking about whether to put some lipstick on. Finally, she decided not to. "It's only a picnic, not a wedding."

There was a knock at the door. Stefan walked in asking, "Are you ready to go, mom?"

"Yes, I am," Mitra answered.

They got to Stefan's home quickly. Everybody was there. They greeted her cordially. They continued normal family chatting—how is this one, how is that one. This went around in the same circle, sometimes changing tone and introducing a little humour while food was being prepared. It was a very fulfilling afternoon because it invoked many pleasant memories from the past.

"You girls look lovely, and you have grown considerably since the last time I I saw you," Mitra greeted Stefan's granddaughters.

"Baba, do you have a picture of yourself when you first landed in Canada?" the girls asked.

"I don't. We didn't have a camera at that time. We bought our first camera when your great-uncle Marko was five years old."

"Oh, you must have been very poor not having enough money to buy a camera."

"No, we did not consider ourselves poor because we did not have money for a camera. It wasn't at the top of our list. We had to pay for a mortgage, food, clothes, and to help relatives back home. Women with children did not work but stayed home with the children."

"Oh, poor women," the younger girl, Julia, said.

"No, we did not feel that way at all. We were very happy to stay home and look after children and do the housework and cooking. It was a happy time being with our children. There were a lot of children playing outside on the street. Mothers were sitting and chatting."

"How can you be so happy with such mundane chores?" Christina, the older girl, said.

"So, you think we did not do anything worthwhile if we did not have a profession. We didn't even think about such things. Not even the Canadian-born mothers, never mind those of us who came mostly from villages and without much education or none at all. Times have changed, my dear great-granddaughters, since I raised your grandfather Stefan. Look at him, isn't he a good man?" Mitra argued.

"Yes, Baba, he is a good man. Are you saying that he turned out so well because you stayed home with him when he was growing up?" asked Christina with a sarcastic tone. It didn't seem a joke.

"I don't know whether my staying home contributed to that, but certainly it did not harm him."

Stefan's wife, Suzan, often didn't agree with Mitra's old-fashioned ways. She would often say, "Mitra's way is very primitive." Usually, she would say this when Stefan wasn't around but this time she did not care. She enjoyed her granddaughters grilling their great-grandma.

Stefan was observing the situation. He noticed how his wife enjoyed their granddaughters' unpleasant behaviour towards his mother. He raised his voice and said, "Enough all of you, leave my mother alone. She doesn't need that. Show some respect for elders, shame on you." This changed the entire atmosphere. Everybody fell silent for a few moments.

You could tell that Alfonso wasn't pleased with his daughters' behaviour and he gave them a very disapproving look, reminding them to stop their present behaviour.

Mitra found herself in a difficult position and was contemplating what to say and finally, to defuse the situation, she said to Stefan, "Don't be angry at the girls and Suzan, they are only joking with me."

But Stefan wasn't going to dismiss his wife's behaviour that easily and he knew that she was quite often mean to his mother. Her daughter, Marianna, behaved like her mother. They usually enjoyed needling Mitra.

The barbecue was done, and the food was put on the table. It was smorgasbord style. Stefan picked up his mother's plate for her. He followed her around the table helping her to the things she wanted. He knew his mother's feelings were hurt and he was sure she wasn't enjoying herself. Mitra didn't eat much claiming that she wasn't hungry, but Stefan knew better.

The atmosphere was quite unpleasant. Then Mitra felt pain in her chest. She did not want anyone to know how she felt, thinking, "Enough trouble for one day." Stefan noticed his mother's face started to lose colour. Mitra was quiet because the girls, their mother and grandmother, stopped conversing with her. They were discussing present fashion trends instead. Mitra was never preoccupied with fashion.

Christina pulled out a picture of a few new trendy pieces. The pants or jeans were shredded with cut out lines that had threads hanging over the cuts as if somebody had chopped it with a saw; the dress had exposed shoulders. Sleeves were hanging at the bottom of an arm pit. Mitra thought, "Who in their right mind would want to wear that?"

Christina suddenly asked Mitra if she liked it. She wasn't going to reveal her honest thinking to Christina, instead she said to her, "It's lovely. You girls would look good in it."

Suzan, Stefan's wife, looked at her mother-in-law with a disbelieving look, knowing full well Mitra could not stand it. The girls laughed. Marianna kept quiet while Stefan again recognized tension in the air. He asked his mother if she wanted to go and rest on the divan in his office, where nobody would disturb her.

Mitra instantly agreed with the suggestion. She asked if he could bring her a bottle of water, "I like to drink lots of water after a good meal."

"You hardly ate anything. What meal are you talking about?" Stefan said.

"Please just bring me a bottle of water," Mitra asked.

"I'll get you a bottle of water, mom," Stefan said.

Stefan led his mother into his study and showed her his divan. He apologized that the room was not very tidy. Stefan had been like that ever since he was small. He was always untidy, unlike Marko and Sava.

Mitra said, "That is all right, son. It doesn't bother me. I won't be here very long."

"Okay, mom, rest and don't worry about anything."

"That is exactly what I intend to do," Mitra answered.

Stefan closed the door. Mitra's hand went into her pocket to find the heart pills prescribed by her doctor after her fall. Dona, the nurse, gave her the pill, just in case she needed it. Mitra took her medication: it was not to be taken before dinner time. She had to take it because she felt heaviness in her chest. She tried to calm down by trying to convince herself that today's young people have a totally different way of thinking, and it should not bother her that much, because at her age she doesn't have any interest in being like them.

She finally felt better after she took her medication. She felt a lot more relaxed. She slightly adjusted her position on the divan and made herself more comfortable. She fell asleep. All of a sudden, she heard a knock on the door. Mitra's sleep was very deep and she could not remember where she was because all around her it was different from her assisted living centre's room and her room in her old house.

Stefan got alarmed and quickly pushed the door open. Her eyes were wide open but to Stefan they had a scary look, "Mom, mom, are you all right?"

Mitra came to herself finally and said, "I'm all right, of course, I'm all right." Then she told him why she had such a look on her face.

"Sorry for scaring you, my son, I didn't mean to."

"That is all right, mom, now that I know that you are okay."

She asked what time it was and when he told her it was almost 4:00 pm.

"No wonder you got scared, I slept for an hour and a half. You thought I was dying."

Stefan smiled now that everything was all right.

"That's true, I was thinking about that."

"Don't worry, son, I'm a tough cookie. I won't go that easily, or that soon."

"I hope not," Stefan added.

When Mitra came out, the four girls were playing some kind of war games.

"Baba, do you want play with us?" Christina asked.

"No, I would not know how to play that. Please continue, I'll talk to the boys."

Everything was nice and quiet again. Stefan reminded the girls about dinner but since they'd had a good lunch around one, dinner would be at six.

"Is that all right with you, mom?"

"Absolutely," Mitra said, "I do not need a heavy dinner, only something light."

Stefan offered his mother a drink, but she said, "I still have water left in your office, if you don't mind getting it please."

Alfonso quickly got up saying, "I'll get that for Baba."

When he left, Mitra said to Stefan, "He is a very nice guy."

"Yes, indeed, he is," Stefan agreed.

The two guys started talking about world markets and financial instability, Mitra wasn't interested in that; instead she was observing the shimmering water on the surface of the pool. The sun's reflection on the water and a gentle breeze were creating an amazing picture of something alive and beautiful. Mitra enjoyed looking at that, imagining that the water was a living thing. No wonder it could swallow living beings when they plunged through the skin of the water. She thought of Petar. So, everything was alive in a different form.

Stefan noticed his mother's interesting expression and asked, "Are you all right, mother? You look like you're deep in thought again. Don't worry now, you know where you are."

"Of course I do. You do not need to worry about me."

The girls finished their games and started preparing dinner, which was mostly leftovers.

The atmosphere was much improved. The girls were talking about how their game ended, each one claiming they did very well and those who lost blamed it on one wrong move. The other side laughed, "Oh, ha-ha-ha, now you look for excuses because you lost," Christina said.

"Aren't you always blaming somebody else for your own mistakes?" Suzan, Stefan's wife, asked.

Mitra thought to herself, "That is absolutely right for those people who do not think that they could be wrong."

The boys were quieter and didn't engage with the girls' discussion. Instead they were occupied with the more serious situation of what was happening in the world. Each said they were not pleased with the talks between Trump and Kim Jong Un of North Korea and the potential nuclear threat.

Suzan said, "Don't worry, these two groups are not serious, and they won't start any conflict. A cartoon in the newspaper the other day portrayed them as playing in sandboxes; Kim Jong Un played with a small toy rocket, while Trump was playing with a huge rocket."

Alfonso said, "It's not a joke; it's a serious business. Can you imagine what power these guys have in their hands to start a nuclear war? I don't think that Kim Jong Un has the resources he claims to have. It is a possibility that the power of domination is shifting in the world. The UN blames China for not cooperating with sanctions, but I don't think it's in

China's interest to comply with that. They would like the UN and America to become weaker and that in return will shift power more to their side. Everybody looks after their own interest."

"You're so right," Stefan agreed.

Alfonso got up and went somewhere. Mitra was finally sitting alone with Stefan. She had been waiting for such a moment, so she could have some private time with him. Stefan looked at Mitra and asked her if she was tired.

"No, I'm not," Mitra answered.

"It's all right, mom. You let me know when you want to go back."

Mitra's thoughts reminded her of her new home away from home. Stefan noticed that Mitra's thoughts had wandered off somewhere and he asked her, "Mom, are you happy in the new place? Because if you are not, we will find a different solution."

"I'm now quite comfortable in my new place. I admit it was a little bit tough for the first few days, but I'm lucky to have met some very nice people. Please do not worry about me, son."

"Fine, mom, if you say so. How is Sofija's project coming along?"

"Good. She asks questions and I tell her what I remember. She is a great girl and has a good head on her shoulders and a tender heart to go with it."

"I'm proud of my great-niece," Stefan said.

"So am I, so am I," Mitra said. "Do you see your brother very much?"

"Yes, I do, mom. I'm seeing him more these days."

"Is there any reason for that?" Mitra asked.

"Not for anything serious, but he has been having some tests lately."

"What tests?" Mitra asked anxiously.

"He was telling me that he does not feel the best. The doctors cannot find anything wrong with him so far. Old age scares him a bit. I should not have mentioned this to you and worry you about it, but I think it is right that you know what's going on in the family."

"Thank you, son. I appreciate it. You have always been an honest and level-headed person."

"Don't worry, mom, I'll keep you informed, and I'm sure Marko will also."

"I'm not so sure," Mitra said. "You know Marko. He never liked talking too much about himself and he always says everything is all right."

"Mom, when I ask him about everything, he is a very private person, too private. He is all right, mom. He just doesn't want to worry you. He is worried for you, ever since your fall."

"Please, children, there is nothing to worry about. I'm fine. I'm at the right place where I get plenty of help and am well looked after. I'm over 90 years old; what can be expected or worried about at my age? Now that we are alone, I want you to know one thing and I want you to share it with your brother and sister. In case of a life-threatening situation, I don't want any drastic measures taken to save me. I'm resigned to meet my end whenever it comes."

Stefan looked at his mother with questioning eyes, "Are you serious, mother?"

"Yes, I'm really serious son."

"I sense you don't like where you are," Stefan said.

"Son, that is not true at all."

Although Mitra's answer wasn't entirely true, she knew there was not a better solution.

"No, son, it has nothing to do with that, but everything to do with reality. Why should I go to great lengths to save myself when my end is near anyway? I would rather go than be bedridden. I don't want that. I prefer death."

"I don't like to hear that, mom, but if that is what you want, we will do as you wish but only in severe circumstances, and if you are in danger of losing your mobility. I promise you, I will talk to Marko and Sava and inform them of your wish."

"Thank you, son," Mitra said.

Dinner was finished. It was already 5:30 pm and Mitra felt tired, even Stefan noticed that. He didn't want to ask her if she wanted to go back; he waited for her to ask.

In the meantime, Alfonso came back with a beer in his hand asking if the two of them wanted anything. Mitra felt tired and asked Stefan to take her back to the residence.

"I will take you back, mom."

After Mitra finished her water, she told Stefan she was ready. Stefan called the girls to come and say goodbye to Mitra.

Mitra expressed her pleasure and how it was wonderful to see them all and spend the whole afternoon with them. Their youthful faces reminded Mitra of her old age, but she was happy for their beautiful young lives.

When they arrived, Stefan stopped the car at the front door, and walked her inside. She sat on the chair and waited for him to come back from the parking lot. They both walked into the elevator and when they came out on the fourth floor, Sandy was coming towards them.

"So, you're back," Sandy said.

"Yes, I am," said Mitra. "This is my younger son, Stefan."

Sandy extended her hand to Stefan saying, "Very pleased to meet you, Mr. Milutinovic."

"Very pleased to meet you too, Mrs. Jonson. Thank you very much for making my mother comfortable. She told me a lot of pleasant things about you. How you chum together and even venture outside for some fun."

Mitra turned around towards Stefan and told him he could leave now if he wanted to.

"Mother, even your son doesn't count when your friend comes," Stefan joked.

"Of course," Mitra said. "My friend is with me all the time, you are only around sometimes."

"Fine, mom, I can see how far you'll go."

All three of them laughed.

Stefan kissed his mother, thanked Sandy again, and he was gone.

Chapter 17

When Stefan left, Mitra asked Sandy, "How is everything with our family, since I've been away all afternoon?"

"We had a little incident with a new guy and your acquaintance Sue."

"What new guy?" Mitra asked. "What did he do to Sue?"

"I didn't see him move into the establishment but when he appeared in the dining room for lunch, he seemed strange. Sue tried to get to her table, but he suddenly turned around and brushed against her. He claimed that Sue pushed him. He turned on her as if she had taken off one of his limbs. She kept quiet, went to her table, and sat down. He walked over to her table and shouted at her using all kinds of obscene, rude words. She told him she was sorry and didn't mean any harm to him. We were all yelling at him to stop it, since she hadn't done anything to him.

"They heard yelling at the front desk and two orderlies and a nurse quickly appeared at the door. They grabbed him from the back because he was going towards Sue; he was going to hit her. They started to wrestle with him, but he fought like a wild animal. We were all scared about what he might to do to us. Finally, the police came and took him away. We were relieved but shaken."

"Where did they take him, hopefully not back to his room?" Mitra said.

"Oh, no."

"What happened with the man? I hope they sent him back home, because he was so aggressive," Mitra said.

"No, they didn't," Sandy said, "Dona, the nurse, told me they didn't because they couldn't locate any of his family. Instead they took him over to the nursing area where there is more security until they can locate somebody from his family. Dona also said that he has some psychological problems, some kind of dementia. She even said the name of it, but it was hard to understand and I didn't want to wrack my brain over it. The less I know the better I feel," said Sandy.

"What happened with Sue, did you check on her?"

"First Dona, the nurse, came and took her to her room. Poor Sue, she was crying a lot. Dona stayed with her for a while and when I met her in the hallway, she told me that Sue was all right now. She gave her something to calm her down and now she was relaxing. I went in to check on her. Everything seemed to be all right with her. And how was your afternoon?" Sandy asked.

"It was very, very nice. You know how nice it is to be with your family."

"I know," Sandy said.

"Sorry, Sandy, for a minute I forgot you people in here are my new family."

"That is all right," Sandy said, "I will forgive you this time, but mind your words next time, lady."

They both laughed and they really needed it in order to take the gloom away from a depressing situation.

"Are you tired?" Sandy asked.

"Yes, I am," Mitra answered. "I think I will go to my room and rest till tomorrow morning."

They said good night and parted.

Mitra went to her room, flopped onto the bed, and quickly dozed off because she was very tired. She slept for an hour and felt her strength had returned. As soon as she thought of her son Marko, her first born child, she felt worried and fearful. She thought she would rather die than hear bad news about Marko.

Her children were her babies and would always remain that way until her death. Mitra remembered Marko growing up. She remembered when they brought him home from the hospital as a baby; she and Petar knew nothing about caring for a baby. They were given some written instructions in the hospital about what to do. Mitra didn't understand the meaning of the instructions, neither did Petar. Petar called their neighbour, Mrs. MacDonald, to show them what to do with the baby. Mrs. MacDonald handled Marko as if he was some kind of a doll. It was easy for her; she'd raised four children. Mrs. MacDonald showed Mitra how to feed, wash, and change baby Marko. Mitra watched for the first and second day and learned how to take care of Marko with the guidance of Mrs. MacDonald.

From then on Mitra slowly took over and did everything for the baby. Petar played with their babies, but didn't change their diapers. It wasn't a man's job at that time, like it is now. Marko was a good baby, very bubbly and smiling all the time. For his first birthday, Mitra made him a round cake without any decorations and stuck one candle in the middle. They bought him a little stuffed giraffe and that was the only toy he grew up with.

They had no money to splash out on different toys; his godfather brought him a three-wheeler bike on his fifth birthday. When he saw his bike, he screamed so loud a neighbour came to our door to see if everything was okay. That special treatment was repeated every five years for each child. They did not spend money on elaborate birthday gifts or parties as most people do at the present time.

He grew up so quickly. When he first started school, he spoke mostly Serbio-Croatian, not much English. Kids at school made fun of him and he would come home crying and upset. At that time, we did not consider kids teasing each other such a big deal but accepted it as normal play among children. He caught up with the language very quickly and everything was all right. He was a very good student and earned a scholarship for university. We were excited and proud of him when the announcer called his name to present him the winning prize.

Mitra thought, "Yes, he was always a good and very smart child. Oh, I pray to God nothing bad will come out of his tests."

She shrugged, "Why would the doctor send him for tests if he thinks everything is all right. No-no, I do not want to think anything negative will happen to my Marko. God won't hurt his family and his mother. No, he would not do that. God is kind."

As Mitra was busy thinking good and bad thoughts, the phone rang. It was Sofija's cheerful voice coming through the phone.

"How was it at uncle Stefan's, Baba?"

"It was very nice. Marianna's girls are so grown up and beautiful."

"Good, did you have a good time?" Sofija asked.

"Yes, of course, very good. Uncle Stefan was asking about your project."

"What project, Baba?"

"You know what project—the story of my growing up," Mitra said.

"Oh, that story."

"Yes, that story," Mitra answered.

"Since we're talking about that, please prepare yourself for tomorrow after your lunch, I'm coming to get some more information."

"I'll be glad to see you, my child, but I don't know what more I can tell you. I think I told you everything I could remember."

"No, no, Baba, there is a lot more about your young life and your life in Canada. Everything about you is interesting."

Mitra had a disturbing night because all her thoughts were of Marko and why he had to have those tests. It was 8:30 am when Sandy knocked on her door and asked if she was ready to head downstairs for breakfast. She told Sandy she was ready and was coming out. When Sandy looked at Mitra, she asked her what was wrong.

"What do you mean what is wrong?" Mitra answered.

"You look as if someone drained all your blood out; you look so yellow and exhausted."

Mitra knew how important Sandy was to her. She felt she should tell her what was bothering her. When Sandy heard about Marko's story, she turned towards Mitra and asked her how old Marko was. After she heard his age, she told Mitra it is normal that people of his age have more check-ups than younger people.

"Come on, don't think the worst. You've got to have faith. Please don't worry so much, just because he's having tests."

Mitra turned towards Sandy and thanked her for the kind words. After they finished breakfast, they went outside to walk around a bit. The morning was so refreshing. All the flowers, grass, and bushes smelled really nice. The fresh air was in sharp contrast to the stuffy air inside the building. There was milkweed in the garden that the butterflies, especially the monarchs, really loved. There were a few on the plants. Mitra and Sandy admired their beautiful wings.

"How wonderful to be in the natural environment, I love it," Mitra exclaimed. At 10:00 am, the temperature was rising rapidly, and they decided to move inside. Sandy went to the exercise room to see what was going on there. Mitra went upstairs to her room. She felt much, much better than earlier and for that she thanked Sandy. She decided to sit in her chair and look outside. The day was clear and bright, she could see as far out as Toronto's CN tower.

Mitra felt sentimental and she thought of her children and their growing years. Marko and Sava were very close in age and they got along very well. Stefan arrived as a surprise. He came five years later. He was not planned for as the other two had been. They thought since they had a boy and a girl, they had a perfect family. Stefan was sent by God to enlarge their family and what a wonderful gift he had been to them, such a precious human being. Thank God for him.

He and Sava played together always. He was a leader and Sava, a follower. She listened to Marko all the time too. She told her mother once, "I have to listen to my brother. He is older than me and he knows a lot more than I do. I love my brother, mom. He protects me in school. Kids won't do anything bad to me because they are afraid of him. I feel so happy he is my brother. Do you feel happy, mom, that he is your son?"

"Of course I do. What makes you ask that?"

"I ask because you don't say, 'I love you' very often, like most mothers do."

"Where is this coming from? Of course I love you. I love you kids more than I love myself. Do you kids feel that you are loved by me and your father?"

"Yes, mom, we know that both of us are loved."

"You know, Sava, when I was growing up, we never looked for or felt we should be told our parents loved us. We knew they loved us without them saying it. We hope you kids believe, without any doubt, that you are the most important people in your father's life, and mine."

"We know, mom, we know. Please forgive me for saying anything about that."

"That is fine. I want you to come and talk to your father or me whenever you need more explanation about anything."

Sandy knocked on the door reminding Mitra not to forget to come down for lunch.

"I'll be down soon," Mitra answered.

After lunch Mitra went to her room. Sofija came shortly after with Tim Horton's coffee and a donut for each. Mitra took only the coffee so Sofija got both donuts.

"I knew you wouldn't take a donut, Baba. That was a perfect excuse for me. I got two donuts," Sofija boasted.

"You sneaky bugger, you like to tease and test me," Mitra said. They both laughed.

"How was your day, dear?" Mitra asked. "Did you see your grandpa Marko today?"

Baba couldn't think about anything but Marko.

"What is this, Baba? You are always thinking of your baby Marko. Think about somebody else sometimes, not always your Marko. No, I have not seen him for few days. You know, I was visiting aunt Sava in Ottawa."

"I know that," Mitra said. "Did you have a good time?"

"Yes, I had an exceptionally good time," said Sofija.

Mitra was asking to find out if she knew anything about his check-ups.

"Why are you always jealous when I ask about my children," Mitra protested.

"I'm jealous because I want you to love only me; nobody else."

"You selfish miserable thing."

They both laughed again.

"Enough joking. let's get to some serious business. Do you remember anything more about your birth country?"

"I don't know what we covered, but I think we talked about most things. If I remember anything more, I will tell you."

"Baba, were you close with your great-grandmother like you and I are?"

"Nobody is close as you and I are. We are more like school friends and quite open to each other's feelings, especially our heart-to-heart friendship," Mitra said.

"I'm also proud and happy about our closeness."

"I was close with my grandmother, but I was not as open with her as you are with me. That is understandable because at that time intimate things were not discussed with elders; it was considered inappropriate, at least in our family. I took care of my grandmother before she died. She wasn't able to move much, and we had to help her to get up for all her needs. She was very grateful for every little thing we did for her. She was especially thankful for my help. She died when I was just 18; like you. She was 90 years old when she died. She used to say to me, 'Please, don't get married before I die.' She wasn't so bright the few months before her death."

"That would indicate that she was not well," Sofija added.

"God rest her soul, she was a good and kind person. My mother always reminded us to be good and respectful to grandma. She would say to us, 'Grandma was more mother to you than me. I had to work in the fields and granny was always home with you. She deserves your love.'"

"It seems that your mother was a very good person."

"Yes, she was. Thank you for saying that. My mother and my grandmother had a very good relationship. My mother highly respected her mother-in-law and she received the same respect from granny."

"Was it customary that the maternal mother lived with you, or was it always from your father's side?"

"It was almost always your paternal grandmother you lived with. In very rare cases, a man married into his wife's family and also assumed his wife's family name. Usually, young men from poor families did that. At that time, it was not easy to start a family, if you did not have the means to provide for them. The only means was land and a place to live. This was done when a girl didn't have any brothers, and her family was much better off than the family of her prospective groom."

"That would have been a good move for a young man," Sofija exclaimed.

"Not really, because his pride would be hurt to give up his family name and assume his bride's family name. People had to do anything to survive," Mitra said.

"How did society react in such cases?" Sofija asked.

"As I already told you, these marriages did not happen very often. The reaction was mixed just as it would be now or any other time. Smart and good people were not judgemental, but some people who were jealous and miserable, or not very smart, would be very judgemental. Let's move on, Sofija, or we will never finish my diary."

"I'm glad that nobody is as close in their relationship as the two of us are, otherwise I would be very jealous."

"That is what you think, young lady," said Mitra smilingly. "Yes, my child, our friendship is the best. I thank God and your good sense for that."

"You've got good sense, Baba," Sofija added.

"I guess we are bragging a little bit too much about how good we are," Mitra admitted.

"But we are, Baba. And when you are good you are good and that's that," Sofija added with laughter.

"Oh my God, how much time we spend goofing around," Mitra said.

"But that is good for our souls. We should not always be serious. That would be boring," Sofija said.

"Yes, you are right my child, you are right as always," Mitra said.

"I agree with you, Baba. I know you've said a lot of things about your past but I'm sure you can add more either from back home or when you came to Canada. Was there anything that you didn't like or that you were afraid of in Canada?"

Mitra thought for a minute and said, "I didn't like going to funeral parlours or going to funerals for burials."

"Why was that?" Sofija asked.

"First of all, I was young, and secondly, children did not view dead bodies back home. We were sheltered by our elders. They didn't let us around the dead too much. Usually older men and women would sit all night long by a dead body. I think I told you when someone died, the body had to be kept by the hearth with a candle burning all night long. They would sit all night and most of the conversation was about the one who passed away. The dead person was completely covered all the time. But when I went to my first funeral in Canada to view the body of a young girl, it felt very scary. You knew that person was dead and yet you saw that person as being alive—and she looked alive, because funerals present dead bodies as if the person was still alive so it looks as if the dead will get up.

"At that time, all the people who we knew were very young immigrants who came after the Second World War, just like my Petar did. So, when you look at that young person, and imagine the earth would swallow him or her and their youthful face and body, that was disturbing and terrifying to me. For days, I would not feel good. I would not be able to sleep or to eat much because I would see the dead person's face in front of me and I imagined myself being in that position."

"Oh, Baba, I'm sorry you went through such terrible times. How do you feel now when you view a dead body?"

"Now I don't feel uncomfortable or scared, neither do I think too much about it, unless that person was close to me or someone else who I was close with," Mitra said.

"So, it looks like you became immune to the things that were awful before and had caused such strong reactions."

"When are you going to have enough of it and leave me alone?" Mitra joked.

"I like to bug you, Baba. You didn't tell me everything. I know there is lot more to tell," Sofija replied.

"Oh, my Lord, I don't know what to say anymore. I think I'm going to start lying to you."

"Oh no, I know you, you don't know how to lie."

"Oh, yes, unless I'm pushed hard enough," Mitra replied.

Sofija got serious and said, "What were funerals like in your village? Do you remember anything about them?"

"I remember when my uncle Todor died. I was still a child. Uncle died during harvest time. That was the death I still remember everything about. I remember a lot of people were in my uncle's house night and day. I heard from my mother that uncle Todor was very sick. She did not say he was dying, so as not to scare us kids.

"I heard from my older brother that people came to watch uncle Todor because someone had to be around a dying person. It would be a sin to let a person die alone. I was extremely curious about what was going on. The previous couple of nights, all the young people from my uncle's house, his son's children, slept at our house. I sensed that something big was going on. My mother warned me not to be too nosy and ask too many questions."

"Why was that? Why couldn't you ask questions?" Sofija asked.

"Old people always said that children should not know too much about dying because it scares them."

"That is true to a point, but it's even worse not knowing what's going on," Sofija said.

"Not really. What you don't know, it doesn't hurt you either," Mitra said.

"My uncle was gravely ill for a couple of days. I heard my cousin, George, and my father working in the room where we stored our winter food. There was a small crack in the wall, and I watched what they were doing through it. I heard them talking about how to prepare a carrier on which they would carry uncle Todor to the cemetery. They made two strong poles about 9 to 10 feet long. The poles were long enough to fit uncle's body and had extra length so four men could carry him.

"They used a strong rope and weaved it around and between the poles to make a bed-like space to fit my uncle's body. On top, they placed a thick blanket, made from our own sheep wool, as if it was a thin mattress. I heard them talking between themselves; when uncle Todor died they would fit him nicely between the poles. They even looked for a white sheet that was prepared for that occasion. I heard my father say, 'Everything is ready; we only need eight strong men to carry him, taking turns.'

"They counted about five places they would have to stop through the village in front of relatives' or close friends' houses."

"Was that a custom?" Sofija asked.

"Yes, it was. Sometimes people told their families whose houses to stop in front of when they died. It was an honour to pay respect to the body.

"The next day my uncle Todor died. We kids were told not to be rowdy or laughing but to be sombre and quiet because our uncle had died. His body was placed by the hearth, mounted on two low stools about a foot off the floor. The burning candle was placed beside his head. The fire at the hearth had to burn continuously while the body was there. They said that fire and light symbolize life and light for the soul to travel to heaven. People were coming and going all day, saying prayers and crying a lot."

"Baba, how come you remember everything so well?"

"I remember it so well because it was harvest time and because of my corn," Mitra replied.

"What did corn have to do with your uncle Todor?"

"It did," said Mitra. "At one time nobody was around my uncle's body. I was hungry, and I grabbed a corn cob and put it on the fire to be roasted beside my uncle's body. I had to go three times to turn the corn cob around to roast all the sides. Each time I went, I felt my uncle was rising up and wanted to grab me."

"Poor you," Sofija said. "Did you roast the corn evenly and enjoy it?"

"You bet I enjoyed it. Perfection isn't that important when you are hungry."

"That means you were really hungry."

"Yes, I was," Mitra said.

"How far was your uncle's house from yours?"

"As far as a half-metre wall, dividing our house in two."

"What do you mean, Baba, how big was your house?"

Mitra was surprised with the Sofija's question.

"Oh, it was so big, we each had a private bedroom, a big dining room, a big sitting room and three toilets. What are you thinking, Sofija? That we lived like you live here? I told you before the size and division of our houses. They were not elaborate or spacious."

"I can see there was no luxury, only bare necessities," Sofija said.

"Measuring by today's standards we were desperate and poor. You must remember that because we didn't know any luxury, we were fine with what we had. We didn't feel poor. Our family was luckier than the rest in the village, because we had a much better house than our neighbours."

"How is that, Baba?"

"It's because our mother's two brothers were builders. Although self-taught, they did good job."

"How would you feel, Baba, if you had to return to such a life now?"

"I must admit I would not feel good after living my life in comfort for many years, but nobody lives the old way there anymore either. Progress has reached everywhere. We are talking about 80 years ago."

"How long was your uncle lying there beside the hearth?"

"He was there only one night. Dead bodies were not kept around more than one day, sometimes not even a day, especially in summer heat. Sometimes if the weather was too severe in winter time and the cemetery was too far, then the body stayed a little longer, but every effort was made to bury the body soon after death."

"Did you cry a lot for your uncle?"

"Yes, I did when he died. After the funeral procession came back from the cemetery, a memorial meal was prepared in uncle Tode's house. There was lots of good food. Everybody enjoyed it, especially children."

"Was it customary to say a eulogy," Sofija asked.

"Not really, not like here, but people did talk about him," Mitra said.

"What did they say about him? Was he a good man?" Sofija asked.

"Ah, not that good to us kids, he was always grumpy, yelling at us for every little thing, complaining about us to our parents and even lying to us sometimes. His children and grandchildren had more love and respect for my father than for him," Mitra said.

"So, you were not terribly sad when he died," Sofija said.

"Ah, yes, in that moment when you see a dead person, somebody you've known all your life, and everybody is shedding tears, you cry too. We were also expected to cry because a member of our family had died. Our parents didn't want us to show disrespect. I heard two women talking about my uncle. They didn't see me behind a stone wall built for privacy."

"What were they talking about?"

"The first woman said she wasn't sorry he died, the other one said, 'Be quiet. God will strike you for talking like that about dead person.'

"'I don't care, he was not a good man,' the first woman said.

"'What did he do to you that you are so mad at him?' the other woman asked.

"The first woman paused for a bit, no doubt wondering whether to say why, or to keep quiet. Then she said, 'I will tell you, but do not tell anybody. Two days after Tode's wife, Todora, had their last child, a boy, I was alone in the woods minding my sheep. All of a sudden Todor appeared from nowhere. As soon as I saw him, I knew there would be trouble. He came at me right away. I pushed him very hard and hit him on the head with my cane. Shepherds usually carried a cane in case a wolf attacked their sheep. I was scared to death and ran home like crazy, leaving my sheep in the woods. I heard that he had a big bump on his head. When people asked what happened, he lied and said a branch had hit him as he was going through the woods. From then on, I never went alone to mind the sheep, but instead went with the other neighbours. That's the kind of garbage he was. God will punish him for his sins. I always felt sorry for his wife, Todora. She was a good soul.'"

"That was a very good explanation about the old funeral customs, thank you, Baba. I know that you have a lot more to tell me about your experiences. It's soon time for me to go home. If you remember anything else, please write it down and tell me when I come next time."

"I promise I will do that. When are you planning to come again?" Mitra asked.

"I don't know. I have some things to do. I will let you know."

"I know what to do. I'm going to call you and tell you that I remembered something very important and you have to come right away."

"All right, you know how to manipulate me. Since you told me about your trick, I will ignore your urgent message."

"Oh my, my, how stupid can I be for telling you my idea? Now, I let the cat out of the bag."

They both laughed again.

"It was fun visiting with you, Baba. We had a lot of laughs."

Sofija bent down, kissed Mitra, and she was gone.

Chapter 18

After Sofija left, Mitra called Marko's place. No one was at home; the answering machine came on. Mitra thought about whether to leave a message or just hang up, but she was afraid that they might think something was wrong because she didn't speak. Mitra left a message asking how their day was. "I just wanted to say hello." Just as Mitra was going to lie down the phone rang.

"Hello, mom."

"Hello, son," Mitra answered.

"We are all good. We were not home when you phoned because we went to see our next-door neighbour, Mike. He asked us to come for a drink."

"How is he now after his hip surgery?" Mitra asked.

"He is good," Marko answered. "He and his wife appreciated our visiting him a couple of times. They wanted to thank us for that. How was your day, mother?"

"It was very pleasant. Sofija visited me."

"Oh, I know you two always have a good time when you are together."

"That is true," Mitra said.

"Stefan told me you spent yesterday afternoon at his place."

"Yes. I had a very good time."

"Stefan told you that I'm going through some tests. I was not happy that he told you that and worried you for nothing."

"I hope it is all for nothing but whether I worry or not, I always want to know the truth about my children. As your mother, I think I have a right to know."

"I know, mom, I understand that, but for now there is nothing to worry about."

"Will you please tell me about the reports when they come back?"

"Yes, mom, I will tell you. You will be informed, I'll make sure of that."

"You must have felt something that made you go for tests."

"I wasn't visiting you very much because I kept getting colds and I didn't want to give one to you; that is why we stayed away from you."

"Nice try, you think it is better not to see your mother because of a cold. No cold is strong enough to divide us."

Mitra meant that as a joke but Marko didn't take it that way.

"Mom, a cold would be too hard on your body. Why would I do that to you when it's not necessary?"

"You are right, son. Sorry about that. I was only making a joke, but it looks like you are not up for jokes."

"Oh, mom, you are imagining things. After persistent cold symptoms, the doctor suggested I go for some tests."

"When are you getting those tests back?"

"I'm going to see the doctor a week from today, so while I have a cold, I won't be seeing you. We will know what is going on next Monday."

"All right, son. I hope everything will be okay. Good luck, son. How is Doris?"

"She is well."

"Is she worried about you?"

"Come on, mom, there is nothing to worry about for now."

"All right, son, I will expect your call."

"Good night, mom."

"Good night, son."

The days for Mitra were spent as usual. Marko was always on her mind. Sofija called to tell her she was going on holidays with some friends.

"Where are you going if I may ask?"

"We are going to Jamaica."

"Take care and have a good holiday, dear."

"Yes, I will have you on my mind. You be a good, Baba. Don't do anything crazy."

"Don't worry I won't, even if I want to."

The week went by slowly. Mitra couldn't stop thinking about Marko's tests, but when she called him, she didn't mention them. She called Stefan to ask if he had seen Marko and how he looked.

"He looks normal; only sometimes he has some coughs."

On Monday, Marko got the news. He didn't want to tell Mitra the same day but on Wednesday he came to see her. Marko told Mitra the truth that he had lung cancer. Mitra asked what kind of treatment they were going to give him.

"Mom, I don't know if I will be going for any treatment, because my cancer is in the fourth stage, and it's already spread everywhere. What is the use of going through such suffering for nothing? I told the doctor I am not going to do anything. I will live the days that are given to me, and that will be it."

For an instant, Mitra held back her tears and hastily said, "Maybe treatment would help. At least it would extend your life."

"What kind of a life. Would you like to see me like that, mother? I certainly don't want to go through such an ordeal.

Don't worry, please, mom; we still have a lot of time left to see each other."

Mitra could not speak. She was choking from sorrow and tears that could not be stopped. Marko sensed that and said, "Mom, we need to accept whatever happens in our lives."

"That is not good, son. I cannot easily accept something like that. I always wanted you, my children, to put me in the ground." Mitra wanted to say, "before I put you in ground," but refrained from that.

"I love you, mom, please don't worry too much."

"I will try my best, son, but I don't think I can do it."

"Please don't worry about me, look after yourself."

"What is Doris doing?" Mitra asked.

"Not much."

"I bet she is crying like me—that is what she is doing," Mitra said.

"Well, she is doing some crying too."

"Please tell her I'm sorry to hear what I just heard," Mitra did not want to repeat terrible news.

"What can you do mom? It is what it is. I don't think we can do anything about it."

The conversation finished, but the terrible news was just beginning to sink in. The worst was yet to come.

"I will come to see you soon, mom. I have to see another doctor tomorrow and hear what he has to say," Marko said.

"What kind of doctor is he?"

"He is a specialist for internal organs."

"Will you please let me know what he says?"

"I will, mom. I will keep you informed about everything. I promise."

"Thank you, son. Good luck to you."

Marko tried to comfort Mitra a little, but there was no comfort for her anymore, after hearing such horrible news.

After Marko hung up the phone, she started to cry even more. She was happy that it was past 8:30 pm and no one would come to her, so she could cry alone in peace. In deep sorrow, people don't need company. The nurse Dona knocked on her door, "I just wanted to say good night, Mrs. Milutinovic."

Mitra didn't want to turn her away because she was very good to her. "Come in, Dona," Mitra said.

When Dona walked in, she saw Mitra in very bad shape. Her eyes were so red, she was still crying.

"Mrs. Milutinovic, I don't like to pry, but I can't help it. What is wrong?"

Mitra looked at Dona not knowing what to say. But then she remembered Dona was a very smart and good person, not a gossiping type.

"I got bad news, very bad news, from home."

"What kind of news?"

"My older son has lung cancer."

Dona said, "I'm sorry, Mrs. Milutinovic. That is not good news for a mother to hear about her child. Hopefully, they can help him—"

Before Dona finished what she wanted to say, Mitra cut in sharply, "No, Dona, they cannot."

She told her what Marko had said. Dona's eyes filled with tears. She said to Mitra that she was very sorry to hear that.

"Would you like me to stay longer with you or do you prefer to be alone?"

"You can sit for a while but please understand how badly I feel; I don't know if it is better to have company or not. Nothing feels right and I can change nothing about his situation."

Mitra did not feel like talking. Dona sat quietly for a while and then got up to leave, saying to Mitra she was going to check up on her later. If she found her sleeping, she wouldn't bother her.

"Sleeping, sleeping," Mitra exclaimed. "How can I sleep? I hope I'm going to fall asleep and never wake up. That would be God's biggest present to me."

"I know, Mrs. Milutinovic, that would be the easiest way out for you but think about your son. What sorrow he would have on top of his illness. He would not be happy to lose you now, believe me. He wants his mother around to comfort him during this hard time. Every grown person feels like a baby towards their parents, especially their mother."

Mitra opened her eyes wide and looked at Dona, "Dona, you are right. What I thought would be good for me is very selfish."

"Sorry, Mrs. Milutinovic, if I hurt your feelings by my saying so."

"No, Dona, don't be sorry. You are so right. It would be the end for me but abandoning my son in his worst pain and suffering would be very selfish. Thank you, Dona, I appreciate what you just said. You are one smart girl."

"Thank you, Mrs. Milutinovic, so are you."

Dona left promising to come back to check on her after she made her rounds.

"Thank you, Dona."

Mitra sat in the chair for quite a while and then decided to go to bed. She thought of what Marko had said, "It is what it is, and we have to face the reality."

"Oh, my dear, dear child, if I could only protect you with my own life I would. This is not a little wound like when you hurt yourself and I took care of it and it healed quickly," Mitra did not want to finish the words, "but this is going to take your life."

That night Mitra said extra prayers, one prayer bowing her head beside the bed and another in the bed. She cried as she prayed until she became exhausted. She dozed off for a while and somehow a peaceful calm came over her. She was wondering whether God was leading her to accept the truth and not to fear death so much.

She heard the door silently being opened and she knew it was Dona. She pretended she was asleep. Dona left and Mitra said prayers again begging God to be kind to Marko and not to let him suffer too much. She dozed off again. When she woke up, she was wondering whether to go downstairs for coffee because she knew she couldn't eat anything.

"After all, I have to move. I cannot sit here night and day. It won't change anything nor help my Marko."

Mitra got ready and went downstairs. Sandy came right after her. She bid Mitra good morning and asked her why she did not call her as usual to go downstairs together. When she looked at Mitra, she was astounded.

"What is wrong, Mitra? Are you all right?"

"Not really," Mitra answered, "I got bad news that my son Marko has lung cancer." She told Sandy how bad Marko's sickness was.

Sandy put her hand on her mouth and said, "Oh my God, Mitra. God help him and you and his family. I'm sorry to hear that, my friend. Your son is such a nice guy."

It was noticeable that Mitra was in pain, but nobody said anything. The others' extra politeness made it obvious what they were thinking. Sandy tried to coax Mitra to have at least a couple bites of food with her coffee. Mitra refused to have anything but coffee. After breakfast Sandy asked Mitra what she would like to do. "Nothing, really nothing," Mitra answered. "I really don't have the desire to do anything. I think I will go upstairs and see if my son Stefan called. I will call him about Marko and what Stefan thinks about the situation."

"That's a good idea," Sandy said. "I will go to the gym to see what they are doing over there."

Since there was no message, Mitra called. Stefan answered the phone.

"Oh, mom is that you already? I didn't call you because I thought you would be downstairs having breakfast."

"Breakfast," said Mitra. "I don't feel like eating this morning."

"I know, mom, I know. It is terrible news. I talked to Marko over the phone and he told me what he had told you. I didn't want to see him yesterday because I wanted his family to comfort him first, but I will go today and stay a little longer with him."

"Please, son, call me and let me know all about his situation. Please, son, you have always been good brothers. Please try to be as supportive of him as you can."

"Yes, mom, you know I will."

"Call me as soon as you come home."

Mitra could not wait. She called Stefan just before supper. She heard from Stefan what she already knew. Mitra waited every day for Marko's visit, but he didn't come for a whole week after he'd told her the bad news. He did call her everyday to tell her that he had many appointments.

"What kind of appointments, son?"

"All kinds, mom."

Mitra didn't want to say anything, but her assumption was that he was arranging his own funeral. Such thoughts shook Mitra. She got off the chair as if a bad voice was coming from under its cushion. "Oh my God, oh my God, I cannot ask him that. No, no, I should not think about that either."

After she put the phone down, she said a prayer. "Sometimes God doesn't hear our pleading, instead he proceeds with his plan. No, I shouldn't think that way. I believe God is good and he listens to our prayers. I have to believe that, otherwise I will lose my mind. Please, God help me and forgive me for my doubts and negative thoughts."

Whenever something new had happened, Mitra always picked up a different picture of her family. She'd hug and kiss it. She has many framed pictures of her family in her room.

Mitra walked up and down her room and sat on her chair again. She picked up a family photo that had been taken two years before Petar's death. Marko was finishing his last year at University and Sava was studying law. Only Stefan was still in high school. "We were really happy," she remembered.

Mitra put the picture on her chest and took a deep breath saying, "My wonderful family. How happy we were. Petar always used to say to us, especially to me, that we should enjoy the life given to us every day because there is no guarantee what will happen tomorrow. How true that was. He said it as if he had a premonition of what would happen in the future."

She lifted the picture off her chest, kissed each one of them in the portrait and thanked God for the wonderful family he had given her. "Sometimes we are not thankful enough for the good God gave us because we're wondering why me? I do not deserve that from God. I have been good. Why is God punishing me?"

The rest of the week went by in anticipation. Mitra still hoped against hope, that somehow things would get better. Sofija was away. Stefan came to see her a couple of times. Sandy was attentive, so was Dona, but Mitra's mind was always on Marko's situation.

After a week of bad news, Marko and his wife came to see Mitra. He looked the same, only his eyes showed the stress he was going through. Those eyes looked a bit sunken. The brightness of his good health visible before, was diminished now. No wonder people believe that eyes are the windows of one's state of health. Mitra hugged her son so tenderly and long, as if to prevent Marko from a future of suffering. The visit wasn't as light-hearted as usual, with occasional cracks of humour. This time, it was sombre and unsettling, even though Marko tried to make it more pleasant.

They didn't stay very long. Doris reminded Marko that they had to go because their son, John, and his wife, Sofija's father and mother, were coming for dinner. Mitra escorted them to the entrance door and after they left, went back to her room to wail with sorrow. Mitra didn't feel like going anywhere, even though she was asked by Sandy and others to go out for a bit. Sofija called to say that she had just come back from her holiday and she would come tomorrow to see her.

Judging by the tone of Sofija's voice, she knew about her grandfather's situation.

The next day was like the rest of them since she'd heard the bad news. She was anxiously waiting for Sofija to come. After dinner Sofija appeared with the usual coffees and two donuts. She came over to sit on Mitra's bed and gave her a big hug and loud kiss, as she asked her how she had been while she was away.

"I was good all the time. What do you think I can't survive without you?" said Mitra jokingly.

"Look at this old lady. I thought she couldn't live without me but looks like I was wrong. Maybe I should go home right away since I'm not wanted around here."

"Sure, if you love me that much or hate me that much you can leave. Enough jokes for one day, Sofija. Did you have good holiday?"

"Yes, Baba, the best," Sofija said.

"I'm glad," Mitra said.

"So, what's happened since I left?"

Sofija's question threw Mitra into confusion and for a minute she did not know what to say.

"I know what is going on with grandpa Marko. My dad told me because he didn't want me to hear it from somebody else. Well, Baba, it's not good news, but what can we do about it? I love my grandpa and despite the odds, I hope he will be around a long time so I can tease him."

"Do you see him very often?" Mitra asked.

"Yes, of course, I do. He is just across the road from us," Sofija replied.

"I hope so," Mitra answered. "Do visit him as much as you can. He told me he likes your company."

"I promise I will. I was wondering if we have some more stories to add to my folder. There is still a lot of room left in it."

Sofija wanted to divert Mitra's attention from Marko's situation.

"Oh, I don't know, Sofija. Right now, I can't think about anything else but my son."

"All right, we will just sit and talk. Is there anything new in your new family? How are your friends?" Sofija asked.

"Good. In the last few days, I haven't been with them much because I don't feel like talking to them, or anybody else for that matter," Mitra said.

"I know, Baba, it's hard for you, but please do not isolate yourself. If you do that for too long, people will back off and then it will be hard to get them back. It's better for you to talk to people. Everybody has some problems, even if they are not willing to talk about them. Please put your mind on something else. It will be better for you and you will be stronger to face the future, whatever comes."

"You are right, my dear, and I promise I'll listen to you. You will start university soon. Are you prepared for such a big step?"

"Oh yes, Baba, I'm ready and look forward to it."

"What do you think you will take, wise girl?"

"I haven't made a definite decision yet. The first year at university is a general one so next year, I will decide. I think it will be either science or astronomy."

"So, you still want to go into space?"

"Oh yes, Baba, I do."

Mitra looked at Sofija and saw that she was tired, "You look tired dear, is that from too much fun on your holiday?"

"I guess so. It's a little bit of everything."

"Maybe you should go home and rest. Don't worry about me, dear, I will take your advice and be more sociable."

"That's good, Baba. I don't know when I will come to visit again but I will come as soon as I can, just to bug you."

"Fine, fine, you just come and bug me, I'll be happy with that."

Sofija got up, kissed Mitra, and was gone. After Sofija left, Mitra threw herself on her bed. Soon, she heard the knock at the door; Dona came in.

"How are you doing, Mrs. Milutinovic?"

"I'm doing well. My great-granddaughter just left. I always enjoy her visits."

"I can tell that. Are you more settled after yesterday?"

"Yes, somewhat."

"I know, Mrs. Milutinovic, it is hard to take bad news."

The way Dona said that Mitra looked at her with questioning eyes, "Is everything well with you, Dona?"

"Not really, Mrs. Milutinovic."

"What is wrong with you? What is happening?"

"It's my son."

"How old is your son, Dona?"

"He is 17."

"Oh, he is too young for anything bad, Dona."

"Yes, he is, but things can happen at any time and at any age. Your son Marko isn't that old either."

"That is true, Dona."

Mitra paused for a while waiting for Dona to speak because she wasn't sure whether Dona wanted to talk about it. Mitra thought, "I should not pry."

Dona knew that Mitra was waiting for her to say something.

"Yes, my son got news four days ago that he has cancer in his right knee."

"Oh my God," said Mitra, "I'm sorry to hear that, Dona."

"My son liked to play football all the time. A couple of years ago, he got banged up pretty badly. He was on crutches for six weeks. We told him not to play football anymore, instead play sports where there wasn't a big chance of severe injuries. He didn't listen. He said he didn't like any other sport. 'Football is my fate,' he would say. What can you say to a 15 year old? He thinks he knows everything and wants to do what he dreams about."

"I know when my children were that age, my husband and I had to work very hard to persuade them not to do something that we knew eventually would be harmful to them."

"Oh, you're talking about different times when children listened to their parents. It's not like that anymore. Kids want to do what they want to do. I remember how I had to listen to my parents, but my kids won't listen to me and my husband."

"There is a lot of influence from outside that encourages kids to do what they want to do. Yeah, things have changed in a big way, but I don't know if it is for better or worse," Mitra added.

"In more ways it is for the worse. It's very, very hard to be a parent today. One isn't sure how to parent effectively. Traditional ideas of parenting are gone from today's system," Dona said. "My son wasn't feeling good with his knee for two months. He started complaining about it. We both believed it was only a temporary problem and would pass. Things got worse progressively. We told him to go for an X-ray in order to know what was going on. The X-ray detected something wrong in the knee. In order to have a better diagnosis, he had an MRI plus some more tests. Our doctor asked to see all three of us: our son, my husband, and me.

"We knew right away something was terribly wrong. Our doctor has a very nice manner but after some small talk, the room fell silent, 'I'm very sorry to deliver bad news but Johnny has cancer in his knee.' We all went silent for a few seconds. My husband asked if there was a chance that there could be some mistake.

"'I know, Mr. Javorsky, you don't want to hear this. Neither would I, but there is no mistake. It has been confirmed over and over again. There is always a possibility that a mistake was made but so far in your son's situation, I'm afraid not.'

"The three of us talked after we went home, and we agreed to keep things as normal as possible. Our son went to school and we went to work. We now have to wait until the doctors decide how to go about the treatment."

"Dona, I'm so, so sorry for you."

"I feel better talking to you about it. I have a feeling that you are a good person and you will not tell others what I told you about my son."

"Please rest assured that I won't say anything to anybody."

"Thank you for listening to my problem. You already have enough of your own," Dona said. "I have to go. They are going to begin looking for me."

After Dona left, Mitra said to herself, "I'm sorry for you, Dona."

Soon Mitra was alone thinking of Marko. He didn't call that day, neither did anybody else.

"I can't bother them by calling all the time. He doesn't want to be reminded of it either, I'm sure," Mitra thought. "Dona's approach makes sense; continue with life as if everything is normal."

Chapter 19

The next two weeks passed normally. Mitra got occasional phone calls from her children and her relatives. Everybody avoided talking about Marko's sickness. Even when he called, the conversation was the same as before. Mitra sensed that Marko's voice was changing; it was a little weaker and less clear.

Every time she wanted to say something to him about his situation, she always remembered Dona's approach, "keep it normal."

Sofija came twice but she didn't stay too long. She was busy between work and preparation for the beginning of the school year.

Both times, Mitra asked about everybody. She sensed that Sofija was avoiding talking about grandpa Marko.

Mitra knew that Sofija knew about it and also that she was thinking about what grandpa was going through. It was obvious that Sofija's mood had changed. When Mitra asked her if she was all right, she would reply, "Yes, Baba, I am."

Marko made excuses for not coming to see his mother. He knew she would be very upset to see the way he looked, only three weeks after he had been diagnosed with cancer.

After three weeks passed, Marko had to go and see his mother. The cancer was growing rapidly, destroying his body. He wasn't sure how long he would be independent. For that reason, he had to go and see his mother. He could not keep her in suspense and avoid telling her the truth.

Marko couldn't go to the residence. Instead he sent his wife and Sofija to bring his mother to him. When Mitra appeared at the door, Marko greeted her. She was shocked when she saw how much he changed. They silently kissed and hugged.

Mitra could not believe such a change in a very short time. Dinner was put on the table, but Mitra had a very hard time swallowing food. She tried not to stare at Marko, but she had a very hard time avoiding it.

Marko finally broke the silence.

"Mom, I can see that you're surprised with how I've changed. I can't hide myself from you. I know it's very hard for you to see me like this. I cannot help it, neither can you. It is what it is, and we have to accept it."

Mitra's eyes filled with tears and they dripped down her face.

"I'm sorry, son. I wish I could have your pain."

"Don't say that," Marko exclaimed. "Everything will be fine, mom."

Marko's wife, Doris, tried to tell a joke, but she too quickly fell silent.

They sat in the sitting room after dinner. Marko sat in the chair close to his mother. The two of them had chamomile tea while Doris and Sofija had coffee.

An hour later, Mitra saw that Marko was very tired. She asked Doris and Sofija to take her back to her place. Marko said, "Mom, you don't have to go yet, it's too early. You were not here that long. Don't worry, mom, you are not tiring me, I'm all right."

Marko moved close to his mother and put his head on Mitra's shoulder, "You are still my dearest mommy and I'm still your baby, right, mom?"

"Yes, son, that is right and always will be right."

Sofija raised her voice, "Oh no, grandpa, you cannot have my Baba for yourself alone, I won't allow it. I must have a big portion of my Baba and I'm willing to fight hard for that."

"Look at my granddaughter; she wants my mother for herself."

"Yes, I do, grandpa," Sofija exclaimed.

"We can all have a share in this wonderful woman—right mom?"

"Right, son, I agree."

Marko looked at his mother and asked whether he would be able to see her soon, or not at all. Mitra wondered the same thing. Both tried to put on happy faces, but at the same time, they could not hide their sadness. The three girls got ready to go. Marko walked them to the door. Doris and Sofija walked out leaving Mitra alone with her son for a while.

Marko started first, "Mom, I'm not sure how things will be with me, or if I will be able to visit you, but please do not think I don't want to. I am losing energy, but I'm still pretty good. Please do not worry about me. Remember how much I love you and that I think about growing up a lot. You were a very good mom. Thank you for that."

Mitra could not listen to these words anymore because of their meaning. His words felt like, "Goodbye, mom."

"Thank you, son, for your kind words. I can say the same thing about you, but I won't for now. We will have a lot more time to see each other."

"I hope so, mom. I hope so," Marko said.

They each tried to assure the other that Marko would have a longer life, but both of them knew that his time was running out. They hugged and kissed many times. They had tears in their eyes. Finally, they let go of each other. That was a very sad goodbye.

Inside the car they all fell silent for a while. Doris started first; she always called Mitra mom, ever since she married Marko 45 years ago. She was closer with Mitra than Stefan's wife, Suzan, who was jealous of Doris and always had something negative to say about her. Doris was not like Suzan. She didn't like to offend people and would always say, "If you don't have something nice to say about people, you're better off not saying anything."

Mitra tried to treat her daughters-in-law the same, even though she preferred to be with Doris because she felt comfortable in her presence. Doris said, "I'm sorry, mom, I think you were surprised to see how much Marko has changed."

Mitra thought for a while and then said, "Yes, I was. I didn't think he would have changed so much."

Mitra asked Doris, "Is Marko eating? Does he have an appetite?"

"Yes and no," Doris answered, "His appetite has gone down; some days he eats better than others."

"How is he sleeping?" Mitra asked.

"That part is a little worse than his appetite. He coughs a lot when he is lying down. If he doesn't sleep for a couple of nights, he has to take sleeping pills. You know Marko; he never likes taking any kind of pills."

"I'm so sorry to ask but I have to know because I want to know. What do the doctors say? Is there any hope that with a new therapy he may get better?"

"I wish that could happen," Doris said, "but the doctors don't have any hope for a cure."

"Did the doctors say how long he has to live?"

Doris swerved the car just to delay the answer. She wanted to reply in a less hurtful way to Mitra. But Marko's days were numbered, and his end was coming very soon.

"Mom, we don't know exactly how long. We have to wait and see. Try to calm down as much as you can, because no matter what you do with your worries you cannot help him, but you can harm yourself. Your son wouldn't like that," Doris said.

"Thank you, Doris, for your daughterly advice. I know I can't change anything, but I cannot be immune to my son's suffering. I have no control over my worries."

Doris helped Mitra get out of the car and helped her up to her room. Mitra kept saying to Doris not to worry about her. She could get to her room without a problem. Doris insisted on helping her because she knew that Mitra was shaken seeing Marko's dreadful change. Doris asked Sofija to stay in the car while she took Mitra upstairs to her room.

Mitra sat down and looked around her room. Her eyes went straight to Marko's picture. She'd framed her children's graduation pictures individually, then she'd framed photos of each of them with their families. Another photo had all the families together with her in the middle.

"We will have to go home, mom. Marko is alone. Are you all right now? Can I leave?" Doris asked.

"Yes, I'm fine. Doris, will you please let me know how things are going with Marko, but please tell me the truth. If there is an emergency, I would like to be with my son and hold his hand."

Doris knew what her mother-in-law was talking about, "Yes, mom I will let you know. I won't lie to you. I'm a mother too, and I know how you feel."

"Thank you very much, dear, for being a good daughter-in-law and a good wife to my son."

"Thank you, mom," she kissed Mitra, and stroked her thinning, grey hair a couple of times and left.

Mitra stood up, took Marko's picture, and after kissing it many times put it on her chest, saying, "Oh, my poor child, my first born, when I imagine what you are going through, I am in pain."

Mitra kept praying and crying. After some time, she fell asleep.

She woke to a knock on the door. "Come in," she said.

Dona was at the door, "Hi, Mrs. Milutinovic, I didn't know you had come back. When did you sneak in?"

Mitra looked at the clock and exclaimed, "Oh my God, I came back at six and now it's eight."

"That is all right. Nothing wrong with resting when you feel tired. Mitra, how was your visit with your son—you went to his place, right?"

"Yes, I did."

"How is he keeping?"

Mitra told Dona everything with a lot of pain and tears.

"I'm very sorry, but you can't do much," Dona said.

"Yes, I know, and that is my biggest pain because I can't do anything."

"Can I do something for you, or would you rather be alone?"

"I don't know what I want, Dona. What I want I can't get, so I don't know what I can tell you. If you have time, you can sit a little. How is your son doing?"

"For now, he is well, thank God. But when you have something bad, one never knows when and how it will come back. My husband and I have lived in fear since we found out about his illness."

"Did you see my companions? Are they back?"

"No, I didn't see them," Dona said, "I don't know if they went somewhere."

"Yes, they went to Niagara Falls and Niagara-on-the-Lake. They did ask me to go with them, but I couldn't because my son invited me to his house. If you happen to see them, don't say anything about me, please. I'd like to be alone tonight. They are very nice people, but I'm not good company tonight."

"No problem, Mrs. Milutinovic. I'll try to avoid them, so they won't be able to ask me."

"Thank you, Dona."

"You are welcome. Why don't you rest now? I will check on you later. Would you like me to bring you something from the kitchen, a cup of coffee or tea?"

"No, thank you, nothing at all. I have some water here."

Mitra's days were slow and sad. She thought incessantly about her son's suffering. Dona, Sandy, and other residents who knew Mitra tried to preoccupy her, but no matter what they did, Mitra's mind was only on her son Marko. Doris called her every day to report Marko's situation. Every time Doris called, Mitra feared what she would hear. Mitra lost her appetite. Often, she didn't go downstairs for meals. Her friends brought her things she liked, either from the kitchen or from a store. They all tried very hard to take care of Mitra.

Sofija left to study at the University of Toronto. Often, she did not come home for the weekend because she had to study. She called Mitra every day, and often tried to crack jokes, but Mitra didn't react to them. Sofija felt guilty for not being closer to home to help out with grandpa Marko. She felt even guiltier for not spending more time with her baba. Sofija had been at university for just two weeks when she asked her parents about taking a year off until the family crisis was settled. Her parents were not in favour of it. They told her there was always that possibility that something could happen next year too.

"Your education is vital for your future. Nobody would encourage you to leave school no matter what," they told her.

Sofija talked to Mitra about it but she too didn't want to hear it.

It had already been three weeks since she visited Marko's house but to Mitra it felt more like a year. In her most recent call, Doris told her that Marko could still sit up sometimes, but he was more often in bed. Mitra didn't insist on visiting because she was afraid it would be even harder on him if Mitra saw his pain and suffering. At the end of September, Marko was completely bedridden. Mitra asked Doris if she could come to visit Marko. She said to Mitra, "You can come, mom, but we will have to wait until he is in a little less pain. Today is not that good. His pain fluctuates up and down, hopefully tomorrow will be better."

September was already gone. October came. Just as Mitra wanted to ask Doris again if she could visit Marko, there was a phone call from Doris. She usually called in the afternoon, but this was in the morning. She usually asked Mitra how she was, but this time she told her that an ambulance had taken Marko to the hospital. He was having a very hard time breathing and was gasping for air.

"I'm at the hospital with Marko but I know you want to come to see him. I cannot pick you up, because I don't want to leave him alone in the hospital."

Mitra said right away that she wanted to see him. "I don't know who to ask to drive me to the hospital," she said.

As Mitra said this, Dona happened to be near Mitra's door. She heard her talking with Doris. She told Mitra that she had a couple of days off. Dona was dressed in regular clothes. Right away, she said to Mitra, "Mrs. Milutinovic, I heard you say you have nobody to take you to the hospital to see your son. I will gladly take you. My shift is over. I'm free now."

Mitra looked surprised, "Are you sure, Dona?"

"Of course, I will gladly take you if you want me to."

"Yes, please," Mitra said, "I will go with anybody who will take me there."

Dona got busy arranging clothes for Mitra to wear.

"Do you need to be sponged?"

"What's that?" Mitra asked.

"You know what it means: washed with a soapy cloth under your arm pits and your private parts."

Dona helped Mitra with everything. Mitra forgot about the shame, because her emotions were drained. She thought only about her son Marko and nothing else.

They quickly arrived at the General Hospital.

Mitra found Marko on a stretcher in the corridor, waiting to be examined. Marko was surprised to see his mother. "Mom, who brought you here so quickly? You shouldn't have rushed to see me. I'm not dying, at least not yet."

"Oh, my son, don't talk like that. Tell me how you are feeling?"

"As you can see, mom, I'm fighting the battle, but I don't know if I am going to win it."

"Yes, son, you will, just keep on fighting."

"I will, mom, I will for both our sakes, and for our family."

Marko felt a terrible pain churning inside his chest. After such pain he had a bad cough, often times with blood in his spittle. Marko didn't want his mother to see that. He put the bloody tissue under his covers, instead of putting it in the waste basket. Mitra and Doris sat beside him. They were quiet for a while just looking around at other patients, coming in and going out. Somebody was groaning.

The nurse came and took Marko away for tests. She told them to go to the waiting lounge. They went there. It took quite a while until Doris was called to the nurses' station. Doris took Mitra with her.

"Mrs. Milutinovic, your husband is in number five. You can go and keep him company. Please wait for the doctor to see you with your husband's reports."

"Thank you," Doris said to the nurse. They both went and sat with Marko. He was sleeping. They sat beside him for more than an hour. Marko slept the whole time. Doris told Mitra that Marko hadn't sleep much last night. He was in a lot of pain.

"That is why he is sleeping now," Mitra added.

Finally, the doctor came with the results. He introduced himself as Dr. Johnson.

"Marko is your husband, right?"

Doris confirmed, "Yes, he is."

"Your husband's results are back. His condition is not so much due to his illness, but the flu. The body has to fight viruses on its own because antibiotics are not effective against viruses. Make sure he drinks a lot of liquid. His upper body should be elevated to breathe easier. If he gets worse, bring him back. But for now, you can take your husband home."

Doris thanked the doctor and turned to Mitra, "You come home with us, mom. Somebody will take you to the residence later, unless you wish to stay with us overnight."

"No, I won't stay overnight, but I would like to stay with you for a while," Mitra said.

When they got to Marko's home, Doris went out to get roast chicken, potatoes, veggies, and spring salad. She returned with the food and two Tim Horton cappuccinos for Mitra and Marko and a coffee for herself. Despite all the pain and sorrow, they enjoyed having a meal together. Mitra thought to herself, "What an unbelievable difference; having a meal with your family instead of with the incapacitated strangers around you."

Marko said, "Thank you, mom, for coming. Sorry I haven't come to see you in almost a month, I won't try to explain myself or make excuses, but lately I've had no energy."

Just after they finished their dinner, Stefan and his wife, Suzan, dropped by. Stefan kissed Mitra first then said their customary greeting to his brother, "Hi, *bratusko*."

"So, you are trying to scare us all."

"I want to test how much I mean to you people," said Marko.

"Okay, smart guy, but be careful do not test our love for you."

They had a little laugh just to ease the tension. Marko explained to Stefan what the doctor said. They all sat together until 9:00 pm. Marko said he was tired and had to go to bed. Mitra asked Stefan to take her back to her place. Doris offered to put her up for the night, but Mitra wanted to go back.

Mitra knew that Doris had her hands full looking after Marko. She didn't want to add more work and worries for Doris. Besides, Marko needed to rest without extra stress. Mitra and Marko kissed and hugged as usual. Stefan yelled out to his brother, "Take care of your wife and don't scare us anymore, *bratusko*." Mitra and Stefan left, but Suzan stayed with Doris, as Marko was already in bed.

After a few minutes, Stefan asked his mother how she was doing.

"Sorry, mom, for not coming to see you more often. The start of the school season involves a lot of preparation before classes begin. I will try to visit you more often."

"Don't worry, son. I'm all right but please visit Marko more often than me. You two, or I should say three, get along very well all the time. He likes yours and Sava's company."

"Does Sava call you, mom? Is she coming to see Marko soon?"

"I don't really know," Mitra answered. "The last time I talked to her she told me she had a very big project to do. She had to finish it."

"I hope Marko will be healthy enough to spend the coming holidays with us."

Mitra knew what Stefan was talking about. She began to cry. She didn't have any tissues left to dry her eyes. Stefan offered her tissues. As she was wiping her eyes, she said, "It's three months until the holidays. That is a long time for Marko to hang on until."

"I know, mom, I know," Stefan said. "But hopefully he will."

They arrived at the centre and Stefan helped his mom to her room. They hugged and kissed.

"Good night for now."

Chapter 20

On the way down, Stefan met Sandy.

"Hi, how are you?" Stefan said.

"I'm good, thank you for asking. How are you Mr. Milutinovic? How is your mother doing? I heard she had a big scare today with your brother."

"Yes, she did, so did the rest of the family."

"How is your brother doing these days?"

"He is trying very hard to hold on to life as much as he can, but he has deteriorated considerably."

"I'm sorry to hear that."

"Thank you for asking, I appreciate it. Please check on my mother from time to time, she appreciates your company very much."

"I will, I promise."

When Stefan left Sandy, he was thinking how much he liked her for no apparent reason. "She has very nice manners and she cheers up my mother a lot."

Mitra lay down on her bed to get some rest. She was exhausted after a day filled with sadness. She tried not to think about how much Marko had changed for the worse since she had seen him a month ago. Tears flowed down her cheeks. She crossed herself and said her prayers. This time, even the prayers didn't help her ease her melancholy and sadness. She started to wonder how she could live watching her son dying.

Oh no, no, she couldn't think about that. God would help her and hopefully she would go before him. She prayed to God to take her before Marko. She remembered how horrible it was to watch Petar die. At least Petar's death was quick. He didn't suffer too long. It happened within a few hours.

Mitra's mind went back and forth until she got very tired and finally fell asleep. She slept until 9:00 pm. When the nurse checked on her, she found her on top of her made up bed all dressed in her good clothes. She touched her gently three or four times to wake her up. Mitra opened her eyes and saw the nurse standing beside her. Mitra jumped when she saw the nurse.

"Is everything okay, nurse? Why are you here? Is my Marko all right?" Mitra asked, still drowsy.

"I'm sorry if I have startled you, Mrs. Milutinovic. I didn't mean to. You were talking about Marko."

The nurse was a new employee and she didn't know anything about Mitra.

"Marko is my oldest son. He isn't feeling well."

The nurse didn't know Mitra and wasn't going to pry. She asked Mitra if she needed any help, and that she would come back with Mitra's medicine. Mitra thanked the nurse and told her she could manage everything herself.

"You are welcome, Mrs. Milutinovic. I have to give you your medication," the nurse said.

Mitra got off the bed when the phone rang.

"Hi, Baba."

"Hi, Sofija, why are you calling so late?"

"No, it's not that late. I know you don't go to sleep before 10 or so. I called you because I wanted to know how you were after you got scared about grandpa Marko. I know uncle Stefan took you back."

"Yes, that is true; he came to see his brother. Suzan came also. Don't worry dear, I'll be all right."

"I will come to see you as soon as I can, but we're already having a lot of tests. It's pretty hard, much harder than high school. They want to weed us out," said Sofija.

"I don't think you will be the one falling out," said Mitra.

"I don't know, Baba, anything is possible," Sofija said.

"Yes, my dear, anything is possible in our lives."

"Baba, I hope you will have some rest and sleep tonight," Sofija said.

"I hope so too, but that is not my biggest concern."

"I know and I'm truly sorry for what is happening with grandpa but what can we do about it?"

"Nothing my dear, nothing."

Sofija paused for a few seconds not knowing what to say. Mitra broke the silence, "Thank you for calling, dear, I love you."

"I love you too, Baba. I love you very much and I'm sorry you have to go through this."

"We all have to go through it. Good night, dear."

"Good night, Baba."

Mitra prepared herself for bed. The nurse came with her medication. The nurse was smart and didn't leave pills with Mitra. She waited until Mitra swallowed them all. Mitra planned on not taking them. She wanted to die before Marko did.

She started thinking about Marko's childhood. She remembered the first steps he took between her and his father. His little arms were straight out, eyes scared. They would extend their arms towards him and as he moved forward to touch their fingers, they would pull slowly back from him. The closer he was to their fingers the more secure he felt. Once he came close and grabbed one of their hands, they would give him a big hug and kiss. His face would light up with a big smile, knowing something good had happened to him.

He was a good baby, not fussy or mischievous. He was little bit delayed with speech. He could say only a few words clearly. They were really worried and took him to the doctor to see if there was a problem. The doctor reassured them that everything was okay because what he was able to say was clear. Once he started speaking, they were surprised how fast he was speaking normally. It looked like he could have spoken long time before, but didn't. He was confused between two languages; Serbo-Croatian and English.

He went to McMaster University, so he could stay home. He always wanted to be a teacher. Throughout university, he had high marks. He was hired full time after he finished his studies. They were very proud of him.

Their first child had a university degree, while Petar and Mitra hadn't even finished public school.

He met Doris at university; she was also studying to be a teacher. When he brought her home to meet his parents, they were disappointed that she was not Serbian, but English. Her good manners won both of them over and they started liking her a lot. They had a beautiful wedding and received very generous gifts. Petar and Mitra paid for the total cost of the wedding.

With the money they saved already from working as teachers plus the money they got from the wedding, Marko and Doris put a sizeable down payment on the house just across the road from Mitra and Petar. When they moved into their house, Marko said to Mitra, "You know, mom, why we bought the house close to you? We want you to babysit our children."

"What about your dad, is he not allowed to watch them?" Mitra asked.

"Of course, mom, but you will be better with that. Dad likes to go and visit his friends. You don't go any farther than across the road to see Stana."

They all laughed.

It wasn't meant for Petar to see his first grandchild; he died soon after they moved into their home. Marko was saddened that his father wasn't around anymore. When Marko was little, Petar would spend a lot of time with him playing games or taking him to the large and beautiful Gage Park to enjoy sand, swings, and a swinging horse. Those were wonderful times in Mitra's life; watching her beautiful, healthy children playing with their father. How could it happen that her life could be so beautiful and fulfilling at one moment and then be full of loss and become heavy with grief and sorrow the next?

While Mitra was thinking about Marko's life and how much joy he brought into their lives, she felt more relaxed. She said her usual prayers and her last words were to leave it all in God's hands. Mitra was very glad that Doris was a good wife and a good person.

That helped especially in Marko's position. Around midnight, the nurse heard something fall in Mitra's room. She came in to see what was going on.

"Are you all right, Mrs. Milutinovic?"

"Yes, my brush holder fell over but I'm all right."

She came in warning Mitra not to bend, she would pick it up.

"Thank you, nurse, very much. I'm sorry for making noise."

"Have you slept at all?" the nurse asked, since it was close to midnight.

"No, not yet, but I will," Mitra said.

"Would you like me to give you something for sleep?"

Mitra thought for a minute and said, "I think it would be a good idea."

"I'll go get it. Are you ready to go to bed?" the nurse asked.

"Yes, I am."

The nurse came back with one sleeping pill. Mitra swallowed it with a few sips of water. She lay back in her bed, thanking the nurse for her kindness and concern. In a few minutes, she became drowsy and fell asleep. When she woke up it was 6:00 am. Her mind was filled with many questions about Marko. She was so restless that she didn't know what to do with herself.

She took some deep breaths to release the pressure of her heart. She was still like that at 8:00 am when Sandy knocked on the door. Mitra said, "Come in, please."

Sandy saw Mitra in a panic.

"Are you all right, Mitra?"

"Yes, I am, but my son Marko isn't."

"Yes, I know, I spoke to your son Stefan and he told me about your son Marko. I was thinking about whether to come in and see you last night but then I thought it could make it worse to talk about it. Sorry, if I made the wrong choice."

Mitra explained what the nurse had done for her and how much it had helped.

"Great. Are you going down for breakfast?" Sandy asked.

"I don't know, I think I won't go," Mitra said.

"It would be good for you to mix with people, but if you really won't go, I can bring you something," Sandy said.

"I don't think I can be in a crowd of people this morning. Would you mind bringing me some juice and coffee? I feel very dry," Mitra said.

Sandy left right away. Within a few minutes, she was back with half of a bagel with cream cheese, a banana, juice, and coffee. Mitra was surprised how quickly Sandy returned.

"I thought you would bring me this after you had your breakfast," Mitra said.

"Don't worry, I'm fine. There is a lot left for me too," Sandy said.

Before Sandy left, she promised Mitra she would come back and keep her company. Mitra was happy for Sandy's friendship once more. After she had the coffee, juice, and banana, she decided to call Marko's house to see how his night had been, and how he was feeling that morning. Just as she was going to pick up the phone and dial, the phone rang. Marko's name was on display.

"Hello, mom," Doris said.

"Hello, dear," Mitra answered.

"I know you're worried about Marko, but first, how was your night and how did you sleep?"

Mitra assured Doris that people were taking really good care of her. Doris knew what Mitra wanted to hear and told her, "Someone wants to talk to you, mom."

When Mitra heard Marko's voice, she became very emotional. She didn't know how to calm her nerves. Marko asked her if she had slept well. She didn't reply instantly but paused a bit, "I'm all right, son, don't worry. I have plenty of time to sleep."

"I have to tell you, mom, I slept pretty good. This morning after I woke up, Doris made a nice breakfast for us. I'm relaxing now with my cup of coffee and newspaper. Did you have breakfast, mom?"

"Yes, I did. Sandy brought me breakfast."

"Why didn't you go down for your breakfast, mom?" Marko asked.

"I just didn't feel like it," Mitra replied.

"Thank her for me, mom. I am glad she is so good to you," Marko said.

"Yes, she really is."

"Mom, please don't be cooped up in your room. Get out and get involved in something. Don't worry so much; your worries won't help me."

"I understand, son. I'll try not to worry, but I'm not promising. Please tell Doris to call me when she has time. It would be better than if I call you."

"I'll do that, mom, but you can also call whenever you want."

"Thank you, son, I will."

"Bye, mom."

"Bye, son."

Mitra was much more relaxed after hearing Marko's voice. Sandy came back to be with Mitra. Mitra asked how the girls were.

"They are well, but they feel bad about your situation. We had a little commotion downstairs in the dining room. You know that tall resident, Bob? He pushed little Jimmy. Jimmy fell to the floor. After he got up, he hit Bob over the head with his cane. Bob looked at Jimmy and called him a little piece of shit. Jimmy yelled back, 'You are a much bigger shit than me, because you are much bigger. Why did you push me?'

"'I didn't mean to push you. It just happened that you turned around unexpectedly.'

"'That's an excuse. You walk around as if you were a big rooster.'

"The nurse heard all of this and said to both men, 'Look guys, since it was an accident and both of you said unpleasant things to each other, can you please apologize to one another? Let's start first with you, Bob.'

"Bob said to Jimmy that he was sorry for his fall, but Jimmy wouldn't accept the apology, 'Yes, I fell, but first you pushed me and made me fall.' They went back and forth. Then I left."

Sandy said to Mitra, "I hope you don't intend to stay in your room all day long. Can I do something for you? Would you like to go for a walk? Can I take you out for lunch or anything else? Today is a beautiful day. It's pretty warm for October."

"Thank you very much, Sandy, for your offer. I appreciate your help and your friendship. I'm waiting for a phone call from my great-granddaughter to let me know whether she will be coming home for the weekend."

"Oh, that's the girl who is writing your memoir."

"Yes, yes, it is," Mitra confirmed. "That is my darling Sofija."

"I don't see her around as often as before," Sandy said.

"That is true," said Mitra and she explained why Sofija wasn't around that much.

"I am going to leave you, Mitra. I'll check on you later to see how you're doing, or whether you want to go somewhere."

"Thank you, Sandy."

Mitra sat in the chair where she had the best view of Hamilton and its vicinity. She remembered how much she enjoyed the city's Confederation Park with her family. They couldn't afford to buy a car until Marko was seven or eight years old. It was a great achievement to have a car at that time. It was a little Ford. She forgets the model because they didn't have it very long. Somebody smashed into it in front of their house.

While they had that car, they would go to the beach all summer long. As soon as Petar would come from work and the kids came from school, they would quickly have dinner and leave right away. They didn't buy another car for two years. They were so shocked when the first one was wrecked. They imagined how tragic it would have been if they were in it. That thought scared Petar and Mitra so much, but the kids begged them to buy another one.

They had wonderful times, especially on Saturdays and Sundays when everybody was off work and school. They used to play beach ball, bocce, and have races. They also spent lots of time in the water. At that time in the late '50s, the beaches had no pollution. Occasionally, they went up north for a week or so, but even though it wasn't that expensive compared to the present, it was still expensive for them. Petar worked alone. They had to cover everything with his pay.

Petar didn't want Mitra to go out and work, leaving their children with somebody else. He always used to say children need their mother at least until they start going to school. No matter what they did together they enjoyed their family.

Mitra took a big sigh, "Oh my God, how wonderful those years were. I should think of happy times, not the sad ones, because I can't do anything about sadness; it brings me only grief and sorrow. When I think of happy times, I feel joy and peace move into my mind and my heart."

As Mitra was reminiscing about the past, her phone rang. She knew it was her darling Sofija.

"Hello, you good-looking lady," the voice said.

"Who is this?"

"Your admirer, that's who… Hi, Baba, it's me, Sofija."

"I knew it was you, but since you were goofing around so was I," Mitra said.

"Oh, Baba, we are good at it," Sofija said.

"Indeed, indeed, we are," Mitra agreed.

After exchanging some small talk, Sofija said that she would come and visit on the weekend.

"After this weekend, I will be preparing for my exams and I won't be able to visit you for quite some time."

They exchanged a few words about Marko and hung up the phones to the sound of each other's kisses.

Marko called his mother again. Mitra was surprised that he was calling her again.

"Is everything all right, son?"

"Yes, it is, mom. I just wanted to know how you're doing, because you didn't sound so good this morning."

"I'm all right, son. How are you?"

"I'm all right. Please, mom, don't confine yourself to your room, go outside in the fresh air. It's a beautiful day. Doris and I are sitting outside having coffee."

Mitra was wondering how that could be; her heart leapt for joy that Marko was able to go outside. There was hope yet that he would get better.

"Hello, mom? Why are you silent?" Marko asked.

"For a moment, I didn't know what to say because I'm so happy that you're enjoying such a beautiful day with your wife," Mitra said.

"Thank you, mom. You better go out with your friends and enjoy it too."

After they got off the phone, Mitra was wondering whether Sandy called him about her confinement, or Sofija phoned him. It really didn't matter whether somebody called him or not, it was nice to hear his voice.

Sandy came back to check on Mitra as she promised.

"How are you feeling now? Have you calmed down a bit?"

"Yes, I have," Mitra answered. "My Sofija called me to say she is coming home for the weekend. My son Marko called me also to check on me and asked me to get out of my room and get some fresh air. I guess I'm going to take you up on it if I'm still invited."

Sandy had a little smile at the corner of her mouth. Mitra knew what that smile was all about or at least she thought so.

"Good idea," Sandy said. "Get dressed and come downstairs. I will let the girls know you're coming with us."

A taxi came to pick them up. Since the weather was so nice and warm, Mary had suggested they go down to Confederation Park, "We can have a nice lunch in the Italian restaurant and walk around for some exercise."

Everybody agreed. Just to see small children and babies would give their heart and mind a great lift. The four of them were sitting on the bench when a married couple with a beautiful girl passed them. The little girl suddenly stopped in front of them and said, "Hi," with a most beautiful smile on her face. They were very surprised at how warmly this lovely child greeted them.

Her parents stopped to call the little one to leave those ladies alone.

"But, mom, they like me."

"Yes, of course, everybody loves you. You will be in trouble one day for trusting strangers."

They were shocked by the differences in behaviour. Here, a little girl had no fear of strangers. She showed the innocent love of a child with no grasp of age in people, but her adult mother saw only useless old people and the rest of the crowd as bad. The little girl stepped away from them, turned around, and blew them a kiss. All four of them sent her more than one. As she left them, she was hopping happily along to reach her parents.

"Oh my God," Sandy said. "Those people don't deserve such a wonderful, innocent angel."

"I wonder who is raising her," Mitra said. "Who would be raising her? Not her mother for sure."

"Surely she does not," Sandy said.

"Somebody else is raising her, judging by her manners," Mary said.

"It doesn't matter who is raising her; they are doing a wonderful job, which will benefit her family and anybody who gets in touch with her. Such good manners," Joan added.

They had been in the park for three hours. They all agreed that they should go home. Sandy called a taxi to come and pick them up. She paid for the taxi. They divided the bill among them. Mitra was glad she went out with the girls. At least it was better than staying home and crying all day long.

The next few days passed very slowly. Mitra was always waiting for a phone call, but she dreaded it. Doris called her twice a day regularly; in the morning and after dinner. Sometimes, she would give the phone to Marko and Mitra would hear his weaker voice. After they finished talking, Mitra cried every time, especially if Doris told her the situation was worsening.

Lots of times, she didn't go downstairs to eat. The girls were very good to her. They always offered to get her whatever she asked for. They even went to the store and bought her some fruit. It was very hard to figure out what one could do in such a difficult situation. The old saying, "Damned if you do, damned if you don't," was how the situation felt for Mitra.

Sofija visited on the weekend. She found her darling Baba depressed and hard to talk to. The good times when they sat, talked, joked, and exchanged points of view were mostly gone. Sofija felt bad seeing how her baba was doing. They didn't talk anymore about Mitra's past; they clung tightly to each other, not knowing what to say.

The next few days continued the same way. Mitra was going downhill along with her son Marko. A couple of weeks after Sofija's visit, Doris called just before lunch to tell Mitra Marko's situation had worsened drastically. She'd called the ambulance. They'd given him oxygen to help him breathe and taken him to the hospital. She was with him at the hospital. He was feeling better now that he could breathe more easily.

"Sorry I didn't call you earlier, mom. There was such a rush and I was only thinking about saving him. I know, mom, you want to come and see Marko, but I cannot pick you up right now because I want to be with him. Everybody is either working or in school. I will call Stefan at work and tell him what's going on. I'm sure somebody will come to drive you, if for some reason Stefan cannot."

When Doris finished talking, she called Mitra's residence to make them aware of Mitra's situation because she couldn't reach Dona or the girls. When Mitra heard all of this she felt numb with fear that these were the last days of her son's life. She felt dizzy; she quickly moved towards her bed and lay down to stabilize herself.

She didn't care if she died, but she had to be strong for her son and she had to see him at least once more. She lay on the bed as tears ran like a stream. There was a knock on the door. Mitra said, "Come in," forgetting to say, "please."

The new nurse came in pretending not to know about her situation. She found Mitra crying. The nurse came over to Mitra and put her hand on Mitra's shoulder, telling her she hadn't seen her downstairs for lunch and was wondering if she wanted her to bring some food or drink.

Through her tears, Mitra answered, "No, thank you, nurse. I can't eat or drink while my son is dying."

Now the nurse gave Mitra a hug, saying, "I'm very sorry to hear that, Mrs. Milutinovic." The nurse admitted to Mitra she'd received a request from her family to check in on her.

Mitra thanked the nurse for her kindness. The nurse offered to stay with her longer, but Mitra said she wanted to be alone. She promised to call if she needed help.

"Please do, Mrs. Milutinovic. We would like to help you."

"Can you please put the phone on my night table, so I can reach it easily if my family calls?"

When the nurse went out, Stefan called his mother to hear how she was coping with Marko's situation. He told her if she wanted to see Marko, he would come to pick her up so they could go together. Mitra got a little bit offended when Stefan asked her if she wanted to see Marko.

"What kind of question is that? Of course I want to see him," Mitra answered abruptly.

"Sorry, mom, I didn't mean to make you mad. It's no problem for me to come and pick you up. I only thought it was too much for you."

Stefan noticed his mother was in a very frail emotional state. He didn't want to say anything more, only that he was coming to pick her up in half an hour.

Mitra answered, "I'm sorry, son, if I was a bit rough."

"That's fine, mom. Don't worry about it, please."

Mitra got up right away. She wasn't sure if she was stable enough. She called the front desk. She needed the nurse to help her dress; her son was coming to pick her up. It took about 10 minutes for the nurse to show up. Mitra sponged herself a bit. She was ready when Stefan showed up.

They exchanged hugs and kisses. This time they took more than the usual time letting go of each other. On the way to the hospital, they didn't talk very much; both of them were crying. When they arrived at the hospital, Marko was lying on his back with intravenous in his arm and an oxygen mask in his mouth. Doris sat beside him.

When Mitra saw her son in that condition, she almost collapsed. Stefan held on to his mother to make her stable. If he hadn't held her, she would have fallen down. She did anyway. The nurse walked in, noticed Mitra's condition and asked if she could get her a drink or something.

Mitra answered before they did, "No, thank you, I don't need anything."

Doris got off her chair and they sat as close to Marko as possible. Marko had changed so much since Mitra had seen him 10 days earlier.

The three of them sat around Marko's bed, having a light conversation. Mitra said a word or two but mostly she kept quiet. Marko was fighting pain and occasionally coughing. Mitra rested her hand on Marko's arm or shoulder. After a couple of hours, Marko's doctor came in to see him. Marko lay sedated. The doctor said to Doris, "Mrs. Milutinovic, can I see you in my office please?"

"Yes, doctor, of course you can."

Doris introduced the doctor to Marko's mother and brother. Doris told the doctor he could tell all three of them about Marko's condition.

"Are you sure, Mrs. Milutinovic?" the doctor asked.

All three of them said, "Yes, we all want to hear it."

They walked into the doctor's office, a small cubicle with a device for blood pressure, a computer, a good office chair, and two others for visitors. Stefan stood while Mitra and Doris sat down in the available chairs.

The doctor opened a page on his computer to show them Marko's situation, then he quickly closed the computer saying, "We can talk without looking at the computer." He bent down towards Doris and Mitra and took each of their hands in his. He looked at them with the saddest expression saying, "I'm really sorry that I have to give you bad news."

The doctor was an older man. "If it is any consolation to you, I lost my son six months ago. I know how dreadful such news is to hear."

He offered them a box of tissues, to which all three helped themselves. He looked at them again and finally said, "I'm sorry but Marko cannot be saved. He is in a lot of pain, and we had to sedate him in order to make it easier for him to bear his pain. I can see on his chart the doctors have tried everything to help him, but the disease has gone too far. For that reason, nothing can be done."

Mitra and Doris burst out crying, holding each other's hands. Stefan stayed in control, but he was angry at the situation. Why did it have to be that way? When Doris stopped crying, she asked the doctor how long Marko had left.

"I would say no more than a week. It will be soon."

All three of them were stunned. They were hoping against all hopes that he could live a little longer. Now, they had to face reality and accept the inevitable whether they liked it or not. Marko's son, John, Sofija's father, called his mother, Doris, to find out how his father was doing. She told him everything the doctor told them.

John was on a business trip. He burst out crying on the phone. He was angry that his mother hadn't told him sooner about his father's condition.

Doris said she was surprised too. She thought he would live much longer. "Sorry, son, I knew you needed to go to Europe for business. I didn't want to stop your trip. It's important for you to keep your job."

"I know, mom, but my dad is more important to me."

"I know, son, I know."

"I'm coming back tomorrow and that's it."

"Fine, if you think so, come. It's better that you come while he can hopefully still see you. He cannot talk."

"When did you last see Sofija?"

"I saw her a few days ago when she came to see Baba. You know we all count less than her great-grandmother."

Doris laughed after saying that and Mitra showed a very faint smile. "See you tomorrow, son. I will stay with your father all night and somebody will stay through the day."

Stefan said, "I will stay with my brother tomorrow."

Mitra said, "I will too, I'm not going back to my place and leave my son to die without me."

John arrived two days later with his wife. Marko's condition was worsening rapidly. Four days had passed since the doctor told them the bad news. The entire family came to see Marko, to say goodbye. Since Marko knew he was dying, he pre-arranged his own funeral with Doris's help. She didn't want to be part of it, but he told her if she could not do it, he would do it by himself. Doris had to help him and be with him.

As they were doing the arrangements step by step, Doris was surprised at feeling that something so dreadful could feel so normal and so important. Marko told Doris the same thing. He told her that he was satisfied with how he was facing his own life's ending with dignity, understanding that life has an end and his end was coming soon.

There were always lots of people coming to see Marko. Mitra stayed by Marko throughout the day. She slept at Stefan's house. Every morning they would come and relieve Doris. Sometimes Marko's son, John, also stayed. It was Friday morning around 7:00 am, when Marko's condition got really bad. They rushed to get there before Marko died, but Mitra couldn't be any faster than she normally was. They got there too late.

Chapter 21

They found Doris slumped over Marko's body, pleading with him to wake up and not to leave her alone. They walked into the room and Mitra's legs gave out when she saw her dead son. Stefan and John were holding Mitra tightly, but for a moment she passed out. They put a cold compress on her face and let her swallow a sip of water, then she came around.

The room was completely packed with family. Everybody was crying, some very loudly, Mitra and Doris especially. There was another patient in the room with Marko, but when the nurses realized that Marko had died, they took that patient to another room. They were sitting around Marko's dead body, which was now serene and peaceful. Death can fool us with its absolute stillness, especially after there has been a stormy fight between life and death.

After an hour, the doctor came and pronounced Marko dead. The nurse asked the orderlies to put the body in the morgue, until a funeral hearse would remove him. The family went to Marko and Doris's home to be there for family and friends who came to pay respect and express condolences to Marko's family. It was a Yugoslavian custom to receive people with good food and drinks, especially plum brandy, slivovica, from the old country.

They were in the funeral parlour for viewing on Sunday night. Monday was the day of Marko's funeral. There was a full service at the church. The priest conducting it gave a short and condensed history of Marko's life. After Marko was buried, all the guests came for Marko's last memorial meal in the hall. A full meal was served for more than 150 people. There were some personal eulogies from the family. That is how Marko's life ended after a very short illness.

Mitra thought her life should also be finished after the death of her first-born son. She stayed with Doris for a week, but realized it was too much for Doris to look after her incapacitated mother-in-law while she was grieving for her husband. Mitra decided to go back to the centre to give Doris some rest. Mitra had lost a lot of her vitality during the process of mourning.

When she came back, she could hardly walk. Everybody was surprised how quickly she had changed. She refused to go downstairs for meals because she wasn't able to do it alone. They brought her food upstairs to her room. She hardly ate anything except bananas and some drinks.

Mitra was going downhill very fast. The staff told her family that she would have to be moved to the nursing side because she needed full-time care. They would wait another week until the nursing side had an empty bed for her.

In the afternoon, the housekeeper was in that area, when she heard a big thump in Mitra's room. She went downstairs to tell Dona about it. Dona went quickly upstairs to Mitra's room. She found her on the floor, unconscious and bleeding from her nose and mouth. She quickly called the ambulance. The paramedics tried to help her regain consciousness but they couldn't. They gave her oxygen. She was breathing without any other visible signs of life.

Dona called Doris because she was in regular contact with Mitra and told her about the situation with Mitra's fall and how the ambulance took her to the General Hospital. As soon as Doris got the news, she called Stefan, and then Sofija in Toronto because she knew Sofija would never forgive her if she wasn't called right away.

Doris told Sofija to stay calm until she called her back after she visited Baba in the hospital.

"Please, call me right away. If Baba is doing poorly, I want to come home right away to see her."

"I will call you. Please don't panic. Hopefully, Baba isn't so bad."

When Doris came to the hospital and saw her mother-in-law lying in bed, similar to the last days of Marko's life, she knew right away it wasn't good. She kept calling her, "Mom, mom, it's Doris. Wake up."

All Doris's calling was to no avail; Mitra's condition didn't change. Mitra's son Stefan came with his wife. There were other relatives and friends whispering, "It's sad for the family to suffer two losses in such a short time."

Stefan asked Doris to go and pick up Sofija after she finished her exam the next day and bring her to the hospital. Mitra's condition remained the same. She was breathing only with the help of the machines.

When Sofija came to see her baba, she had been in the same condition for three days. When Sofija saw her baba motionless, she put her head on Mitra's chest pleading with her to wake up.

"Sofija is here, wake up, Baba. We haven't said everything we wanted to. Baba, please wake up, please, we haven't completed your diary. We have to do it. That is why you have to wake up. What can I do without you here? Come on, I want to hear that happy voice of yours and that wonderful sense of humour you always entertained me with. I love you, Baba, I love you so much, please don't leave me. My life won't be the same without you."

As Sofija said this, tears poured out of her swollen eyes. But her pleading didn't have any effect. Mitra didn't give any sign she'd heard. The doctor knew of Mitra's tragedy. The family met with the doctor to make some decisions about what could be done for Mitra, if anything. The doctor's opinion was that she would not get better if she didn't get better in the first five days after her accident. "I believe her subconscious does not want her to come back and on top of that, her vitality at 90 isn't that of a younger person."

The family members gave each other questioning looks. Sofija spoke first, "I would like it if we give Baba a few more days. Then if she doesn't get better, we will make a decision."

Sofija's family, especially her parents, didn't want Sofija to stop going to her classes, "You know that Baba wanted us to do the right thing and do things that are beneficial to us especially to our future. Please do not disappoint her. Remember how much she loved you unselfishly."

Sofija travelled back and forth to school every day just to be with her baba, as long as she could. She even brought pen and paper pretending that she was ready to continue with the diary. "There is still some gravel left." She reminded her baba about all the wonderful things they'd done together.

MItra didn't react to any of her pleadings. After five days in the same condition, the doctor and the family made the decision to take her off the machine and let Mitra follow her son. Stefan told the family and the doctor that his mother had expressed the wish her family would not take drastic measures to keep her alive, if she was in the situation she was in now. "She told me that on her last visit to my home a couple of months ago."

Everybody agreed to let Baba go, but Sofija still wanted her baba to stay around. For a couple more days, they worked on Sofija and finally she came to understand that she had to let go of her hope for Baba to get better. She had to agree with the family and let her go. They decided that the coming Wednesday, they would do that on October 12th at 10:00 am.

Sava arrived from Ottawa with her partner two days after her mother's accident. She was there all the time beside her mother's bed. On Tuesday, the room was full of family members. One by one they said goodbye to Mitra. The three last ones were Sava, Stefan, and Sofija. They let Sofija be the last one to say goodbye to her baba because of their exceptional relationship and closeness.

When Sofija came out from the room, she was sobbing and crying hysterically. In the morning, they all came an hour before the scheduled time. They waited a few minutes for the nurse to fix the room nicely. The family brought a nice embroidered cover that Mitra always liked and spread it over her body.

They also brought two beautiful flower arrangements to put on each side of her bed. The doctor came in and shook hands with all the members of the family. He said a few words and complimented the family for making the right decision.

Father Nikola came in at 8:00 am and prayed to God for Mitra to forgive all her sins and take her soul to His heavenly Kingdom. Everything was ready. Sava, Stefan, Doris, and Sofija stood closest to Mitra holding her hands. Together, the family said a prayer and crossed themselves. When everything was ready, the doctor disconnected the machine.

After he disconnected the machine, Mitra slightly opened her eyes and looked around. There was a faint smile on her face before her last breath.

Mitra knew that for the last moment of her life, her family was with her. She left the world with a smile knowing she didn't die alone, even though it was not in her home.

Acknowledgements

Many people deserve to be acknowledged for helping me put my novel together.

The most deserving of these is my brother Branko Vinčíć, who was tireless in reading and editing this manuscript. Also, many thanks to Mr. George Budimir, my friend Professor Julia Frankel, Mary-Anne Kenney, and my niece and nephew, Nada and Simo Katić, who refreshed my memories of back home.